Colter woke in the middle of the night.

He'd been dreaming about Karen. Again. She was so close, right in the next room, and he couldn't forget it. He was waging a war within himself, and he was losing.

Suddenly the door to the bedroom opened, and Colter shut his eyes, feigning sleep. She was stoking the fire.

He slitted his eyes and looked at her through his lashes. What he saw froze him, and he hardly dared to breathe.

Karen was wearing a floor-length batiste nightgown, but as she stood in front of the fire, the light shone through it, making it seem almost transparent. Colter swallowed hard.

Karen finished with the fire and turned, stopping when she noticed the pile of his clothes on the floor. Her eyes moved upward to his face, and she gave a visible start when she saw that he was awake.

"Come here," he said huskily.

Dear Reader,

When two people fall in love, the world is suddenly new and exciting, and it's that same excitement we bring to you in Silhouette Intimate Moments. These are stories with scope, with grandeur. The characters lead the lives we all dream of, and everything they do reflects the wonder of being in love.

Longer and more sensuous than most romances, Silhouette Intimate Moments novels take you away from everyday life and let you share the magic of love. Adventure, glamour, drama, even suspense—these are the passwords that let you into a world where love has a power beyond the ordinary, where the best authors in the field today create stories of love and commitment that will stay with you always.

In coming months look for novels by your favorite authors: Maura Seger, Parris Afton Bonds, Linda Howard, and Nora Roberts, to name just a few. And whenever you buy books, look for all the Silhouette Intimate Moments, love stories *for* today's women *by* today's women.

Leslie J. Wainger
Senior Editor
Silhouette Books

Doreen Owens Malek
Danger Zone

Silhouette Intimate Moments
Published by Silhouette Books New York
America's Publisher of Contemporary Romance

SILHOUETTE BOOKS
300 East 42nd St., New York, N.Y. 10017

Copyright © 1987 by Doreen Owens Malek

ISBN: 0-373-07204-X

First Silhouette Books printing August 1987

America's Publisher of Contemporary Romance

Printed in the U.S.A.

Books by Doreen Owens Malek

Silhouette Romance

The Crystal Unicorn #363

Silhouette Special Edition

A Ruling Passion #154

Silhouette Desire

Native Season #86
Reckless Moon #222
Winter Meeting #240
Desperado #260
Firestorm #290
Bright River #343

Silhouette Intimate Moments

The Eden Tree #88
Devil's Deception #105
Montega's Mistress #169
Danger Zone #204

DOREEN OWENS MALEK

is an attorney and former teacher, who decided on her current career when she sold her fledgling novel to the first editor who read it. She has been writing ever since. Born and raised in New Jersey, she has lived throughout the northeast and now makes her home in Pennsylvania.

Chapter 1

Karen Walsh looked around at her fellow hostages and wondered how much longer they would be held. She knew that in the end they'd either be released or killed, but the waiting had them demoralized to the point that even the latter fate would almost be welcome. After five days of captivity the underground supply room that served as their prison seemed like hell, where hope was abandoned and all dreams ended in a formless, pointless despair.

The heat in the basement was intolerable. Karen pushed her damp hair back from her brow and pulled her clinging blouse away from her midriff. The women around her were no longer even exchanging glances with one another, but slept fitfully or stared at the floor. Like shocked rats in a cage, they had given up and merely marked time until something—anything—happened to relieve the tedium of their incarceration.

Karen was no happier than her companions, but felt they could have been treated worse. They received food and water at intervals and were permitted to sleep undisturbed on the floor. To her knowledge no one had been beaten or molested, but she couldn't speak for the men, who had been taken to another part of the building. Karen's group, an assortment of secretaries, clerks and minor functionaries, had an armed guard posted outside the closed door of their improvised jail. They could hear him pacing back and forth, back and forth, a metronomic counterpart to the heavy silence that filled the stifling, airless room.

Karen was a translator at the government offices on the island of Almeria, a British colony off the northeast coast of South America. Located between the U.S. Virgin Islands to the north and Grenada and Trinidad to the south, Almeria had been a favorite vacation spot until it became the scene of increasing unrest during the previous decade. The natives had been trying for years to oust the British and establish home rule. Finally a militant group had taken over the Government House in the capital city of Ascension. They had captured eighteen of the employees and held them hostage, with Karen among them. The insurgents demanded a meeting with the governor-general to draw up a new constitution and turn the government over to the Almerians. If their demands were not met by eight o'clock the next morning, they would start executing the hostages one by one.

Karen leaned back against the rough cement wall of the cellar and closed her eyes. She thought about the course her life had taken to bring her to that moment, which might be close to her last, and considered whether she would have done anything differently. She had never imagined that she'd be involved in such a drama, but supposed that no one did. She had done the best she could with her life and realized that she had no regrets.

She had married an older man in the British foreign service when she was twenty-one and had traveled with him to Almeria. She was divorced three years later. When her former husband was transferred, she stayed on and kept her job, translating official documents into Spanish for the consumption of the native population. She had been happy in her position until the day less than a week ago when her whole world had changed.

She shifted her weight on the hard floor and tried to relax. Her clothes were filthy, and she was filthy, and she'd hardly slept since the ordeal had begun, but she was better off than some of the other women whose nerves were close to shattering. At night she could hear their muffled sobbing and was grateful that so far she had remained calm. She was as frightened as anyone else, certainly, but at least outwardly composed, and she found it helpful to put her mind on other things to forget where she was and what was happening.

She thought about her family. She was worried about her sister, Grace, who was married and lived in New Jersey. Grace had probably heard of the crisis in Almeria on the news and was terrified for Karen. The two women were close; their parents had died when they were children and Grace and Karen had gone to live with an aunt, who was now also dead. Their father had been a Chaucerian scholar with friends in British academic circles, and some of them kept in touch with the girls after the accident that killed the senior Walshes. One of the men introduced Karen to his brother, Ian, whom she later married.

Karen tucked her skirt around her legs and lifted the hair off the back of her neck, thinking about her husband. Their marriage had been more a union of convenience than love. She knew that now; at the time she'd been too young to appreciate the difference. She'd understood only that Ian was kind to her, and she'd wanted to get away from her aunt's stolid existence and see some of the world. Ian's career had offered what she thought was an opportunity for travel and excitement, and she'd been truly fond of him. To her sheltered eyes his English accent and his age had made him seem wise and sophisticated. He was a far cry from the boys who'd pawed her at high-school dances and had little ambition beyond making it to the next weekend to blow their paychecks. So she was happy to accept Ian's proposal and journey with him to his next assignment, the governor-general's office in Almeria.

But Karen soon realized that the marriage was a mistake. Her husband treated her like the child he thought she was,

and although tolerant and indulgent, he had little time for
her outside of his bed—and in fact made few demands on
her there, either. His business kept him occupied almost
constantly, and he and his associates were old enough to be
her father. Their British wives had teenage children and
nothing in common with an American girl barely out of her
teens herself. Karen was bored, lonely and miserable. Desperate to do something constructive, and against her husband's wishes, she got a job at the document office in
Ascension. When the marriage finally broke up, she decided to start her new life on Almeria, where she had a job
she liked and friends she had made through her work. At the
time of the government house takeover she'd been on Almeria almost five years.

Now she sighed and tried to guess what time it was. The
cellar was windowless, and without the arrival and departure of daylight it was impossible to tell. The guards changed
shifts regularly, but if she took naps and missed the movement outside the door, she lost track.

Karen tapped the shoulder of the woman sitting in front
of her. When Linda, who was the assistant to the governor-
general and one of Karen's friends, turned to look at her,
Karen tapped her wrist.

"Eight o'clock," Linda whispered, "p.m."

Karen nodded dully. They had half a day left.

Suddenly they heard a loud commotion in the basement
corridor outside their prison. The steel-plated door to the
hallway crashed open, and a man burst into the room. He
was dressed in combat fatigues and holding a submachine
gun at the ready. The hostages cowered in fear, thinking that
their fate had been decided twelve hours early.

But as Karen looked at the intruder, she realized that he
was physically different from their captors, who were uniformly dark and slight, definitely Latin. This man was big,
over six feet tall, and very tan, with hair the color of lemon
peel and brows bleached almost white by the sun. His light
blue eyes raked the group as its members shrank against the
walls and stared at him in horror. In the background, they

could see the guard lying at the tall man's feet, unconscious and bleeding from a head wound.

The man lowered his gun cautiously, taking in the scene before him, and raised his free hand in a placating gesture. "Ladies," he said in English, with an unmistakable Southern drawl, "calm down. I'm on your side; I'm not going to hurt you."

Karen's mind raced as she tried to determine the reason for his arrival. What on earth was another American doing in the middle of this mess? She could see the rest of the women looking around, wondering the same thing. They were still immobilized with fear and at this point wouldn't trust anyone, no matter what he said.

The man was already scanning their prison, checking the blank featureless walls, the single exit that had been barred by their captors. "Just keep cool and do what I say," he added, narrowing his eyes at the air shaft near the door. He took a step closer to it, and his weapon swung in a circle as he moved, almost touching one of the mail clerks who sat in front. She covered her face with her hands and began to cry with a soft mewing sound that was pathetic to hear.

The gunman stopped his inspection of the shaft and looked around impatiently until he found the offender.

"Keep quiet, will you?" he said shortly. "Unless you cooperate, I'm not going to get you out of here."

There was a slight noise outside, and he whirled for the door, lifting his weapon purposefully. The crying woman screamed.

"Will somebody shut her up?" he said rudely, turning back and indicating the terrified clerk with the barrel of his gun. "She's going to get us all killed."

Karen got up and moved through the group to her colleague's side to put a comforting arm around her shoulder. "Shh," she said to the woman, who was as rigid as wood, frozen with apprehension. "I really think he's here to help us."

Another man, dressed like the blonde, dashed through the door and barked something to his companion, departing almost as quickly as he had arrived. The gunman faced the trapped women and announced rapidly, "Look, ladies, we've got about ten minutes to pull this off. Every one of us is going to die right here unless you listen to me and can the hysterics."

"So far," Karen replied clearly, the first one of the group to speak, "the only person who seems close to hysterics is you."

The man whipped his head around to look at her, his pale eyes meeting hers over the intervening distance. After a silence lasting a couple of seconds he grinned and said, "You'll do. Come with me."

Karen stared back at him, shocked into silence. Sorry that she had called attention to herself, she had no choice but to do as he said. She picked her way over the sprawled limbs of the other hostages and stood before the intruder, her gaze wary.

He grabbed her wrist and hauled her after him into the corridor with such strength that her feet barely seemed to touch the floor. He called over his shoulder to the women left behind in the basement, "The rest of you stay put. I'll be back."

Karen almost tripped over the prone guard on the way out. She halted, pulling the gunman up short.

"Is he dead?" she whispered.

Her companion looked down at the guerrilla, insensible on the floor.

"Nah," he said dismissively. "Don't worry about him. He'll have a shiner and a headache tomorrow, that's all. In a few months he'll be showing his scar to the girls and telling them what a glorious hero of the revolution he is."

He took off again, pulling Karen in his wake. They fled up a flight of stairs and into an outer room with a view of the street.

"Who do you work for?" Karen asked as he left her to go to the window. He flattened himself against the wall next to it.

"I work for me," he replied, ducking forward and taking a quick look at the road. He glanced back at her and gestured to the hall they'd just left. "Where does that corridor lead?" he asked.

"To the staircase running down to the main lobby." The Government House was a converted mansion from the British settlement period and featured the central staircase common to many of those homes.

She watched as he pulled a folded piece of paper out of his breast pocket and studied it. She could see that it was a floor plan of the building. His profile was very clean, very sharp, as he bent over the blueprint; he looked like a seasoned professional athlete studying a game plan, rather than the soldier he obviously was.

"Good," he said, replacing the map in his pocket. He looked at her again and said, "You're an American?"

"Yes."

"So am I," he offered unnecessarily, pushing the curtain back from the window with the saber point of his rifle and taking another look at the street. The sun had set and dusk was spreading over the landscape. "Where you from?"

"New Jersey."

"Oh, yeah? I'm from Florida myself but I know Jersey. I spent the night in jail once near Newark—you know that part of the state?"

Karen stared at him. Were they really having this singles' bar conversation while the Government House was under siege? And why had he abducted her away from the other women?

The second question was answered as he said, "As soon as I see the trucks coming to pick you up, I want you to go back downstairs. You herd those other women out to the emergency exit by the kitchen loading dock and get them ready to go. I'll meet you there after I make sure these floors are clear. Got it?"

"I think so," Karen replied faintly. "We're being rescued?"

"That's the idea." He peered at her closely, wondering if he had misjudged her mettle. "I need you to help me, now," he said warningly. "Can I count on you to do that?"

Karen nodded briskly, with more certainty than she felt.

"What's your name?" he fired at her, taking another covert glance at the street. A shot from below glanced off the window frame with an eerie, whistling sound, and a scattering of wood chips spattered against the glass pane.

"I knew we hadn't taken them all out down there," he muttered to himself, falling back against the wall.

"Karen Walsh," Karen said, swallowing hard.

"Steve Colter. Pleased to meet you," he replied, with another wicked grin. Now that the initial shock of their meeting was receding, Karen could acknowledge to herself that he was very attractive. He had a disturbing physical presence, and a disarming manner that made itself felt even under these less than favorable circumstances.

"Mr. Colter, uh, what's going on?" she asked him. "Why are you here?"

"The Brits hired me to get you people out. We're taking you to their embassy in Caracas."

"Venezuela?"

He winked. "You know another one?"

"But why?"

"Closest British embassy around here."

"Now, why are *you* doing this?"

He checked the magazine on his weapon, releasing the cartridge and then reloading it with a sharp metallic sound. "For money, honey."

"Oh, you're a mercenary."

"That's me," he said, leaning forward and raising his head to peer into the distance, "a summer soldier. I go anywhere the weather's warm and the pay is good." He straightened suddenly, alerted by some action in the courtyard and said urgently, "The trucks are here. You know what to do. Are you ready?"

"I'm ready," Karen said breathlessly.

"Good girl. Go, now. Run!"

Karen dashed back to the cellar supply room and ushered her band of ex-prisoners to the appointed spot.

"Where are we going?" Linda Folsom, the governor-general's assistant, asked Karen as they hurried through the labyrinth of passageways that led to the loading dock. All ten of the women had followed Karen's direction without objection, her bravery in speaking up to Colter apparently having convinced them that she should be in charge.

"To the loading dock," Karen replied. "Colter is going to meet us there."

"Is that his name, Colter?"

"Yes. He's an American."

"I gathered that," Linda said crisply. She was British, and her father was a government official. "Is that Yank supposed to be rescuing us?"

"Yes, he has some other men with him, too."

"Well, I must say," Linda observed breathlessly as they rounded a corner, "he seems perfectly capable of doing it by himself. And as for me, I'd follow him anywhere, into or out of a civil war."

This was such an unexpected statement for Linda to make under the circumstances that Karen stopped short, causing the other woman to crash into her.

"What do you mean?"

Linda made a face. "Don't be dense. Surely you noticed that the man is gorgeous."

"I did, but at first I was a little more concerned about what side he was on."

Their conversation came to an end as they approached the dock, a large flat area like an airplane hangar with a huge roll-up garage door at the back. Supplies and deliveries were received at this point, and Colter evidently planned on taking them out of the building through the spacious rear exit.

They were joined shortly by the men, who looked as if they had not fared quite as well as their female counterparts. Some were cut and bruised, as if they had been physically abused, and one of the security guards was supporting his bandaged arm. Karen and Linda exchanged glances. They didn't want to think what might have happened if Colter and his men hadn't shown up when they did. And it was far from over; they still had to get away.

During the next minute or so, Colter's eight men assembled at the loading dock from all parts of the building. They were dressed in khakis, T-shirts, camouflage pants, denim vests—a motley assortment of clothing—but uniformly, they carried Israeli Uzi submachine guns, the most efficient assault weapon in their deadly business. They fell into line behind Colter as he appeared from Karen's left and ran to the steel door. He held his gun down at his side, reducing the kick, and shot off the lock holding the door in place. Then, slinging his rifle over his shoulder, he threw up the door to reveal a trio of military transports waiting for them to board.

Everything seemed to be moving at the speed of light. The hostages ran to the trucks as Colter and two other men directed them, separating them into three groups for boarding purposes. Colter stretched out his arm and caught Karen as she ran past him.

"You're going with me," he said. "Get into the third truck."

Karen obeyed, looking back at Linda, who was heading for the first one. There was no time to object, Karen realized as she ducked under the canvas flap and took her place on one of the side benches. She didn't mind, anyway; Colter's confidence was contagious. Already she felt safe with him.

An armed man rode with the driver in each transport, and the two other mercenaries jumped into an accompanying jeep. Colter vaulted into Karen's truck at the last possible second, grabbing a hand pull just inside the back flap, and the little caravan careened wildly down the access lane and into the street.

Everything had been done in the space of a minute, with the efficiency of long practice. The band of hired soldiers probably did this sort of thing all the time. But Karen didn't. She found that her hands were trembling so badly she had to clasp them between her knees to keep them still.

"Got the shakes?" Colter asked, looking down at her.

Karen nodded, ashamed that he'd noticed.

"Don't worry, it'll pass," he said, with more sympathy in his tone than she would have expected. He wasn't inured to the physical effects of fear, then. Perhaps he had even felt them himself. But then she looked at the set of his broad shoulders as he stared out the back of the truck, the way he held his weapon as if it were an extension of his body, and she doubted it.

Suddenly he began to curse under his breath. He levered his gun into his hands and yelled, "Hit the deck, everybody. We've got company."

Karen flung herself to the floor, crossing her arms over her head. The moving truck was rocked by a series of explosions. Colter knelt and, steadying his weapon on his upraised knee, fired several rounds from his position at the rear. Karen could hear what sounded like little bombs going off around them; someone was lobbing grenades at the transport. The noise was deafening and the smell of cordite choking, overpowering.

Through it all the driver roared on and even seemed to pick up speed, taking the turns through the narrow downtown streets at breakneck pace. Karen could only assume that reinforcements had arrived and the rebels were making a final effort to recover their fleeing hostages.

A charge went off right behind them, and Colter turned and threw himself down, seizing Karen and sheltering her under him. She was conscious of a second flash of light, followed by a thunderous detonation, but was more aware of the man who lay on top of her, pinning her to the metal floor of the transport with his body. He was heavy, but not uncomfortably so, and once again she felt protected, even though she knew that anything hitting him would probably injure her as well. Her face was crushed against his chest, and she inhaled the clean male smell of him, detectable through the odors of sweat on his skin and the starch in his shirt. She could feel his heart beating under her ear, and its deep, steady thud was comforting. She noticed that it was not racing, as hers was. She wondered what it would take to get it pumping wildly. World War III, maybe. Or the right woman. Then all at once she was ashamed of herself for having frivolous thoughts at such a time, and she closed her eyes willing them to stop.

The firing from outside fell off dramatically, and Colter sat up. Karen scurried away from him as soon as he released her and huddled against the curved wall of the truck.

He leaned forward, concerned, and put a large hand on her shoulder.

"Are you all right?" he asked.

Karen nodded mutely, more shaken by his recent closeness than the rebel attack.

"You sure? You jumped up like you were on fire."

Karen looked away, disturbed by the unintentional accuracy of his analogy. She wondered wildly if the confinement in the cellar, followed by the theatrical rescue, was unseating her reason. She had been fantasizing about a man whose only thought was to save her life. He would have done the same for anyone else on the truck, and she knew it.

"I'm fine," she murmured, and he stood, satisfied. He made his way back to the door and then looked around at the rest of his passengers. Some were mute with shock, others weeping openly. He alone seemed unaffected; it was another day's work to him.

Karen waited for the onslaught to resume, but nothing happened, and the truck plummeted on toward its destination. She hoped the worst was over.

Colter crooked his finger at Karen, and she rose unsteadily. When she reached him, he put his arm up behind her, sheltering them from view, and spoke to her in a low tone.

"Do you have any psychological training?" he asked. His eyes, the color of Karen's aquamarine birthstone, searched her face.

"I, uh, no," Karen replied, thinking it an odd question for him to ask.

He nodded resignedly. "It was just a hunch. I thought you might, from the way you took charge back at the Government House. These people are pretty shaken up, and we're going to have to hold them together until I can get them where they're supposed to go."

She liked the way he spoke of it as a cooperative effort. "I'll do what I can," she said.

She grabbed for a handhold as the truck hit a pothole and pitched her forward. Colter put an arm around her and steadied her against his side. She had an overwhelming temptation to relax into his embrace, let him take care of everything. But she had promised to help him, and this wasn't the way to go about it. She straightened and eyed him alertly.

"The situation isn't good," he said shortly. "I saw one of the jeeps get hit, and I think we've got some injured people in another truck. We're taking you to a ship waiting in the Ascension harbor. It's supposed to be outfitted with trained staff and medical supplies, but it will be an overnight trip to Caracas. We've got to keep the injured, and anybody who's on the verge of losing it mentally, going long enough to get them to a hospital there."

"Can't we leave them at the hospital here?" Karen asked. "Surely the Almerian authorities will cooperate; the rebels were acting on their own." She glanced over her shoulder at the rest of the passengers; some of them were taking an interest in her conversation, clearly wondering what she was saying to the mercenary.

Colter shook his head. "The government here is too unstable, and the rebels are everywhere. We have to sneak you out on a tuna boat because the locals didn't want to risk an international incident at their airport. I can't vouch for the safety of any of these people if we leave them in Almeria. I'm being paid to get them to Venezuela, and that's what I'm going to do. Now are you with me?"

"Of course," Karen whispered, her dark eyes locked with his pale ones.

He curled his right hand into a fist and tapped her on the chin with it.

"Good girl," he said again, and she wondered why such a casual salutation from an obviously distracted man should mean so much to her.

The truck bumped to a stop, and Colter jumped down from its open back while it was still moving. Karen was the first of the hostages to get out; he reached up and put his hands on either side of her waist, lifting her to the ground.

They were at the harbor, and another time Karen would have been able to appreciate the beauty of the warm tropical evening. The stars were out, glittering against the blue velvet expanse of sky. A full moon hung above Sangre de Cristo Bay, illuminating the sea below with the iridescent light of a Chinese lantern. All the little boats bobbed at anchor, the water slapping against their hulls with the rhythmic motion of the waves, as a salt wind blew in from the ocean, stirring Karen's hair. It was a soft, lovely night.

Colter and his men hustled the hostages onto the boat as quickly as they could move. Karen noticed Colter turning from side to side as she went up the gangway, and she realized he was on the lookout for the harbor police. She saw two men with stretchers come down from the boat to pick up the injured, and she was glad she had made it through unscathed.

But it wasn't finished yet. They could still be stopped on the way out, and she tried not to think about their tenuous situation as she went below deck with the others. They were gathered in the dining room by the medical staff, who handed out tea and sandwiches with unflappable British calm. She couldn't see the boat depart from the dock, but she felt its motion as it left the slip and sailed out into the bay. She knew that Colter and the other mercenaries had remained on deck, and she guessed they had stayed above to deal with any trouble that might arise.

Karen was reunited with Linda, and the two women spent the next several hours working with the medical personnel, a doctor and two nurses, performing any service that didn't require professional training. They unwrapped bandages and washed utensils, fetched and carried as the wounded were tended. Three of the mercenaries had been shot, and one of the government workers had suffered a heart attack. In addition, several of the male hostages had sustained injuries during their confinement, so there was plenty to do.

And when Karen wasn't with the nurses, she was talking to the shock victims: the mail clerk who couldn't stop crying and the security guard with the bad arm who kept insisting that they were all going to die, despite repeated assurances to the contrary.

By the time she took a break it was close to midnight, and their vessel was far out to sea. She sat down on a cot next to Linda and accepted a cup of tea from the younger of the nurses, an English rose with vivid red hair who called everybody "sweeting."

"You'd better not let your handsome friend catch sight of 'sweeting' there, or he might just emigrate to Britain," Linda said dryly as Karen took off one of her shoes and rubbed her foot.

"What friend?" Karen asked confusedly. She was so tired she could hardly follow the conversation.

"Our savior, dearie, the big blonde with the big gun. By the way, where is he?"

"I don't know. I haven't seen any of them since we boarded."

"You don't suppose they've jumped ship and left us to fend for ourselves?" Linda asked in a stage whisper.

"Don't be silly. They're being paid to take us to Venezuela, and I don't think they can collect unless they deliver us in person." Karen took a sip of tea and glanced at Linda. "Do you think you'll go back to England now?"

"I suppose I shall have to," Linda replied, sighing, "though I can't say I'm looking forward to facing my stepmother over the breakfast table every morning. Father got me the job on Almeria to take me away from her, but he might be in difficulties now with all of this, so I should think everything will be rather uncertain for a while. What will you do?"

"Stay with my sister in New Jersey, I guess."

"Isn't that near New York?"

"Yes, right across the river, on the east coast."

"I would love to see New York. I hear it's unforgettable."

"That's one way of putting it."

"Is it true that everyone gets mugged there?"

Karen laughed. "Where did you get that idea?"

"I read the American newspapers," Linda replied airily.

The older nurse stopped in front of them and said, "Ladies, you may take a shower if you like. We've rigged a hand-held job in the head just down the hall, and there are fresh clothes on a stand outside the door."

"Ooh, lovely," Linda said, standing up. "I could certainly do with a good wash. Do you mind if I go first?"

"Fine with me," Karen replied. She could hardly move. She took a ten-minute nap while Linda was gone, and then revived enough to stumble down to the tiny metal-appointed bathroom. The soap was some fragrant, hand-milled British variety, and there didn't appear to be any shampoo, so she washed her hair with it, too. After she dried off, she dropped her ruined outfit into the steel wastebasket provided and dressed in the proffered clothes, which turned out to be a pair of seaman's baggies and a loose cotton blouse. She didn't want to consider the picture she made as she emerged with a wet head, wearing her borrowed togs, which fit her like a pair of boxing gloves.

Karen made her way back to the dining room and asked the nurse who had suggested her shower if she could go up on deck.

"I still have cabin fever from that basement," she explained. "I would love to get a breath of fresh air."

"I don't see why not—we're too far out now for any trouble," the nurse said. "But I'd better check."

She returned shortly and told Karen that she could go up if she felt like it. Most of the other passengers were sleeping on the cots and air mattresses the crew had provided. Karen felt rejuvenated in her clean skin and clean clothes, and walked past them briskly, eager to escape the confines of the lower level.

Out on deck the air was chilly, and a stiff breeze whipped her oversize shirt around her body. The boat was old. The warped floorboards beneath her feet creaked as she walked, and through the dated glass screen she could see the pilot leaning on his wheel and checking his instruments. She seemed to be alone. Everybody was probably too exhausted from the ordeal to feel like taking a stroll. Above her was the tower where the lookout scouted for frolicking porpoise, indicating a school of tuna below them. Karen went to the polished wooden railing and leaned over it, letting the fresh wind blow her hair back from her face. She stood there for a long time. She was out of Almeria. She was safe and on her way to freedom. She had never felt so good.

"Cigarette?" said a masculine voice behind her.

She turned to find Colter with his back to the water, his elbows propped against the railing, offering her a pack of Camels.

She shook her head.

He lit up and said, "Great outfit. You look like Nellie Forbush in *South Pacific*."

Karen glanced down at herself. "Anything would have been an improvement over what I was wearing."

"Oh, I don't know," he said, exhaling a stream of smoke. "I kind of thought that little beige skirt you had on was cute."

"It was no longer beige by the time I took it off," Karen said dryly.

"You did very well in there," he told her seriously, tilting his head as he examined her. "I know you were as tired and drained as anybody else, but you pitched right in and worked side by side with the nurses."

Karen looked at him. His deep voice seemed almost disembodied. In the faint light all she could see was the pale eyes and the flash of teeth in his tanned face. "How do you know?" she asked.

"I was watching you."

"You were? I didn't see you."

"But I saw you. You must be beat; you didn't sit down once. Why did you work so hard?"

"You asked me to," she answered simply.

There was a silence, during which the only sound they could hear was the froth of waves breaking against the bow of the ship. Finally Colter said, "So why aren't you passed out below deck with the others?"

"I did take a short nap, but now I feel keyed up, alert. I don't think I could sleep."

He nodded. "It affects some people that way."

"What does?"

"Danger. The adrenaline will keep pumping for a while. You'll need a few days to settle down."

Karen shivered suddenly as a salty gust flattened her shirt against her, and Colter said, "You're cold. Do you want to go below?"

"Oh, no," she replied. "That cellar was so hot and stuffy, and it seemed like we were trapped in there for a year. This is wonderful, really."

"Then let me get you something," he said, straightening up from the railing.

"Don't go to any trouble," Karen began, but he held up his hand.

"No trouble," he said. "Just stay right where you are."

Karen did as he said, closing her eyes, content to wait for his return. He was back in no time, handing her a light denim jacket that, judging from its size and the tobacco scent clinging to it, had to be his. She put it on, and the sleeves cascaded to her hips.

"You'd better grow if you want to fit the clothes around here," he observed. "That looks almost as good as the sailor suit you're wearing."

"It's warm," she said, rolling up the sleeves. "Where did you get it?"

"I brought a pack with me," he explained.

"I shouldn't keep you up," Karen said apologetically. "Don't you want to get some sleep yourself?"

"Oh, I don't sleep much," he said vaguely. "Don't seem to need it." He drew on the cigarette he held until the tip glowed. "And I'd always rather talk to a pretty girl."

"Will you go home for a rest now?" Karen asked him.

"I'll go home until they call me," he replied flatly.

"Where is home?"

"Anastasia Island. It's right off the coast of Saint Augustine, Florida," he said. He finished his cigarette and threw the butt overboard.

"Do you have family there?" she asked.

"No," he said shortly. "I have no family anywhere."

He was answering her questions directly, but with a noticeable lack of enthusiasm. Karen surmised that she was moving into a sensitive area and dropped the subject.

"Did those guys mistreat you?" he suddenly asked in a hard tone.

It was a moment before she realized that he was talking about the Almerian revolutionaries.

"No," she answered truthfully. "We barely saw them. The guards stayed outside the door."

"Some of the men weren't so lucky," he said bluntly.

"I saw that they were injured. The doctor didn't seem to be too worried, though. I don't think they were hurt badly."

"Not as bad as some I've seen," he said grimly. "They're all alive."

"Three of your team were shot, too," Karen said.

"That's different—it's part of the job, part of the chance you take. You people at the Government House were helpless victims."

Karen didn't know how to respond to that. She burrowed deeper into his jacket as he leaned forward to close the lapels over her neck. He bent his head abruptly and then started to chuckle.

"What is it?" she asked uncomfortably.

"What did you do to your hair? It smells like after-shave lotion," he said, chuckling.

"All they had to wash with was some lavender shaving soap, and they didn't have any shampoo, so..."

"I see," he said grinning. "I'm just relieved to hear that you don't shave."

"I'm glad you think it's so funny," she retorted, offended.

"Come and sit down," he said, extending his hand. "There are some deck chairs over here and a blanket."

Karen's fingers were swallowed up in his large callused palm as he led her to a seat and dropped into the ancient wooden lounge next to it. He unfolded a striped woolen blanket from the back of his chair and spread it over both of them.

"Better?" he said.

"Mm-hmm," she replied, snuggling into the well-worn softness of the lap robe and stretching out her legs.

"I was surprised to see this stuff here," he said. "This isn't exactly a cruise ship."

"I imagine even Portuguese fishermen like to take a little nap on deck now and then."

"I guess." He leaned back and folded his arms on his chest, turning his head to look at her. "So," he said. "What the hell was a nice New Jersey girl doing on that sun-blasted rock in the middle of the West Indies? You look like you should be teaching kindergarten in Bergen County." He dug in his pocket for another cigarette and lit it.

"I came to Almeria with my husband five years ago, for his job," Karen explained.

Colter froze in the act of lifting his cigarette to his lips. His eyes traveled to her bare left hand, dimly visible in the light from the deck lantern behind them.

"You're married?" he said.

"Divorced."

His hand resumed its motion. "So why were you still in Ascension?"

"I stayed on after my ex-husband was transferred. I liked my job and saw no reason to give it up, and I had my apartment and my friends."

"Your parents are dead?"

He asked the question as though he already knew the answer.

"Yes. I have a sister, but she's married and has her own family. I didn't want to intrude."

"So you stuck it out on your own, huh?" he said. "You must be a loner."

"Like you?" Karen suggested.

He didn't answer. She saw the bright arc his cigarette made as he tossed it away.

"Steven?"

She saw his profile move in her direction. "'Steven?'" he said.

"Isn't that your name?" she asked, confused.

He shrugged. "Everybody calls me Colter, sometimes Steve. No one has called me Steven since—" He stopped abruptly.

"Since?" she prompted.

"I was a kid," he finished gruffly. "A long time ago."

"Do you mind if I do?"

"Why?"

"Well, you look like a Steven to me. And I don't want to call you what everyone else does. I want to be different."

"You already are," he said huskily.

"Steven," she said firmly.

"Yes?" he said brightly, like a contestant on a quiz show.

She giggled. "I want to ask you something."

"Ask away."

Karen hesitated. She was intensely curious about how he'd gotten into his line of work, but she'd already seen how he resisted personal questions. So she attacked the problem philosophically, saying, "Isn't it difficult to risk your life all the time?"

"Not if you haven't much to lose," he replied promptly.

His answer, stated in that flat, matter-of-fact tone, chilled her. She could tell that his fatalism wasn't a pose, but a reflection of deep inner conviction. She had never heard such resignation in a man's voice.

"But surely you want to live?" she whispered.

"Well, I don't want to die," he answered reasonably, but it was too late to negate the impression he'd already created. A warning signal went off in the most primitive part of her brain: this man was trouble. But with the contrary instincts that had frustrated her parents and driven her poor husband to distraction, she was intrigued rather than frightened.

"Did you live in the U.S. until you got married?" Colter asked her, breaking the silence.

"Yes, with an aunt, my mother's sister," she answered. Karen went on, filling him in about her background. She found that it was remarkably easy to talk to him, despite their unorthodox meeting and current unsettled circumstances. Or maybe that *was* the reason conversation was so relaxed. Stripped of the artificiality of social convention and still elated by her recent rescue, she told Colter things she would be embarrassed to recall in the morning. And in the deepest part of the night, suspended in time on the vast ocean, he listened. He was a good listener. He seemed content to smoke and stare up at the bowl of stars suspended overhead, asking an occasional quiet question. In a powerful, unspoken way Karen found his presence comforting, and when toward dawn she finally drifted into sleep, she was completely comfortable and unafraid for the first time in a week.

When the ship docked in Caracas, she was jolted awake. The lap robe fell to the floor as she stood. Sometime during the night Colter had left it folded carefully around her, tucked under her chin, and he'd added his fatigue jacket to combat the predawn chill. Wearing one of his garments and carrying the other, Karen went in search of him, but he was nowhere to be found.

The first thing she saw as the crew scurried through the docking procedure was the crowd of reporters waiting to meet the boat. She went below, where Linda seized her as she rounded the corner toward the dining room.

"Where on earth have you been?" Linda whispered. "You were gone all night."

"I fell asleep in a deck chair."

"You fell asleep in a deck chair. Well, it may have escaped your notice, milady, but we are *not* arriving in Hamilton, Bermuda, and the Queen Mother's equerry is not waiting to greet us. There is, however, a screaming mob of press people intending to pounce the minute we disembark."

"I saw them. What are we going to do?"

"I know what I'm going to do. The embassy is sending over an escort to get us to a hotel in Caracas, and I will attach myself to them like the tail on Lady Astor's horse. I suggest you do the same."

Linda had just finished speaking when the embassy people arrived. Two impeccably dressed Englishmen advised the group that there were cars waiting to take them into Caracas. They would be housed at the Hotel Miramar as guests of Her Majesty's government. A formal statement would be issued that day, and a press conference held in the afternoon. They expressed deep regret for the "inconvenience" the refugees had suffered and hoped that they would be comfortable in their new accommodations.

"I had bloody well better be comfortable, after all this," Linda muttered to Karen. "Hang on—I want to see if one of them knows my father. I might be able to wangle a little something—one never can tell."

Karen stood in the middle of the bedraggled group and wondered where Colter was. She hadn't seen any of the mercenaries since she'd awakened. She was attempting to comb her hair with her fingers when Linda returned, wearing a secretive smile.

"What are you up to?" Karen asked knowingly.

Linda handed her a laminated card. "An embassy chit," she said. "Good at the hotel for food, clothing, whatever you like. Have a ball."

"You mean I just show this, and any purchase will be charged to the embassy account?"

"Right you are. Better than American Express. Who needs money, I say."

"Did you hear from your father?"

"Oh, yes. He says stiff upper lip and all that. Something tells me my next job will be around the corner from his office in Berkely Street."

They were ushered up onto the deck of the boat into warm weather and a bright morning, then herded down the gangway toward the waiting vehicles.

The reporters attacked as soon as they caught sight of the hostages. Karen turned her face away as they shouted questions and tried to shove microphones at anyone who passed. It was like running a gauntlet. She and Linda, along with two of the other women, collapsed into the back seat of a stretch limousine bearing the embassy seal, gasping for breath. The driver took off almost before the doors had closed behind them.

Karen's first sight of downtown Caracas was a blur of old buildings and shiny new shops, narrow streets thronged with traffic, and dark handsome people bearing the marks of both Indian ancestry and the later Spanish settlement. They bypassed the impressive front entrance of the hotel, where more reporters were waiting, and pulled up to the service door at the back.

"Good Lord, what a ghastly experience," Linda said. "No wonder everyone hates the press. How on earth did they find out where we were and where we were going?"

"Who knows?" Karen answered. "They always do."

They were led through the kitchen and up the service passage to the second floor, which had apparently been cleared for them.

"I must arrive this way again," Linda said, as they waited in a conference chamber at the end of the corridor to be assigned their rooms. "It always takes so long to register in a foreign hotel."

Finally they were given their keys, and a warning that if they wandered about the premises they would be easy targets for the press. She and Linda took adjoining rooms, and Karen collapsed on the bed as soon as she had fastened the lock and pulled the shades to shut out the blinding equatorial sunlight.

Her room, like the rest of the hotel, was ostentatiously overdecorated. The curtains and the spread on her bed were a cabbage-rose chintz, the red of which matched the wall-to-wall carpeting and the tasseled lamp shades. A gold and crystal chandelier overhead complemented a gold-flecked fleur-de-lis wallpaper, and she could see that the adjacent bathroom carried out the gold and red motif, with gold fixtures on the sink and tub and deep red plush towels. She expected Lily Langtry and Edward the Seventh to walk in at any moment and supposed that the bill presented to the British embassy would reflect the Regency decor.

Her telephone rang, and she didn't know whether to answer it. But if it were a reporter, she could always hang up.

"Hello?" she said.

"My word," Linda's voice exclaimed, "what do you think of this place? A bit much, isn't it?"

"I guess it's nice, if you like such an ornate style."

"Darling, it's as dated as the Dave Clark Five. I'm sure it hasn't been renovated since Jack the Ripper was on the prowl. Did you order from room service?"

"I will later. I feel kind of tired. I couldn't sleep last night, and I think I'll take a nap. Do you know when we're going to be flying out of here?"

"They're supposed to come around and take ticket orders, ship us all back where we came from on the earliest plane. I was just told that many of the rebels are still at large, and the Government House has been closed indefinitely. I guess returning to Almeria will be out of the question for a while, maybe permanently."

Karen thought about that for a moment. It was difficult to realize that everything was changed: her home for the past five years, her job, her life.

"Karen, you there?" Linda said.

"Yes. Look, I'm going to sign off and get some rest. I'll call you later, okay?"

"Fine. Bye-bye."

"Goodbye."

Karen hung up the phone and lay back on the bed, limp with exhaustion. She fell asleep in minutes. When she woke up, late afternoon sun was seeping through the shades and slanting across her bed.

There were two slips of paper under her door. They were cables, one from her sister and one from Ian, expressing concern about her captivity and relief that she was all right. Wire services had carried the news of the rescue, and Grace said her story was on television constantly.

Karen smiled to herself as she put the telegrams on the dressing table. This was the closest she would ever come to celebrity.

There was a knock at her door.

"Who is it?" she called.

"Delivery for you, *señorita*," an accented voice said in English.

Karen opened the door to a uniformed bellboy who presented her with a huge wicker basket of pastel gladioli. The thing was almost bigger than she was.

"Are you sure this is for me?" she asked the boy, who deposited the flowers on the carved writing desk in her room. He peeled off the yellow cellophane wrapping to expose the dewy blooms, then stood back to admire the effect.

"Oh, yes," the boy told her. "Señorita Walsh from the Almerian group, the order to our florist was very clear." He handed her a small white card and made for the door.

"Wait, oh, I haven't any money," she said, dismayed.

"*De nada, señorita,* I already get," the boy said mysteriously and left.

Karen looked at the card, wondering what the bellboy "already got."

"Thanks for your help," she read. "I'd like to take you to dinner to show my appreciation. I'll be by for you at eight." It was signed "Colter."

Karen stared at the bold masculine handwriting, thinking that the delivery boy's remark was now explained. Colter had tipped him in advance, which accounted for his solicitousness with the flowers, and now the mercenary was going to arrive for her in three hours.

She had nothing to wear.

Chapter 2

Karen bolted into the corridor, pausing a moment to look up and down, but the lavishly appointed hallway was empty. She almost tripped over a gilt curio stand as she hurried to Linda's door and knocked loudly.

"Linda, are you in there? Open up, it's Karen."

Linda flung open the door with a flourish, and then stared at Karen as the other woman flew past her and stopped, wide-eyed, in the middle of the room.

"What is it?" Linda asked. "Nuclear war?"

"I have a date in three hours," Karen said breathlessly.

"With whom?" Linda demanded. "That embassy person seems very nice, but he *is* old enough to be your grandfather."

"With Steve Colter."

"The American who rescued us?" Linda said, instantly alert. "Where is he?" She eyed Karen as if she were concealing him in her shoe.

"I don't know where he is. He sent flowers to my room and said he would be by to pick me up at eight. What am I going to do?"

"Well, the first thing you're going to do is change out of those dreadful rags. You look like one of the pickpocket waifs in *Oliver Twist*."

"That's the problem. This is all I have."

"You mean you haven't been downstairs? There's a lovely boutique and salon on the mezzanine."

For the first time Karen noticed that Linda's blond hair was freshly frosted and perfectly coiffed, her nails were done, and she was wearing a chic navy sheath, a definite post-captivity purchase. "I spent the afternoon sleeping," Karen said.

"Darling, who sleeps? I can see that my work is cut out for me with you. Come along, and bring that plastic golden goose I gave you. It's time for a little shopping spree." She took Karen by the hand and led her into the hall.

"Do you think any reporters will bother us?" Karen asked as they descended in the thickly carpeted elevator. Samba music came from an overhead loudspeaker as Linda replied, "They tried with me today, and I beat them off with a stick. I don't think they'll be back. They're probably all at dinner, anyway."

Karen grinned suddenly as a thought struck her. "I just realized that a short time ago we were afraid of being shot at any minute, and now our biggest problem is buying me a dress."

"A sign of good mental health—not to worry. We're recovering from an unspeakable experience, and we need a distraction. Several of them, in fact. We'll get you shoes, and a bag, and some makeup, too."

They remembered Linda at the Miramar Boutique. Salesladies descended like locusts as they entered the shop, and Linda started issuing orders in staccato Spanish before Karen could open her mouth. Karen was whisked off to a mirrored booth while Linda went through the racks like a tornado, flinging silks and wool crepes and polished cottons about as the boutique employees tried to keep up with her. A tiny clerk named Maria arrived at the drawn curtain outside Karen's cubicle with an armful of garments and said, in hesitant English, "Your friend say to try these, *señorita*."

Karen looked at the price tags, which were marked in bolivares, pounds, and dollars, and almost fainted. The news was bad in all three currencies.

She cleared her throat. "Maria," she said calmly, "would you ask my friend to come and speak to me, please?"

"Certainly, *señorita*." Seconds later Linda's head poked through the curtain.

"What is it?" she said impatiently. "I'm busy."

"Linda, do you know how much these clothes cost?"

"Of course, silly, I just bought mine here a few hours ago."

"Linda, these prices are outrageous. This blouse, for example, is two hundred dollars, or fifteen hundred bolivares, whichever makes the more staggering impression."

"And a very good value, too; that's fine quality silk."

"Linda, I can't charge this stuff to your embassy. It's robbery!"

Linda sniffed. "Don't be absurd, the government can afford it. Do you know the kind of taxes we pay at home?"

"That's no excuse for taking such obscene advantage."

Linda fixed her with a frosty "we of the upper classes don't discuss money" stare. "Do you want to look smashing, or not?"

"Yes, but . . ."

Linda held up a manicured hand. "But me no buts. You have two and one-half hours left; now get cracking."

She disappeared, and Karen sighed, thinking that Linda's long history of nannies and lawn parties and public schools had left an indelible impression. Growing up in New Jersey just didn't compare. Karen would always worry about the cost of everything, while Linda considered it déclassé to refer to it.

"Here you go," Linda announced, shoving a black silk jersey dress through the curtained partition that separated them. "Just the thing. I'd like to catch his expression when he sees you in that. What size shoe do you wear?"

"Six and a half, American."

"God knows what that means here; you'll just have to try them on," Linda muttered and hurried off again.

The silk jersey dress was stunning. It clung to Karen's curves in all the right places, with an overskirt that flared at the hips and a deep scooped neckline that showed off her light summer tan. One glance, and Karen knew that she had to have it.

She walked out of the cubicle and turned in front of the three-way mirror on the floor. The salespeople murmured appreciatively.

"What did I tell you?" Linda said triumphantly behind her. "Now for the shoes. Put these on."

Linda handed her a pair of black peau de soie sandals with three-inch heels.

"I don't know," Karen said doubtfully, looking at them.

Linda sighed dramatically. "What is the matter with you?" she said irritably. "You can't be worried about dwarfing him; the man is the size of a great sequoia. If I had your legs, I'd go jogging in shoes like those."

"I doubt it," Karen said dryly. "I just think they're impractical."

"Of course they're impractical—that's the whole idea." She put her hands on Karen's shoulders and turned her around. "Look," she said. "When was the last time you had a dinner engagement with such a gorgeous, fascinating man?"

Karen didn't have to think long. "Never."

Linda extended her hands, palms up, in an I-rest-my-case gesture. "Then why are we having this conversation? If he'd asked me to dinner, I wouldn't be standing about nattering, frittering away precious time—that I can tell you. But, unfortunately, he didn't send *me* flowers, or invite *me* out, and I will probably spend the evening doing the *Times* crossword puzzle and watching reruns of 'The Avengers' dubbed in Spanish. Now will you *please* stop trying my rapidly dwindling patience and *take* the damned shoes?"

"Okay," Karen said, laughing.

"Good, now that's settled. On to the undies and the makeup."

Linda supervised purchases for another hour until they had Karen outfitted from head to toe. As the clerk was ringing up the shocking bill, Linda appeared, carrying a pair of beige cotton twill slacks with a tan silk blouse and a pair of espadrilles.

"What are those?" Karen asked fearfully.

"Well, darling, you don't propose to wear that black tango number back home on the plane, do you? The pilot will have a heart attack and miss the runway, and you'll end up in the marshlands."

"The Meadowlands, Linda, but I get the idea. Just throw that stuff on the counter; I won't even look at the tags."

"You're learning," Linda replied, satisfied.

They left with several large bags stuffed with goodies, and as they lurched back to the elevator, Linda noticed that the beauty salon was still open. Karen was grateful that there wasn't time for her to get her hair done, but Linda did manage to slip inside and wheedle a bottle of nail polish out of the manicurist. It was obvious that she had also hit the salon hard earlier in the day; the manicurist followed her into the hall and waved merrily as they got onto the elevator.

"Charming girl," Linda commented as they rose to the second floor, this time accompanied by a Venezuelan businessman and a bossa nova band on the intercom. "I did have a bit of a communications problem with her, though. All I wanted was a bottle of rosewood nail polish, one such as a mute could buy at Harrods in thirty seconds, but this afternoon she kept coming up with these flaming reds, totally inappropriate for my coloring. I don't think subtlety is their long suit around here."

The elevator doors slid open soundlessly, and they bustled into Karen's room.

"Now you just hop into the bath," Linda instructed, "and Mother will set out all your things neat and tidy. Too bad we don't have those wonderful American rollers that you heat up; they give you such lovely curls in, and for, ten minutes."

"I never set my hair," Karen said as she undressed. "It's too heavy, and it just pulls out all the curl."

"Yes, indeed, that must be a terrible problem," Linda replied sarcastically. "Speaking as one who is practically bald, I can give you very little sympathy, I'm afraid."

Linda busied herself unpacking their purchases as Karen took a shower and emerged, dripping, a few minutes later. The new clothes were set out, valet style, on the bed, and the shoes lined up next to each other like tin soldiers on the floor.

"Now into those duds, and Bob's your uncle," Linda said, picking up the phone. "I'll order up some tea to my room. Shopping always makes me parched. With the service in this place it should arrive long after you're gone."

Karen slipped the expensive garments on, loving the feel of the rich material next to her skin. She bent and fastened the straps of the shoes around her ankles and then straightened, smoothing the dress over her hips as she did so.

"Now isn't that a dainty dish to set before the king," Linda said with relish, watching her. "Or the Yank, in this case." She rubbed her palms together, chortling. "Now sit in this chair, my darling, and we'll put the finishing touches on the chocolate soufflé."

"You make me sound like a dessert," Karen said, giggling, as she sat at the marble vanity table in the bathroom.

"You look edible in that outfit, and unless I mistake my American adventurers, he'll think so, too."

Linda brushed Karen's black hair as Karen applied liner and mascara to her dark brown eyes and lipstick to her full mouth. Then Linda did Karen's nails with the recently acquired polish, a Venezuelan brand named "Tentacion" in a shade called "Rojo Prohibido" (Forbidden Red). At last they realized it was ten minutes to eight, and Karen didn't have any perfume.

"Forget it," Karen said. "I'll do without it."

Linda was horrified. "You can't see a heavy-duty number like Colter and not wear any scent. It would be like leaving off your...skirt."

"Not quite, Linda."

"Stay right there," she said to Karen as if the latter were about to take off for parts unknown. "I'll be back in a jiffy."

She returned in seconds with an ornate bottle equipped with a glass atomizer. "I bought it this afternoon," she said, displaying her treasure. "Eight hundred bolivares an ounce. Couldn't resist it."

It seemed like Linda couldn't resist much. She sprayed the air, and Karen sniffed appreciatively.

"What's it called?" Karen asked.

"Encantadora," Linda replied. "Enchantress. Don't you love it?"

"It's very nice."

"Hold out your hands," Linda said.

Karen obeyed, and she sprayed the back of Karen's wrists, then behind her knees.

"Won't do to wear too much," she said to Karen, putting down the bottle. "Can't have you smelling like a Covent Garden tart." She glanced at the clock on the nightstand and grabbed her purse. "I must fly, don't want to be here when he arrives. Though I would love to see him out of those tacky fatigues."

"I wonder what he looks like in a dinner jacket," Karen said.

"No, darling, out of the fatigues and out of everything, if you take my meaning," Linda drawled.

Karen laughed. "Linda, you're awful."

"Yes, I know." She hugged Karen briefly. "I haven't had so much fun since I was at school. You look a perfect peach in that outfit. I only hope he doesn't pass out at your feet when he sees you." She went to the hall and called back as she left, "Tell me all about it in the morning."

Once Karen was left alone in her room, she began to fidget. She opened the empty closet and threw all the wrappers and bags from her purchases onto the floor, slamming the door closed behind them. Out of sight, out of mind. She slipped her new lipstick and other cosmetics into the black embroidered envelope purse she was carrying and checked her hair in the mirror. It fell in a loose shining arc to her shoulders, and she patted it routinely. She was as attractive as she could make herself under such impromptu conditions, but she still felt the quivering of butterflies in her stomach, the attack of nerves that always presaged an important event in her life. She hadn't realized until this moment how very much she wanted Steve Colter to respond to her. She'd never felt such an instant, total attraction to any other man, and the feeling both exhilarated and frightened her.

The knock came at her door at two minutes after eight.

"Who is it?" Karen called. Her voice sounded funny, trembly and uncertain. Annoyed, she resolved to steady it.

"Colter," came the response. By contrast, he sounded cool and very sure of himself.

She opened the door, and he froze on the threshold of her room, staring at her.

"Wow," he finally said, clearing his throat. "That's quite a transformation."

"I could say the same of you," Karen replied, pleased that he appreciated her efforts.

He was dressed in an eggshell linen jacket with an off-white shirt, dark slacks, and a striped silk tie. His thick blond hair had been recently cut and styled, and he was clean-shaven, shorn of the light beard he'd had when they met. His blue eyes held hers with unwavering interest, and she felt as if he were seeing her for the first time.

"The dress is a knockout," he said, his gaze traveling downward from her face, over her body to her legs, and then back up again. Her skin grew warm; she felt as if he'd undressed her.

"It isn't too much?" she asked worriedly.

"I'd like to see a little less of it," he replied, grinning, and her flush intensified, spreading over her cheeks and neck.

"I mean that I didn't know where we were going, and I was afraid I'd be overdressed." Then she realized that this was worse, and she closed her eyes, mortified.

When she opened them again, he was leaning against the wall, laughing silently.

"You look perfect," he said, putting her out of her misery. He straightened and extended his arm, and she slipped her hand through it.

"How did you know where to find me?" Karen asked as she locked her door behind her and put the key in her purse.

"I have a contact at the embassy. He told me where they'd taken you," he replied.

"Where are you staying?" she asked.

"At a friend's apartment," he answered vaguely.

"I guess you come to Caracas often enough that you know people in town," Karen suggested.

"I pass through now and again," he said.

His evasiveness was maddening, but nothing short of a rude inquisition would elicit more direct information, so Karen changed the subject.

"Is the restaurant near here?" she asked as they emerged from the elevator into the rococo lobby, filled with scrolled mirrors and heavily upholstered brocade furniture.

"Just a walk across the square," he said.

"What do you call that decorating style?" Karen said, nodding backward as they passed through the revolving door into the warm, late summer night.

"Reign of Terror?" he said, casting her a sidelong glance.

Karen laughed. "I don't know, but I can't get used to it."

"I can see why," he said. "You probably feel like Boris Karloff is going to jump out of a closet and hand you a severed head."

"It does sort of look like one of those overdone mansions in horror movies," she said, smiling. "Have you ever been to the Miramar before?"

"Nah," he said dismissively. "It's a tourist trap."

"Oh."

They were walking across a Spanish-style square with a splashing fountain in the middle, surrounded by adobe brick buildings crenellated along the top and fronted by Moorish arches.

"The Caribbean Sea is right back there," Colter said, pointing to the rear of the hotel they'd just left.

"I can smell it," Karen said, inhaling deeply.

"The settlers used to post lookouts on the roofs facing the water," he added, indicating the open spaces between the battlements. "There was a lot of piracy in those days; the Caribbean coast of Venezuela was the famous Spanish Main."

They were approaching a softly lit restaurant, and as they passed through the ivy-covered front door, Karen read above it, in fancy script, La Casa Americana.

"Does the name mean we can get American food here?" she asked Colter hopefully.

"No, they called it that because they serve only Tasmanian food," he replied soberly.

She looked at him, and he smiled.

"Would you tease a starving woman?" she asked him archly.

"Never. You can get American, Spanish, or Carib Indian dishes. They serve all three."

"Oh, good."

The maître d' greeted Colter by name and led them up a flight of steps to a rooftop terrace overlooking the ocean. They were seated at a table for two next to a half wall made of native fieldstone. It was decorated with clusters of bougainvillea, the showy pink and white flowers giving off a heady, heavenly fragrance. The waves soughed against the sand below them, and Karen could see the froth of whitecaps in the distance. Above them the night sky was slightly overcast, with a three-quarter moon hiding behind a cover of shifting, diaphanous clouds.

"What a lovely spot," Karen said as Colter held her chair and she sat in it.

"It's the prettiest sight in Caracas, for my money," Colter replied. He sat across from her and signaled the steward to come to their table.

"What would you like to drink?" he asked.

"I don't know... whatever you're having," Karen replied.

"Are you sure?" he asked. "I'm having a double margarita."

"Oh, no, in that case..." She stopped, nonplussed.

"Double margarita for me, and white wine for the lady," he said in Spanish to the waiter. He turned to Karen. "Is that all right?"

"Fine," Karen said, relieved.

"Most of the staff here understand English," Colter said to her, "but I find you get better service if you speak to them in Spanish." He shrugged. "They hate the tourists."

"I can't blame them," Karen said, sighing.

A waiter approached them and lit the hurricane lamp sitting in the middle of their table, then stood at attention, waiting to take their order.

"I don't see a menu," Karen whispered to Colter, leaning across the table.

He grinned. "There isn't one. You just ask for what you want, and they tell you if they can make it."

"That's original."

"How about a prawn cocktail to start?" he asked her.

"Prawn?" she said doubtfully.

"They're like shrimp, but they gravitate to warmer waters."

"Okay."

He ordered and the waiter scribbled.

"*Y dos melones con carne,*" Colter added. "That's like a honeydew, hollowed out with a meat filling," he explained to Karen. "It's good—you'll like it."

She nodded.

"And for the main course?" Colter asked.

"Scallops?" she said wishfully.

"*Ondas con migas de pan,*" Colter told the waiter. "Breaded scallops, sautéed in butter," he said to Karen.

"Wonderful," she said.

Colter ordered vegetables and a main dish for himself while Karen studied the view, and, covertly, him. He was very fluent in Spanish, conversing with the waiter like a native, and she wondered how many other languages he could speak as well. For all his cosmopolitan air, there was a certain rootlessness about him that disturbed her; it was as if he worked at remaining aloof and uninvolved, in the world but not of it.

"So," he said, when the waiter left, "I guess you got off the boat okay this morning?"

"Yes, but I wandered where you were when I woke up and found you gone."

"I had things to take care of in town," he said, "and I knew the embassy people would look after you."

She wondered if the "things" he had to take care of involved collecting his fee for delivering the Almerians to Caracas. "I have your jacket and that other vest thing in my room," she said.

"Is that an invitation?" he asked lazily.

"No, I just meant to remind me to give them to you," she said hastily.

He let that pass, but his intense gaze scorched her, conveying a message he didn't have to send in words.

The steward arrived with their drinks. Colter took a bite of his lime slice, then licked the salt from the rim of his glass as he took a deep swallow of the liquor.

"Are you from Florida originally?" Karen asked brightly, taking a sip of her wine, desperate to distract him.

"I guess so," he replied.

That baffled her into silence, but she recovered momentarily and said, "Your parents lived in Florida, then?"

"I don't know where my parents lived, Karen. I was a foundling, and I was raised in an orphanage," he said flatly.

She stared at him, her throat closing. She could have cut out her tongue.

"I'm sorry," she finally managed to whisper. "I didn't know."

"Of course you didn't, and you needn't look so upset. It was a long time ago. I just thought I'd better tell you up front so we could skip the chitchat."

"The orphanage was in Florida?" she murmured.

"That's right. It was the Colter Street Children's Home in Crescent Beach, Florida, and the janitor who found me in the vestibule was named Steve. Now are there any further questions, or can we get by my tragic past and talk about something more interesting?''

Karen couldn't think of anything more interesting than his background, but it was obvious that he didn't want to discuss it. She was saved from having to reply by their waiter, who brought the prawn cocktails. Instead of the red sauce that usually garnished shrimp at home, a spicy mustard relish was served with the shellfish, and Karen found it delicious. She looked up from a bite of the delightful dish and found that Colter was watching her with obvious enjoyment.

"Was it the right choice?" he asked.

"Oh, yes, it's wonderful. What's in the sauce, do you know?"

He grinned. "I know, but I don't think I'd better tell. It's a Carib recipe and liable to shock you."

Karen chewed with somewhat less enthusiasm, and he chuckled.

"What do you mean?" she asked warily.

"Are you sure you want to hear?"

She stared at him balefully.

"All right. One of the main ingredients is clay."

Karen coughed and put down her fork. "Clay? As in dirt?"

"That's right, but take it easy. The Indians have been eating it for centuries, so I don't think it's going to poison you."

Karen pushed the crystal dish a little further away from her on the table. "You won't mind if I don't take that chance, will you?"

He shrugged. "Chicken."

Karen folded her arms on the table. "Steven Colter, you don't mean to sit there and tell me you think it's a good idea to consume *mud*."

"You thought it tasted fine until I told you what was in it."

"That's beside the point. It can't be healthful."

"I'm told the Indians around here live to be over one hundred," he said in reply.

The waiter came to clear, and Karen indicated that she was finished. When the melons arrived seconds later, she surveyed her portion cautiously and said, "Is there anything I should know about this before I eat it?"

"The filling is just chopped beef," Colter said, smiling. "Nothing that you wouldn't encounter in your average American hamburger."

"And the melon? Anything weird involved there?"

"Does it look like a honeydew?"

"Yes, but . . ."

"Does it smell like a honeydew?"

She sighed.

"Well," he said, spreading his hands, "you know the old expression; if it looks like a duck, and it quacks like a duck . . ."

"All right, all right," she muttered, taking a bite. It was, of course, delectable.

"Well? Any shooting pains? Nausea? Double vision?" Colter inquired.

"Very funny," Karen said darkly.

"I'll bet you were one of those kids who made your mother cut the crusts off sandwich bread and wouldn't eat tomatos unless the seeds were removed," he said, grinning.

"I am not a fussbudget," she said defensively. "Any normal, thinking person would object to swallowing stuff that should be part of an adobe hut."

He shook his head. "You can take the girl out of New Jersey, but you can't take . . ."

"Oh, shut up," Karen said, interrupting him.

They both glanced around as music began behind them. A guitarist accompanied a singer dressed in a long skirt and a colorful off-the-shoulder peasant blouse. She began a tune so laden with sorrow that, even though Karen couldn't quite understand her, it was clear the song was detailing a ruined love affair or an insurmountable loss of some kind.

"That isn't Spanish, but it sounds familiar," Karen whispered.

"Portuguese," he answered quietly. "If you listen closely, you can probably make out some of it."

The woman continued her song. Karen found the mournful notes so disturbing that she sat in silence for several seconds after the singer had finished and retired. The diners applauded politely.

"She's a fado singer," Colter clarified, when Karen met his glance. "Fado means 'fate.' They sing about the sorrows of a life ruled by relentless, remorseless destiny man can neither control nor avoid."

Karen shuddered. "No wonder she sounded so sad."

"Sad, but true," he said as the waiter took away the fruit and brought the main course.

"Do you believe that?" Karen asked him soberly. "That we're all in the grip of some predetermined fortune and have no power over our own lives?"

"Seems that way, doesn't it?" he asked her.

She shook her head. "I'll never accept that. And I must say it seems a strange philosophy for you to espouse. Aren't you the man who rescued me from a bunch of terrorists? Weren't you trying to intervene in my fate then?"

"I was trying to collect a paycheck," he said harshly. "Don't confuse the issue."

"But why do you do it at all?" Karen asked, unable to stop herself.

"What?"

"The mercenary work. Why do you do it?"

"Got to do something," he answered evenly. "I'm in the habit of eating."

"But surely you could find another job, a man like you."

They were staring at each other across the dimly lit table, their food, and their surroundings, forgotten.

"What do you mean," he said curtly, "a man like me. You don't even know me."

"I can tell that you're intelligent and capable; you don't have to..."

"Sell myself to the highest bidder?" he suggested.

"I didn't say that," Karen backtracked hastily.

"But you thought it. Maybe I like it, did you consider that? Maybe I like seeing the world, being in a different place every couple of months. Can you really picture me sitting in an office in a pin-striped suit peering at a calculator all day?''

"But you wouldn't have to do that," Karen protested. "There are lots of jobs you could take without risking your life all the time for money."

"That's what bothers you, isn't it?" he said quietly. "That I risk my life, not for a noble ideal or a country, but for money."

"You have no loyalties, no allegiance. If you fight, it should be for a cause other than yourself, shouldn't it?''

"If you say so. As for me, I'm the best cause I know," he answered.

He threw down his napkin and stood up. "Spare me the speech, I've heard it. Stargazers like you are always full of idealistic jargon. What do you know about anything, anyway? All your life you've had your parents, then your husband, and now your sister to hold your hand. Just let me live my way and you live yours." He turned and strode off the terrace, descending an exterior stairway that took him out of sight.

Karen sat frozen in abject misery, almost at the point of tears. How on earth had their lovely dinner degenerated into such an ugly scene? And when was she ever going to learn to keep her big mouth shut? He was perfectly correct; she had no right to badger him about his choices, and that knowledge did not make her feel any better.

She remained motionless, staring at the flickering candle inside the glass bell of the hurricane lamp, until the waiter came up to her and pointed to the exit.

"What is it?" she said, startled.

"Mr. Colter, he is down on the beach," he said in English, because she had spoken in that language. "Do you want me to show you?"

Karen hesitated, then nodded. The very least she owed Colter was an apology.

The waiter took her to a flight of stairs that led directly to the strand below the restaurant. Karen removed her shoes and crept onto the sand in her stocking feet, walking toward the shadowy outline of a man she could see in the distance.

Colter was leaning against the sea wall, smoking a cigarette and staring out at the ocean. He turned at her approach.

"I thought you had left," he said softly, watching her come closer.

"Steven, I'm sorry," she said hastily, before he could go on. "You're right. We just met, and your career is none of my business. In fact I should be grateful you've chosen your line of work; you probably saved my life back on Almeria. Please forgive me."

He waited so long to reply that she thought he was dismissing her, and she almost turned to leave. Then he said quietly, "You know, I didn't think you would go out with me tonight."

Karen stared at him. "What?"

She saw the lift and fall of his shoulders in the darkness. "I thought that when I got to your hotel there would be a message saying you were otherwise engaged or something. I was surprised when you answered your door and you were dressed and ready."

"Why?" she asked softly.

"Oh, we were sort of trapped together on the boat, and you were still scared and eager for company. But I figured once the worst was over you would take stock and realize that you didn't owe me a social occasion."

"I owe you my life, Steven," she said quietly. "So does everyone else who was held hostage in Government House."

"Is that why you came with me tonight?" he asked quietly. "Out of gratitude?"

"No, of course not," she said, shaking her head. "Why would you even think that?"

He lifted his hand expressively, and the cigarette he held made a fiery arc against the night sky. "You're a nice girl. It's been a long time since I spent an evening with a nice girl, as you may have gathered from my behavior tonight. In my line of work I don't get to meet too many of them."

"Who do you meet?" Karen whispered, taking a step closer to him.

He laughed shortly. "Good-timers, bar girls, hustlers of various types. The opposite side of my own coin, you might say. A lot of people are quick to make judgments. They regard men like me as little better than whores." He tossed his cigarette away. "Upstairs I thought you were one of the judges."

"Oh, Steven, no," she said, reaching out to him, and in the next instant she was in his arms.

He held her tightly against his shoulder for a few seconds, and over the washing of the surf behind them, she heard him say in her ear, "Karen, forget the way I sounded off at dinner. I didn't mean it. I was just..."

"Hurt?" she suggested, looking up at him.

He didn't reply, but she could read the answer in his face. He looked into her eyes for a long moment, then bent his head and kissed her.

His lips held a faint taste of salt from the margarita, and the bitter tinge of tobacco. They were firm and cool on hers. Strands of Karen's hair lifted and blew against his face as he pulled her closer, slipping one arm around her and drawing her against his body. His mouth took hers more hungrily as the embrace deepened, and Karen wound her arms about his neck, hanging on him while his tongue probed hers. She could feel the tension increase in his large frame.

Colter made an involuntary sound of pleasure as his free hand roamed down her back, past her waist, forcing her into the cradle of his hips. Karen gasped against his mouth and pulled back.

He released her instantly, turning to the side, not looking at her.

Neither of them spoke as he lit a cigarette. "I guess I got carried away," he finally muttered. "Do you want to go back to the terrace?"

Karen nodded, glad of an excuse to rejoin the other diners. It was dangerous to be alone with him. They went back toward the stairs, and she stumbled trying to walk in the damp sand. Without a word he took the shoes she was holding and put one in each of his pockets, then scooped her up and carried her to the landing.

"Thank you," she murmured as he deposited her on the bottom step, still a little startled by the abrupt change in transportation.

He gave her the shoes and then took her hand when she was ready, leading her back to their table.

There was only one other couple still in the restaurant, and their waiter was hovering anxiously, wondering what had become of them.

"You can take this away," Colter said to him as they resumed their seats, waving his hand at their abandoned plates. He looked at Karen. "Would you like anything else?"

"Just coffee," she said.

"Dos cafés," Colter told the waiter, and then settled back in his chair, his blue eyes searching Karen's face.

"I want to tell you something," he said.

"Yes?"

"You were right about my being able to do something else. I joined the army at sixteen, and they trained me in electronics. I tried it but couldn't stay; it was just too boring sitting at an instrument panel hour after hour. So when I left the service I started to hire myself out for the other skills I'd learned there, and I've been doing that ever since."

"Why are you saying this now?" Karen asked quietly.

"I blew up because you touched a nerve," he answered. "I don't like being reminded how people like you see me."

"Now *you're* making generalizations," Karen said. "I know I sounded like I was criticizing you, but I was really just trying to understand." She stopped for a moment and then added, "I don't know how you cope with the isolation. You're all alone in the world."

He shrugged. "Why not? I don't need anybody."

Karen sighed. "I'm afraid I do. I'm always in touch with my sister, and even though Ian and I are divorced, we still write and try to see each other when we can. I just can't let go of the people I care for. I never could. I'm sure Ian loved me, but it was more like a father's love, and when he saw that it was best, he was able to let me go.''

Colter turned his head. "I wouldn't know about that," he said bluntly. "Nobody ever loved me that much."

Karen didn't know what to say. He was such a curious combination, seemingly aloof yet given to sudden offhand remarks that were oddly revealing. It kept her constantly off balance.

The coffee came, and they sat drinking it, intensely aware of each other and what had passed between them on the beach. Finally the restaurant was closing, and they got up to go. As they walked outside, Karen saw by the church tower clock across the square that it was after midnight.

"I didn't realize it was so late," she said. They were passing a lilac bush, and she paused to inhale the fragrance of the lush blooms.

"Time flies when you're fighting," he said dryly. He picked a purple cluster and tucked it behind her ear, arranging her hair to accommodate it.

"How do I look?" she asked, striking a pose.

"Like the heroine in a Bizet opera," he replied. "You know, with your coloring you could almost be Latin."

Karen shook her head. "Black Irish. The skin is the give-away. All my life I've wanted that lovely matt olive complexion that's supposed to go with dark eyes and dark hair, but what did I get instead? Irish linen. I burn in the sun and chap in the cold."

He chuckled. "Remind me not to bring you along on a camping trip."

"Camping? Oh, camping is my specialty. Contact dermatitis from the hard water and terminal poison ivy. I was the only Girl Scout who never went on the jamboree; the counselors refused to take me. My mother said the sensitive skin ran in my father's family."

Colter was grinning, swinging her hand in his as they walked along.

"Walsh is your maiden name, then?"

"Yes, I went back to it after my divorce."

"Well, at least you know what your real name is," he said as he pushed the door of the hotel open and she preceded him through it.

She stopped walking and looked up at him.

"Did you ever try to find your parents?" she asked quietly.

His jaw hardened. "No. They didn't want me, and as far as I'm concerned that's the end of it."

They ascended to the second floor and walked down the corridor, stopping outside Karen's door. There was a silence while they both tried to decide what to say.

"I'm never going to see you again, am I?" Karen finally whispered.

"Hey," he said, tipping her chin up with his forefinger, "never say never." He kissed her cheek lightly, then turned his head and captured her mouth with his.

This time he pressed her right from the start, pushing her back against the wall and enveloping her with his body. Lowering his head, he dragged his lips across her throat and tongued the hollow between her breasts. Karen arched into him, sinking her fingers in his hair and closing her eyes. She was certain she should stop him, but was unwilling to end the delicious sensation of his hands and mouth on her skin. When he kissed her again, more urgently, she swayed on her feet, clinging to him for support as her defenses dissolved.

"Let's go inside," he said huskily, his breath fanning her face. He took her key from her hand.

"No," she replied, with surprising strength.

"Come on," he urged in a low tone, caressing her. "You want me."

She did, but at the instant that she almost gave in she had a sudden image of every other woman he had said the same thing to, women who'd responded to his undeniable allure in the way she was responding now. She knew that he was a womanizer, forced by his inclination as well as his life-style to take his pleasure where he found it. And she couldn't join a list of forgotten conquests. She needed him to remember her, if only because she was the one who got away.

"I want you," she said quietly, "but I'm not going to bed with you."

He stared down at her, still breathing hard, his hair mussed by her hands, his gaze heated, incandescent. Then, when he realized she meant it, he sighed heavily and leaned against the wall, closing his eyes.

"I don't believe this," he said. "Remember me? I'm the guy that saved you."

Karen smiled. "As I recall, I already thanked you for that."

He shook his head, half laughing. "This can't be happening," he said. "Women are crazy about me."

Karen didn't doubt it. She reached up and touched his cheek, and he opened his eyes.

"Can I give you my sister's address and phone number?" she asked softly.

"Why?" he inquired, studying her, his expression sober now.

"In case you ever feel like you want to talk to somebody."

" 'Talk?' " he asked.

"Talk."

She took a slip of paper from her purse and wrote down the information. He folded the sheet in half and stuck it into his breast pocket.

"I have to tell you that, 'talking' isn't the reason I usually take a girl's number," he said dryly.

"I know that," Karen replied. "Make an exception in my case." She felt the sting of tears behind her eyes and was suddenly afraid she was going to cry. "Steven, please take care of yourself."

"I always do."

"Who else was it who used to call you Steven?" she asked, delaying his departure. She didn't want to let him go.

"One of the nuns at the foundling home. She was…good to me."

"Do you ever see her now?"

He shook his head once. "She's dead."

Karen put her arms around him and laid her head on his shoulder. "I'll be thinking about you," she murmured.

He tucked his hand under her hair, lifting it off her neck. "Don't think about me, Karen. Go back to New Jersey and get married and have a couple of kids. Years from now I'll be that guy you kissed on a beach someplace. You probably won't even remember my name."

"I'll remember," she whispered.

He took hold of her arms and held her off, disengaging her embrace. "Good night, sweetheart," he said, kissing her forehead.

"Goodbye, Steven." Karen was blinking rapidly, seeing him through a mist of unshed tears.

"Goodbye." She watched him walk to the elevator, which responded instantly when he pressed the button. He saluted as he stepped through the doors, and she didn't go into her room until he was out of sight.

Karen sat on the edge of her bed and tried to swallow the lump in her throat. Had she done the right thing? She told herself that she had, but already she was regretting her loss.

It was several seconds before she noticed that the red call light on her phone was blinking. She picked up the receiver and asked for the message.

Her plane ticket and traveling papers were being held for her at the desk. She asked for them to be sent up to her room and had just hung up the phone when someone tapped at her door.

"Darling, it's me," Linda's voice said. "May I come in?"

Karen got up and opened the door. Linda breezed past her in an elaborate lace peignoir set and high-heeled lounge slippers. She was carrying a tray holding a teapot and a plate covered by a cloth napkin.

"So how was the big date?" she asked, setting down her burden on the end table. "Tell Mother all about it."

Karen faced her.

"Oh dear," Linda said, observing her friend's expression. "He really got to you, didn't he?"

"I guess so."

"What happened?"

"We ate dinner, and he ordered me some fish dish with clay in it, and then we had a fight, and he kissed me on the beach, and then he wanted to sleep with me but I said no."

Linda nodded with relish. "Well," she said briskly. "I knew he wouldn't be dull. Was that 'clay,' darling, or is my hearing failing?"

"Yeah, but it's not worth going into," Karen replied wearily.

Linda poured herself a cup of tea and settled comfortably on the bed. "Why did you say no? To sleeping with him, I mean. Just as a matter of academic interest, you understand."

"He's so alone. It seemed like it would add to that loneliness if I became another sexual statistic in his life. Does that make sense?"

"Don't ask me," Linda said dismissively. "You don't make sense half the time, but I love you, anyway. What was the fight about?"

"I asked why he was a mercenary when there were so many other things he could do."

"My, that was impertinent. What did he say?"

"He told me to mind my own business."

"Quite right, too. Advice I never take, by the way, but well worth repeating." She removed the cloth from the plate of biscuits and held one out to Karen. "These are very good. They're something called *dulcettas*, which as near as I can make out means 'sweeties.' I've been eating them all evening while watching a Brazilian soap opera on television. I didn't even know they had soap operas in Brazil—did you? How about some tea?"

"Okay, thanks."

A bellboy knocked and delivered Karen's envelope as Linda was pouring her drink. She was booked on the noon plane back to Newark, nonstop, the next day.

"British efficiency," Linda said when she saw what Karen had received. "I got mine this evening. They're certainly giving us the boot in short order, aren't they?"

"I guess they figure that the sooner we're home, the sooner all of this will be forgotten."

"I picked up a little tidbit about your friend Colter after you left tonight," Linda said mysteriously as she handed Karen her cup.

Karen stared at her. "What?"

Linda batted her eyelashes.

"Linda, tell me."

"Well, you know that man from the embassy, the friend of my father's?"

"Yes?" Karen said impatiently.

"He told me that Colter is a specialist in the type of rescue work he did for us, going into siege situations and breaking hostages out. Apparently he's called in on that sort of thing constantly, and it's about all he does. As you can imagine with the state of the world these days, he's in great demand."

"He never told me that," Karen said, almost to herself. "Even when I questioned his ethics, he didn't say a word about it. He led me to believe he was just a soldier of fortune—you know, a guy who would do anything if the price were right."

"Well, darling, I'm sure he's well paid. I doubt if he's running a charity bazaar for the antiterrorist set."

"Still, it's not the same. He's really an expert at getting people out of trouble, isn't he?"

Linda studied her closely and sighed. "Better drink that cuppa, Karen; this could be worse than I thought. This may, indeed, be *love*, the big one, with a capital *L*."

"Oh, stop making fun of me," Karen said impatiently, "and listen. If what you're telling me is the truth, I can't understand why he would deliberately let me think the worst of him."

"Testing you, perhaps?" Linda asked.

"Maybe," Karen replied thoughtfully. "You could be right. He's a complex man."

"That," Linda said, sitting up and setting her cup in its saucer, "I gathered."

"I get the impression he's afraid to want things, or people, too much, because that would make him vulnerable."

"You figured out a lot about him in one evening," Linda observed.

"He's not as clever as he thinks. He gives some things away if you watch for them. And I was watching. Besides, it was two evenings. I spent the night on the boat with him, too."

Linda's green eyes widened. "So that's where you were! And you told me you fell asleep on deck. Naughty girl."

"I did fall asleep. When I woke up in the morning, he was gone. You see what I mean? We had kind of an intense conversation, and I think it took him by surprise, made him uncomfortable. He ran from it then, but later he asked me out. He was drawn to me, but not enough to overcome his past experiences. He believes that if he remains aloof, he'll never have to let down his guard."

"He's right, isn't he?"

"Sometimes you have to take that chance."

"No, you don't," Linda replied simply. "You can choose to be alone."

"That's what he's done," Karen said. "Or maybe it wasn't a choice at first. He was an orphan and raised in a home. That might be why he's so wary. I volunteered to give him my address, something I've never done before, because I knew he wouldn't ask for it. And at the same time I could tell he really liked me, but he wasn't willing to get that involved."

"Sounds like you might have gotten to him, too," Linda said quietly. "That's a pretty defensive reaction for a man who doesn't care."

Karen shook her head sadly. "He won't call me. I just know it."

Linda stood and put her cup down on the tray. "I would love to continue this fascinating conversation," she said, "but I have to be up at a beastly hour to catch my plane." She went to the desk in the corner of the room and picked up a blank notepad. "This is where you can reach me, both in town and at our place in Sussex. Ring up any time, or come and visit. I shall miss you. I doubt if things in Almeria will ever return to what they were, so we probably won't get together on the job again. Promise me you'll keep in touch, now."

"I promise," Karen said dutifully.

Linda kissed the air next to her cheek. "I must run, good night." She paused in the doorway to look back at Karen. "Darling, I know he's damnably attractive, but you'd best forget him. He sounds like walking heartbreak to me."

Karen didn't answer.

Linda sighed. "Well, off to the wars. I'll have to whip these people into shape early if I'm to make my flight."

Karen smiled to herself. Linda would make her flight. With her imperious voice and "Rule Britannia" manner, she always got the staff scrambling to perform for her in hotels and restaurants. Karen, on the other hand, stood in lines, lost her luggage and could never get a sandwich sent to her room before she fell asleep waiting for it.

"Goodbye." Linda waved and pulled the door closed behind her.

"Goodbye," Karen murmured. It was her second farewell of the evening. She undressed slowly, thinking about Colter and her conversation with Linda.

She knew Linda was right about him, but it would be difficult to put him out of her mind.

Karen climbed into bed and left a wake-up call at the desk. She had thought she wouldn't be able to sleep, but the events of the past few days caught up with her. She fell into a deep, dreamless slumber that wasn't broken until the phone rang in the morning.

She dressed quickly and sent a cable to her sister telling her when she would arrive at Newark. There was no message from Colter. She had a late breakfast in the hotel dining room and then left by taxi for the airport.

In a couple of hours she was on her way home.

Chapter 3

Karen's sister Grace was waiting at the arrival gate in Newark, her face a mask of anxiety. When she saw Karen making her way through the crush of people, she surged forward and threw her arms around her younger sibling.

"Oh, Karen, are you all right?" she said worriedly. "Ken and I were just frantic when we heard the news." She drew back and peered at Karen closely, biting her lower lip.

"I'm fine, Grace; just let's get out of here," Karen replied, glancing around her furtively. "I really don't feel like running into a reporter who wants an interview with the returning native. You never can tell who might have gotten wind of my flight schedule."

"Of course," Grace said hurriedly, almost running to keep up with Karen's brisk pace. "But what about your things?" She glanced toward the crowd waiting for the luggage return.

"There are no things, Grace. Just what's on my back, and in this tote. I didn't even have my passport, the British embassy in Caracas arranged my travel visa."

"Oh, you poor dear," Grace said, overcome again. "Ken and I watched it every day on TV. I couldn't believe the story when I first heard it. I was at the supermarket, and when I came out and got in the car, the report was on the radio. Then on the five o'clock news there was a film of it, and later they started interrupting the programming to give special bulletins.''

"Grace," Karen said patiently, "I don't mean to be rude, but I really don't want to talk about it. I lived it for five days, and I'd rather forget it, okay?''

"Fine, fine," Grace said hastily. "I understand. We're just glad you're home safe and sound.''

Since her marriage Grace had a tendency to use the editorial "we," including her husband and two children in her opinions.

"Where are the kids?" Karen asked, remembering them. Tommy, five, and Mary, three, were conspicuously absent.

"Oh, Tom's in school and I got a sitter for Mary. I figured you might not need her Big Bird imitations today.''

"Thanks," Karen said, "I appreciate it. You know how much I love her, but a peaceful ride back would be nice.''

"I made up the spare room," Grace said as they passed through the outer doors and headed for the short-term parking lot. "You feel free to stay just as long as you want. Do you have any plans about what you're going to do?''

"Well," Karen said dryly, "it's pretty obvious that I'm out of a job.''

"You don't think you'll go back to Almeria?''

"I'm a little afraid to go back," Karen answered frankly. "Even if this crisis is settled, the unrest is going to keep on indefinitely. And if they ask me to return, working at Government House would keep me right in the thick of it.''

"Thank God," Grace said, relieved. "I was afraid you would be determined to stay on there.''

"Not after the past week," Karen said, subdued. "America looks pretty good to me right now. I think I'll try for a job around here, then get my own place.''

"What about your apartment in Ascension?" Grace asked. She was scanning the numbers on the metal fence, looking for the section where she'd parked her car.

"I don't know. I guess I'll close it up and ask my land-lady to send me my things, the clothes and personal stuff, anyway. The furniture isn't worth transporting; she can sell it."

"This way," Grace said, spotting her station wagon. They walked in silence for a while until she went on, "Karen, I know you said you didn't want to discuss the kidnapping, but if you just answer one question, I'll forget it, okay?"

"Okay. What's the question?"

"You weren't hurt, were you? I mean, physically?"

"No, not at all," Karen replied reassuringly. "Some of the men were, but they left the women alone."

"Gallantry?" Grace asked sarcastically.

"Who knows?" Karen answered wearily. "But I can tell you the worst that happened to me was that I got a terrible scare."

"That makes me feel a lot better," Grace said, sighing. They reached her car and she unlocked the passenger door for Karen. "Still, it must have been awful." Then, realizing that she was still pursuing a subject she had promised to drop, she fell silent and walked around her car, getting in on her side.

Karen slid into her seat and buckled her seat belt, look-ing around at the familiar green New Jersey turnpike signs, feeling as though she had just returned from another world.

"Now, there's no rush about getting your own place," Grace said, starting the car and pulling out of her space. "Take all the time you want. We have plenty of room, and Ken and the kids are looking forward to having you in the house."

Karen almost winced. She knew that Grace was sincere, but the role of dependent relative was not one Karen in-tended to play for long. At the moment she had no choice, but her first order of business would be to get out on her own.

"What about money?" Grace asked. "Do you have any? We can lend you some if it's necessary." She pulled up to the lot monitor's booth and paid her parking fee.

"That's thoughtful of you, but I still have that bank account at Federal Trust in Manhattan. My share of the money Dad left us is in it."

"It's a blessing you never moved it to Almeria, or you might never have seen it again. Do you have any real idea of what's going on there now?" She steered the station wagon onto the access road for the turnpike.

"Nobody seems to know. The rebels have been arrested, but the group supporting them is still acting up, and nothing is settled. Believe me, Grace, I don't care. By the time we were rescued all I wanted concerning Almeria was to be out of it."

"Who rescued you?" Grace asked curiously. "I heard something about it on the news, but the reporter wasn't very clear. They weren't police, were they, or government agents?"

"They were a team of mercenaries," Karen said. "They were paid to go into Government House and get us out."

"They must have been good at it," Grace observed, gliding up to the northbound entrance for the turnpike and taking her ticket from the machine. "The report said it was all over in fifteen minutes."

"Yes," Karen replied evenly. "They were very good." She shifted in her seat and rolled down the window. "How does Tom like kindergarten?" she asked.

"He wasn't too keen on it at first, but he's getting used to it," Grace replied.

"I can't wait to see him," Karen said. "Does he still look like Aunt Elizabeth?"

Grace grinned. "More than ever. She'll never be dead as long as Tom is around to stare at me with those district-attorney eyes. I swear, sometimes I think she's come back in that little body to tell me to clean up my room and do my homework."

"I know what you mean," Karen sympathized. Grace's son resembled their aunt in an uncanny, almost supernatural fashion. It was difficult to look at him and completely dismiss the theory of reincarnation. "And how is Mary? Charming everybody at nursery school?"

"Sure," Grace said. "She's charming as long as she gets her way. Cross her and the charm fades very fast."

"She's only three, Grace."

Grace shook her head. "You indulge that girl too much."

"My godchild, after all."

Karen settled back in her seat and watched the exits pass in a blur of off-ramps and overpasses. Grace lived in the Passaic County suburb of Wayne in a development of ranch houses and split-levels, built twenty years earlier, when Wayne was still rural and the township mostly farmland. Now it was a crowded, bustling hodgepodge of shopping malls, professional offices and industrial complexes, and the house Grace and Ken had purchased when they were first married was worth four times what they'd paid for it. Ken worked as a chemist for a pharmaceutical company in one of the corporate parks, and their two children attended local schools. Grace was on the PTA and took exercise classes with her neighbors; Ken was a member of the Elks and played golf. They were the perfect nuclear family, and always made Karen feel as if she had traveled backward in time and landed on "Father Knows Best."

"It's been a while, huh?" Grace said.

Karen turned to look at her. "What?"

"It's been a long time since you passed through here."

Karen nodded. "It's busier than I remember it."

Grace grimaced. "It gets busier every day. Ken says if any more New York commuters relocate to this area he's going to write his congressman about moving Wall Street to North Jersey. It would save everybody a lot of traveling."

"Do you remember Alice Dunphy? Her parents had a farm just outside of Oakland. I wonder if it's still there."

"I doubt it. Probably ten colonials are sitting on it now."

"Her father used to say it was just forty-five minutes from Broadway, like the song."

Grace snorted. "That was never true. The only thing that's forty-five minutes from Broadway is the corner of Broadway and Thirty-third Street."

"I love New York," Karen sang softly, like the tourism advertisements, and Grace laughed.

Conversation flagged, and Karen put her head back against the headrest, closing her eyes and thinking about her forthcoming job search. She would get the Sunday papers with the full classified sections that weekend, and type up a résumé to be printed for distribution. As Grace drove she made her plans, unaware that her employment prospects would turn out to be much narrower than she had suspected.

In the weeks that followed, Karen discovered that getting a job was a problem. With no local references and little demand for a Spanish language translator in affluent suburbia, she sent out a lot of unanswered queries and made quite a few fruitless phone calls. She continued to respond to want ads, and finally got a written referral from the Almerian attaché, but the opportunities presenting themselves were still few. She came to see that her skills would be more in demand in an urban environment with a bilingual population, and she expanded her horizons to include cities like Paterson and Passaic. She resolved, regretfully, to include a car in her increasingly alarming budget calculations, and routinely sent résumés to people she had little hope of hearing from in return.

More than a month passed, and she was still unemployed. She helped Grace with the kids, read, took long walks, composed what she hoped were riveting cover letters, and meditated on the meaning of life. Nothing worked. She still couldn't forget Steven Colter.

One afternoon Grace came into the paneled rec room with the mail and handed Karen a letter.

"England," she said, indicating the postmark. "Must be from your friend Linda."

It was, and Karen put it in her jeans to read later, staring out at the lawn and the turning October trees.

"What's the word on the job search?" Grace asked, sitting down and glancing at her watch. She had to pick up Mary from the nursery school's morning session in twenty minutes.

"Discouraging," Karen replied. "I'm thinking of buying a pistol and holding some of these personnel people at gunpoint."

Grace smiled slightly. "I wouldn't adopt such drastic measures just yet." She paused thoughtfully and then said, "Karen, tell me if I'm being too nosy, but I get the definite impression that something is still wrong."

"Of course something is still wrong. I can't get a job."

Grace shook her head. "That's not what I mean." She twisted a lock of hair around her finger and went on cautiously. "Maybe you should see a counselor."

Karen stared at her. "What?"

"I've read about people having delayed reactions to these hostage situations," Grace added hastily, in a rush now to get it all out, "and I think maybe it would help you to talk to somebody, a professional who would know what to do."

"Grace, have you been raiding the local library, playing psychologist again?"

Grace's pale complexion turned pink. "I'm only trying to do what's best for you," she mumbled.

Karen got up and hugged her sister, then sat on the floor at her feet. "I know I haven't been my old self, Grace, and it's sweet that you're concerned about me. But the problem has nothing to do with my captivity in Almeria. It's not even the job situation, really, though I must admit that feeling I was accomplishing something would help to take my mind off it."

"Off what?" Grace said. She looked down at her with the dark eyes that were the mirror image of Karen's own, and their mother's.

"I met a man on Almeria."

"Oh," Grace said softly, nodding. "I see. Was he one of the government workers?"

"No."

"Then who? A native?"

Karen shook her head. "The leader of the team who rescued us. An American."

Grace studied her. "Well?"

Karen shrugged. "I haven't heard from him since I left."

"Does he have this address?"

Karen nodded. "I gave it to him."

Grace stood and walked to the sliding doors, rubbing at a finger mark on one of the glass panels with the tail of her shirt. "Did you think you would hear from him?"

"Not really," Karen sighed. "But I guess somewhere inside I must have been hoping, or I wouldn't be this disappointed."

Grace turned and faced her. "Do you want to tell me about it?"

While they went to get Mary, Karen filled Grace in on what had happened with Colter. Grace listened carefully, asking few questions. It wasn't until they had returned to the house and Mary had settled in front of the television to watch "Mr. Rogers' Neighborhood" that Grace asked, "Are you sure you want to get involved with a man like that?"

"A man like what?" Karen asked, looking up from the latest version of her résumé, which made her sound like a cross between Joan of Arc and Joan Lunden.

"Well, he must be about as far from Ian as anyone could possibly imagine," Grace said reasonably.

"Maybe that's a good thing," Karen responded. "Ian and I weren't exactly compatible, if you recall."

"But a man who traipses around the globe putting himself into dangerous situations all the time, a man who could be killed at any moment?" Grace said. "Why set yourself up for that?"

"It's a pull I've never felt before," Karen replied quietly. "There's just something about him."

"Oh, no," Grace said, holding up her hand. "Don't tell me. I know what this is. I remember all those wild boys you were always trying to 'help' before you settled down with Ian. This guy Colter is just an older version of Billy Sykes."

"I didn't settle down with Ian—I just settled. Into boredom. And Billy Sykes has nothing to do with this."

"Maybe not as an individual," Grace said, "but the pattern is still there. You always felt sorry for the lost and lonely ones. You were always going to change their lives. And all you ever got from it was trouble.''

"There wouldn't have been any trouble with Billy if Aunt Elizabeth had been reasonable. Reporting him to the juvenile authorities just put him on the wrong path, and it went downhill from there.''

"He would have wound up on that path anyway and finished in prison just like he did. And this Colter has all the Sykes trademarks: no family and no friends, combined with the good looks and that aloof personality you seem to find so irresistible.''

"He's not aloof. He's actually quite charming.''

"You know what I mean; personally aloof, hard to get close to, withdrawn. I don't know why that type fascinates you, Karen. Anyone else would have appreciated Ian and still been with him. He's really a good person.''

"I know he's a good person!'' Karen said heatedly. She would never be able to make her sister understand. Grace valued having a family above all else and thought anything was worth enduring to achieve that goal. Her husband Ken, who was also a good person and the proverbial "good provider'' their aunt had always recommended to them, put Karen to sleep. She could no more imagine being married to him than she could imagine still being married to Ian.

"I don't want to fight,'' Grace said, lowering her voice and glancing at her daughter, who had turned to look at them when their voices rose. "All I'm saying is that I don't think you should chase after this . . . whatever he is. Adventurer.''

"I'm not chasing after anybody,'' Karen said darkly, looking away.

"Probably because you don't know where to find him.''

"I know where he lives. Saint Augustine, Florida.''

"Oh, so you're planning to fly south for the winter?''

Karen shot her sister a disgusted look. "Is that supposed to be funny?''

"What's the problem? You don't think he's there, right?''

"I don't think he spends a lot of time at home, no.''

"So what are you going to do? Sit around here staring into space like a catatonic?"

"I have not been sitting around!" Karen protested, standing up abruptly and letting her papers slip to the floor. "You know very well I've been trying hard to find a job, and I'm sorry if I can't seem to get interested in all the suitable bachelors you've been parading through here during the past month. If I hear one more word about the stock market or insurance rates or municipal bond funds, I am going to throw a screaming fit at your next cocktail party and start pelting your neighbors with the hors d'oeuvres. Now leave me alone." She stormed up the stairs and slammed the door of the guest room behind her, perilously close to tears.

It wasn't long before Grace was tapping at the door. "Karen, let me in. Come on—I want to talk to you."

Karen got up resignedly and opened the door, going back to sit on the edge of the bed as Grace followed her inside.

"I'm sorry," Grace said. "The last thing you need right now is your sister giving you a bad time."

"It's all right," Karen replied. "It's just that I want you and Ken to see that arranging these little get-togethers to find me a husband is transparent, and embarrassing. I feel like the prize mare at a horse auction."

"We were only trying to help," Grace said in a small voice.

"I know, I know," Karen said. "You think that if I could find a suitable husband I wouldn't need a job or anything else. But Karen, I'm not like you. That didn't work for me with Ian, and it won't work for me now."

"But then what are you going to do?" Grace asked. "Employers aren't exactly lining up to engage your services."

"You noticed that," Karen said dryly. "I guess I'll keep trying, maybe go back to school for some further training. I'm not sure. But I'm certainly not going to rush into marriage to cure what ails me. I made that mistake once, and I will never do it again."

"All right," Grace said flatly. "No more parties, I promise. You're on your own. But if you need any help, just ask, okay?"

"I will. And thanks, Grace. I do know you mean well."

Grace nodded and left the room, pulling the door closed quietly behind her. Karen rolled over on the bed and stared at the ceiling for a while, then remembered Linda's letter and took it from her pocket, unfolding the scented pages to reveal the Englishwoman's patrician scrawl. It seemed that Linda was doing a good job of enlivening the Sussex countryside, and when Karen finished her letter, she was even more depressed than she had been after arguing with Grace. She felt sorry for herself for about five minutes, then dug in the drawer of her bedside stand for the list of job calls she still had to make. Preparing herself to deal with the blandishments of obstructionist secretaries, she lifted the receiver and dialed the first number.

Karen was sitting in the kitchen after breakfast several days later when the phone rang. Ken was at work, the kids were at school, and Grace was making a second pot of coffee at the counter, so Karen answered it.

"Hello?" she said absently, filling in the crossword puzzle on the back page of the newspaper.

"I'd like to speak with Miss Karen Walsh, please," a female voice said. Startled, Karen didn't respond for a second. The caller had an accent, and she couldn't place it immediately. Then she realized that the woman sounded like a relative of her father's who'd died when Karen was small; she had a brogue.

"This is Karen Walsh," she replied.

"Miss Walsh, this is Mrs. Schanley from Mercy Hospital in Belfast calling."

"Belfast, Ireland?" Karen said loudly. The line was crackling.

"Northern Ireland," came the crisp reply.

Karen's mind raced. Did her father have any long-lost family member who might have surfaced across the water and wanted her for some reason? She couldn't think of anybody.

"Yes, what is it?" she said. The line calmed down suddenly, and she could hear clearly.

"We've a patient here on the critical list. He's in a bad way and seems to have no relations, poor man. He's been in the intensive care unit since he was brought in several hours ago, and in cases like this we try to contact whoever the patient requests."

"Yes?" Karen whispered, closing her eyes.

"Well, just before he lost consciousness, he asked for you, miss."

"Me?" Karen said faintly.

"He said your name and told me your address was in his wallet, and so it was."

Karen's fingers tightened on the receiver. "Who is it?" she whispered.

"A Steven Colter, U.S. citizen, miss. Resident of Saint Augustine, Florida, by his papers." She pronounced the state Flo-ree-da.

"Is he... What's wrong with him?" Karen asked shakily.

"Gunshot wound to the chest. We had a bit of trouble hereabouts last night, and he was mixed up in it somehow."

Karen could guess the rest. "Did he say anything else?" she asked, swallowing.

"Yes, miss. Said you were to have his effects if he passed on." The woman's voice dropped an octave, took on a confidential note. "There doesn't seem to be anyone else, if you take my meaning."

"Is he dying?" Karen could barely get the words out.

Mrs. Schanley resumed her official tone. "I don't know as to that, miss; it would be for doctor to say. There was massive bleeding, according to my notes, but he's a young buck, isn't he, hale and strong."

"Yes," Karen agreed. Very strong, but in a moment of weakness he'd called for her.

"It would help if we had someone to consult about his case," the woman said gently. "He's right out of his head and may be that way for a good while."

"I'll get there as soon as I can," Karen said firmly, making an instant decision.

"Will you take responsibility?" Mrs. Schanley asked eagerly, anxious to dump her problem in Karen's lap.

"Yes, yes," Karen said impatiently. "I'll be on the next plane, and I'll sign anything you want."

"Just as you say, miss." Relief was evident in her delivery. "For my records," she added, "what is your relationship to Mr. Colter?"

Karen thought for a moment. "Friend," she said. Then she turned the newspaper she still held in one hand to find the blank margin. "What is your address there?"

"Mercy Hospital in Donegall Place. All the cabbies know it; you can come straight through from the airport or the quay."

"And what is your position at the hospital?" Karen asked, scribbling madly.

"Oh, beg pardon, didn't I say? I'm the administrative assistant here. You'll find me on the first floor, just forninst the admissions office."

Forninst? Must mean nearby, Karen thought. "Thank you, Mrs. Schanley, thank you very much. I'll be seeing you within a day or so."

They said their goodbyes, and as Karen hung up the phone, she caught sight of her sister, who was frozen with the unfilled coffeepot in her hand, the water running in the sink behind her.

"Please tell me that wasn't what it sounded like," Grace said.

"It's Steven. He's been hurt in Belfast, and I have to go to him."

"Now wait a minute," Grace said, reaching behind her to turn off the water. "Wait just a damn minute. You're not going anywhere."

"He doesn't have anybody else, Grace," Karen said, ripping off the corner of the newspaper page and putting the scrap into her pocket.

"For heaven's sake, Karen, he doesn't have *you* either. By your own admission you went out with him *once* in Caracas, and now you're ready to run off to Europe after him like some...camp follower. It's insane."

"I have to go," Karen said stubbornly, looking around for her purse.

"I knew it," Grace groaned. "I knew something like this would happen."

"Grace, if you start up with that Billy Sykes nonsense again, I swear I'll tie you to the stove."

"But Karen, Northern Ireland! The whole place ignites every night on the six o'clock news."

"Grace," Karen said briskly, "do us both a favor and stop watching the news." She was rifling through her purse, looking for her bankbook. "What time does the bank open? Nine o'clock? I have to get some traveler's checks."

"Are you going to use Dad's money for this trip?" Grace demanded.

"What do you suggest I use? Wampum? The New York account is all I have. I'll stop off at the bank on the way to the airport." She punched the buttons on the phone for information. "I have to book the next flight for Belfast."

Grace sank into a seat at the table, watching Karen. "This is a nightmare," she said. "You just left Almeria, and now you're going to Belfast. Doesn't this guy Colter ever hang out anyplace quiet?"

Karen put her hand over the mouthpiece and looked at her sister.

"Grace, he may be dying," she said quietly. "He thought he was, or he never would have asked for me. I know that." When the operator came on the line, she took her hand away and spoke into the phone.

Grace fell silent. She listened to Karen dialing the airline and making the flight arrangements, mentally shaking her head. Karen would never change. Her marriage to Ian, which Grace had hoped would tame her wildly romantic nature, only seemed to inflame it. She was now more determined than ever to chase an elusive dream, bound up in her mind with this injured mercenary who had so clearly captured her imagination.

"Well," Grace said as Karen hung up the phone, "I can see that, as usual, you're not going to listen to me."

"The flights to Aldergrove Airport outside Belfast don't run too frequently, and the connections are bad," Karen said, as if Grace hadn't spoken. "The fastest way to get there is to fly to Liverpool and then take the ferry across the Irish Sea."

"How very interesting," Grace said sarcastically. "Ken is going to lose his mind when he hears this."

"Then don't tell him," Karen replied.

"I think he'll notice your absence, don't you?" Grace said. "Where am I supposed to say you've gone?"

"Tell him I went to England to visit a friend," Karen said piously. "That's not a lie."

"Except you're not staying in England, and the friend isn't Linda."

"Details," Karen replied. "I have to get some clothes together. Where did I put that stuff that arrived last week from Almeria?"

"It's in the basement," Grace said, standing up. "Come on. I'll do the laundry so you can pack."

"You'll help me?" Karen said, brightening.

"I can't think of any way to stop you," her sister replied darkly.

They went down the stairs to the cellar, and by early that afternoon Karen was on a plane out of Kennedy in New York to Liverpool, England.

She slept during most of the five-hour flight and didn't see much of industrial Liverpool, about which she knew nothing except that the Beatles had originated there. In the autumn dusk it seemed to be a gray, grimy city, filled with working-class people and brick factories spewing black dust into the damp, chilly air. Karen took a cab directly from the airport to the waterfront, passing rows of long, low tenements where children played in the narrow streets or in the fenced, postage-stamp yards. Laundry lines flying multi-colored flags were strung from one house to the other like utility wires, and the factory wives gossiped over the barriers to their adjoining properties as they took in their wash. Karen looked around as they drove, taking it all in, fascinated with this glimpse of life in a town she had never seen before and probably never would see again.

The docks were crowded at the end of the business day, and she almost lost her way because, incredibly, she could barely understand the directions she was given. Although the people ostensibly spoke English, their accent was so thick it made her native tongue seem like a foreign language. She finally found signs saying: Belfast Ferry, Queue Up Here, and got in line behind a group of people waiting for the boat.

When the ropes were taken down and they could get on board, British policemen checked the papers of all the passengers very carefully, examining Karen's newly reissued American passport with particular interest. When they held her aside and let the other travelers go ahead, she knew that she was in for trouble.

"What's the problem?" she asked as one of the harbor policemen picked up a phone inside his little booth and made a call.

"Just making a security check, miss," he replied politely. "Not to worry."

"But why the delay? I'm going to visit a hospital patient in Belfast, and this is the last run of the day. Time is very important."

"Won't take a moment," he answered and then lowered his voice as he spoke into the phone.

Karen tapped her foot restlessly, staring out at the rolling, brackish water as the ferry's engines idled, waiting for the run it looked like she was going to miss.

The policeman hung up the phone and returned to her, handing back her passport and then touching his cap politely.

"There you go, miss," he said. "Sorry to have troubled you." He smiled slightly, looking into her eyes. He was young, his speech mercifully comprehensible, clipped and clear.

"What was all that about?" she asked, annoyed, as she stowed her passport in her purse.

"You're an American with an Irish surname," he said, shrugging.

"So?" she asked, bewildered.

He glanced around him, as if making sure he would not be overheard, and then answered quietly, "Let's just say that sometimes such people aren't crossing the water just to see the sights."

Karen stared at him for a long moment before she realized what he meant. They'd been checking to see if she had any terrorist connections.

The idea was so outrageous that she almost laughed, and then realized that to do so would be in bad taste. It was a serious matter and not entirely implausible; she'd read that antigovernment groups in Ulster frequently used women as couriers and that they had a following in the States.

"I see," she replied neutrally. "May I go now?"

"Step right for the lower level," he said, nodding. Karen followed his directive and was the last passenger to cross the makeshift gangway before it was removed. She felt the ferry's throttle open as the boat began to inch forward. When she looked around to pay her fare, she saw that someone came to take it after the trip was underway, as they did on the London buses. She fished in her bag for the British pounds she'd gotten for dollars at the airport, wondering what the passage was and hoping they didn't require the exact amount, as in New York. She was so ill prepared for this sudden trip that she hadn't even stopped to check the rate of exchange for the money. Karen couldn't believe anybody would cheat her. The British people were associated in her mind with wartime newsreels featuring Winston Churchill's bulwark integrity. She supposed there had to be a few criminals in the mix somewhere, but was confident she wouldn't run into any of them.

The ferry had an enclosed central mall on both levels, featuring rows of seats and glass windows allowing a view of the water all the way around. Encircling this middle portion was a promenade with a wooden deck and a railing that permitted those passengers who wished to remain outside to make the trip in the open air. Karen climbed to the top and hung over the railing, watching the English coastline vanish into the gathering dark behind her and letting the cool, damp breeze caress her face. She tried to remember that it was less than twelve hours since she'd received the call from Mrs. Schanley in Grace's kitchen, but the distance she had come made the passage of time meaningless. Fog rolled in, and she turned up the collar of her coat, blinking as the heavy dew settled on her lashes, obscuring her vision. Somewhere over the water the mist condensed even further, and when she arrived in Belfast, it was raining.

She would soon discover that in Belfast it was usually raining. She walked through the large open dockside building, which reminded her of an airplane hangar, carrying her single bag in one hand and her purse over her shoulder. There was a cab stand just outside the exit, which opened onto a cobbled street, the main thoroughfare for the shipyard district. Karen flagged a taxi, a Ford Cortina that sported a sign advertising Livery, and the cabbie jumped out, grabbing her bag before she had a chance to say a word. He stowed it in the boot of the car and then turned to face her, his face lined and weary, but his brown eyes intelligent, aware.

"And where would you be going, miss?" he asked. He had an accent like Mrs. Schanley's, just a touch different from the "Mr. Gallagher-Mr. Sheehan" brogue she associated with the Irish. His speech reminded her that his country was part of the United Kingdom, entirely separate now from the Republic, its neighbor to the South.

"Mercy Hospital, Donegall Place," she answered. "I hope it isn't far."

"Certainly not," he answered, opening the back door and holding it for her. "Get in."

Karen obeyed, and he took off almost before her feet were inside the car. She soon discovered why the Irish were frontline claimants for the dubious title of worst drivers in

Europe; he pulled in front of oncoming traffic and dodged lorries three times the size of his taxi with suicidal aplomb. She was cringing, hanging on to her seat with both hands, when he said, "You'd be an American, by the sound of you."

"Yes," she whispered as they shot across an intersection, barely missing a double decker bus. Its driver shook his fist and screamed epithets that they mercifully could not hear.

"And what's your business here?" he asked, glancing in the rearview mirror at her. The light at the next crossing changed as they approached it, and he jammed on the brakes, hurling Karen's purse onto the floor.

"I'm visiting someone in the hospital," she managed to say, scrabbling for her bag and praying for a quick end to her perilous journey.

"That's a terrible pity," he sympathized. "Is this your first time in the North?"

"Yes."

"Well, you should be ready for some fearful sights," he advised. "We'll be passing the roundabout in a bit. The post office there went up like a Jerry bomb just yesterday. They had a Tory dignitary visiting, I'm told, an M.P. who'd made quite a few killing speeches against the IRA. A bunch of provos took the station over and held him till some hired boyos broke him out. Couple of them got it, though; I saw the pictures on the telly." He pointed suddenly. "Look sharp—there you go. The coppers still have the lines up."

Karen looked where he pointed, her throat closing. This had to be where Steven was hurt. The rubble from a recent conflagration littered the street, and the area was roped off from pedestrian traffic, the entrance blocked by a police van. Even in the dark and the rain, she could see the aftermath of conflict in the scene.

"Not exactly like home, is it?" the cabbie asked dryly.

"We have our problems too," Karen answered quietly.

"Will you be staying the night?" he said as he pulled up to the hospital entrance.

"Yes."

"I'd mind where you go," he cautioned her. "This district is no place for a young lady the likes of you to be larking about at night."

Karen had no idea what "larking about" was, but she didn't think she'd be doing it. "Can you recommend a hotel?" she asked.

He thought about it as he shifted into neutral and the little car idled under him. "The Ulster Arms is a decent place," he said. "Not too dear, and respectable."

She liked the way he pronounced "decent," as if it were spelled "day cent." "Thanks for the advice," she said, getting out and handing him a fistful of bills. "Take your fare, and a tip for yourself."

"Meela murder," he groaned, "never tell a working man to set his own price. Did you not look at the meter?"

Karen did, but it was all in pounds and pence, the sum a mystery.

Seeing her confusion, he separated two bills from the rest and handed her the difference. "Good luck to you, miss," he said fervently. "I've a mind you'll be needing it."

"Good night," Karen called after him as he peeled off into the rainy night, his tires protesting.

The stone facade of the hospital loomed before her, its entry lit by Grecian-style electric torches on either side of the main door. It looked solidly built, but old, like Bellevue in New York, and, also like Bellevue, took up critical space in the heart of a city. She walked up the wide steps, which were flanked on either side by large religious statues, and went in the front door, stopping by a desk marked Patient Information.

The woman seated there glanced up politely. "Yes?"

"I'd like to know where Steven Colter's room is," Karen said. "He was admitted, oh, I guess last night or early this morning."

The woman, who wore a name tag marked Mrs. Dunphy, looked through a box of index cards on the desk before her. No personal computers for Mercy Hospital.

"What would that spelling be?" Mrs. Dunphy asked.

Karen realized she didn't know. Hoping that it looked the way it sounded, she took a guess.

Mrs. Dunphy removed a card from her collection. "Here he is," she said, "but he's in critical care, miss. He can't be having any visitors."

"Oh, but Mrs. Schanley called me and told me to come," Karen said, not to be denied her goal after a transatlantic trip in search of it. "She said he asked for me."

"That well may be," said Mrs. Dunphy, who knew her hospital procedure as well as her King James Bible. "But visitors are not permitted . . ."

"Can I see Mrs. Schanley?" Karen interrupted anxiously.

"Mrs. Schanley went home at five," Mrs. Dunphy informed her primly.

Karen closed her eyes. Of course. It was after 8:00 p.m.

"Will she be in tomorrow?" Karen asked.

"Certainly. Nine o'clock."

"Thank you," Karen said hastily. "Thank you very much." She turned and went toward the door again, waiting until Mrs. Dunphy became occupied with another questioner. Then she fled to the bank of elevators she had spotted around the corner, stopping a uniformed nurse who walked out of one as the doors opened.

"Could you tell me where the intensive care ward is?" Karen asked her.

"Cardiac, postnatal, postsurgical?" the nurse said briskly.

"Uh, postsurgical," Karen replied.

"Third floor, step left as you leave the lift," the woman replied. "You can ask at the desk. You'll see it right enough."

Karen thanked her and took her place on the old-fashioned elevator, which actually closed with a grille, something she'd seen only in movies. The "lift" creaked and groaned as it rose, and Karen hoped that the inspection sticker fixed to the wall was recent. She didn't have the nerve to check.

The nurse's station was in plain view as Karen reached the third floor. She went to the desk and waited. One of the nurses, a middle-aged matronly blonde, finished making notes on a chart and looked up at Karen. The woman was attired in a pale blue uniform with a full white apron and a pleated gauzy cap that looked like an inverted muffin cup.

"Yes, miss?" she said.

"Is this the intensive care ward?" Karen asked, praying that she would be able to talk her way past this starched bastion of her profession.

"It is. May I help you?"

"I want to see Steven Colter," Karen said baldly, deciding on the direct, confrontational approach. The woman, whose name was Miss Mandeville, didn't look susceptible to the anguished pleas of a weary traveler. She looked, in fact, like she arm wrestled the all-Ulster rugby team before breakfast.

"The American?" Miss Mandeville said. "The one brought in from the trouble in Castlebar Street?"

"Yes. Please, I know it's against the rules, but I'm very concerned, and it would really help if I could just see him...."

"And have you come all the way from the States?" Miss Mandeville asked. She crossed her arms over her full bosom and peered at Karen narrowly, her pale blue eyes missing nothing.

Karen nodded wearily. She was tired and hungry and so worried that if they didn't let her see him soon she was ready to take on Miss Mandeville with a club.

"Well, then, you must have a look," Miss Mandeville said, bustling out from behind the waist-high counter and motioning to Karen to follow.

Karen stared for a moment, disbelieving, then almost ran to keep up with her.

"Is he," she began, then stopped. "What's his condition?" she amended quietly, as they walked down the white-tiled hall.

"Rallying, I should think," Miss Mandeville said. "It was a bit dicey at first, I must say. I was on duty when he arrived, and he'd lost so much blood that surgery had to be postponed until he could be transfused. But his color's good now, and his blood pressure's back up, with a nice strong pulse." She turned to Karen as she opened the door of a private room, isolated at a bend in the corridor. "I've an idea he's a tough Yank."

"Not as tough as he thinks," Karen replied. "No one is."

Miss Mandeville stepped aside and let Karen precede her into the room.

Karen halted at the foot of the wrought-iron bed and tried not to show what she was feeling. But Miss Mandeville had been around hospital visitors far too long.

"Not given to fainting, are you?" she asked Karen sharply.

"I have never fainted in my life," Karen replied calmly, thinking that she hoped she wasn't about to break that tradition now.

Colter was hooked up to so many tubes and machines that he looked like a large, tanned, severely damaged android under repair. A heart monitor beeped on one side of the bed while intravenous fluids, blood and saline and glucose, dripped into his arm from a stand on the other. He was naked to the waist, his brown skin contrasting sharply with the white sheets. A large gauze dressing covered the left side of his torso, extending to his midsection, just below the electrodes taped to his chest. The nurse had said his color was good, but his skin had a sallow cast beneath the tan that Karen found alarming, and he was so still that he seemed strapped to the bed, immobilized by all the equipment. His bright hair, usually so shiny and smooth, was matted and dull, spread on the pillow like dirty straw. His long sandy lashes lay lifelessly on his cheeks, and his lips were parted slightly, dry and pale. But even the injury and all the indignities modern medical science had inflicted on him couldn't make him ugly. He was still beautiful.

"He isn't in a coma, is he?" Karen asked fearfully.

"No, no, don't fret yourself about that," Miss Mandeville replied. "He's just sedated, it's the drugs keeping him under. He should come out of it within a day or so."

"Will he be in a lot of pain?" Karen murmured.

Miss Mandeville didn't answer, and Karen wished she hadn't asked.

"Can I stay in here with him for a while?"

The nurse shook her head firmly. "I'm afraid not. This has to be it for tonight."

"What about tomorrow?" Karen asked anxiously.

Miss Mandeville thought about it for a moment. "I'll leave word that you can see him for a brief bit."

"You won't get into trouble, will you?" Karen said, for the first time remembering that the woman had broken the rules to help her.

Miss Mandeville drew herself up to her full five feet two inches and announced, "I'm the nursing supervisor on this floor, miss. Only doctor can change my orders, and he'll permit it if I will."

"Oh, thank you, thank you," Karen said, effusively grateful. "I'm sure you're taking very good care of him, of course, but I imagined all sorts of things, and it means so much to be able to see him."

"You're very fond of him, aren't you?" Miss Mandeville asked.

Karen met her eyes, then looked away. "It's crazy," she answered. "The truth of it is I hardly know him."

"Well, that's the way of it sometimes," Miss Mandeville answered softly, and Karen glanced at her sharply. The other woman's expression was wise, and Karen realized that her sober, no-nonsense appearance now didn't preclude a youth that had been far different.

"Come away, now," Miss Mandeville said, and they left the room together, pausing outside in the corridor.

"I'll be back in the morning," Karen said.

"I'll leave the orders," Miss Mandeville replied.

"I appreciate what you're doing, Miss Mandeville," Karen said.

"Not at all, not at all. Good night to you, and don't fret. He's on his way back. You can rest easy about that."

Karen left the hospital feeling better than she had since before Mrs. Schanley's phone call. She fled past Mrs. Dunphy at the reception desk and emerged into a chill, light rain, glancing down the street for the sign indicating the Ulster Arms.

She found it half a block away and walked into the lobby just before nine in the evening. The place looked slightly threadbare but very clean, and the desk clerk showed her to a room on the third floor overlooking the street.

"Can I get anything to eat?" she asked him as he put her bag on the floor next to the bed.

"Dining room's closed, miss. Would you be wanting a snack?"

"That'll be fine. What's available?"

"Biscuits and tea, toasted cheese sandwich?" he suggested.

"Great, send that up to the room, please." Since she'd seen Colter alive and apparently on the mend, her appetite had returned.

"Just as you say." He bowed out, and Karen went to the window to look down at the rainy thoroughfare below.

Maybe tomorrow she could talk to him, tell him that she'd come as he'd requested, that everything would soon be all right.

Karen turned back to the bed and took off the spread, exposing a woolen blanket and thick, ribbed sheets. She undressed and put on her robe and was washing her face in the bathroom when the clerk knocked with her tray.

The same man delivered it; she had the eerie feeling he was the only staff member in the place. She ate lightly and then climbed into the bed, turning out the light.

In the morning she would see Colter again.

When Karen awoke, the rain had stopped, but the sky was still overcast and the weather damp and blustery, a typical autumn day in the British Isles. She had breakfast—a thick porridge called "stirabout" for obvious reasons, in the paneled red-carpeted hotel dining room—and presented herself at the third-floor desk of the hospital before 9 a.m. The nurse who listened to her request to see Colter unpinned a note from his chart and said, "Oh, yes, Miss

Walsh, we've instructions to let you visit Mr. Colter. He's been a bit restless, coming out of his sleep, but I think you ought to see our Mrs. Schanley first. She left word she'd like to talk to you."

When Karen hesitated, the nurse said gently, "It won't take but a moment. He'll be fine until then."

"Mrs. Schanley is on the first floor, by the admissions office?"

"She is. You'll see her name on the door."

Karen took the elevator downstairs and found Mrs. Schanley without any trouble. She looked up from her desk as Karen walked through her open door.

"Mrs. Schanley, I'm Karen Walsh," Karen greeted her. "You called me about Steven Colter, and when I went up to visit him just now, the nurse said you wanted to see me."

Mrs. Schanley, who was a slim woman in her forties with short stylish hair the color of orange Nehi, got up and took Karen's hands in both of hers.

"I'm so very glad to see you," she said. "It was good of you to come all this way. We were quite worried about your friend just a short while ago."

"Yes, I understand that," Karen said impatiently. "I don't mean to be rude, Mrs. Schanley, but the nurse said he was waking up, and I'm anxious to talk to him. Can you tell me why you sent for me?"

Mrs. Schanley suddenly looked abashed, and Karen wondered what was coming.

"Mr. Colter is not a U.K. citizen, Miss Walsh. He's not on the National Health."

Karen gazed at her, stymied, until she realized they were talking about Colter's hospital fees.

"I'll pay his bill," she said recklessly, terrified that they would refuse him further treatment because he was uninsured. She hoped that she had a bank balance sufficient to follow through on the boast.

"Oh, is that so?" Mrs. Schanley said, obviously doubtful about the nature of Karen's relationship with Colter.

"He's my... fiancé," Karen lied boldly.

"I thought you said you were friends."

"Well, we are. I mean, we were about to get engaged when all of this happened, and we will. Very shortly. So you have nothing to worry about, Mrs. Schanley, everything will be taken care of, I assure you."

Mrs. Schanley, who, in her position, had heard all sorts of tall tales from better liars than Karen, still looked suspicious, but mercifully decided to let the issue pass for the moment.

"I'll go up with you, then," she said to Karen, picking up her notes and following Karen out into the hall. Karen had no choice but to let the woman accompany her back to the third floor. The nurse Karen had spoken to earlier took them to Colter's room.

"He's drifting in and out just now," she confided to Karen. "You can only stay a moment, so call him if he seems asleep—he should respond."

Karen nodded and opened the door, with Mrs. Schanley on her heels.

Colter looked almost the same as he had the last time she saw him. His eyes were closed and his limbs still, but even in repose he seemed less out of it, more alert.

"He's looking better," Karen murmured.

"That he is," Mrs. Schanley confirmed. "What a beautiful man. The nurses must be fighting over him."

Karen walked to the side of the bed and leaned over the railing.

"Steven," she said. "Steven, wake up."

His lashes fluttered, and then his lids lifted and the blue eyes looked into hers. He seemed to gaze for a moment, register her presence, and then his eyes closed again.

"Steven," she called again.

His eyes opened once more, and this time they held hers.

"Karen," he murmured. His voice sounded hoarse, unused.

"Yes, it's me."

He licked his lips and blinked.

"What are you doing here?"

Chapter 4

Karen and Mrs. Schanley exchanged glances.

"You sent for me," Karen said.

Colter moved his head back and forth on the pillow. "No," he muttered. "No."

Karen could see that Mrs. Schanley didn't want to agitate a man in his condition, yet felt duty bound to clear up the matter.

"But Mr. Colter," she said gently, "you told me to contact Miss Walsh...."

"If I died," he rasped, raising his head with an effort. "Am I dead?"

Mrs. Schanley fell silent.

"Go home, Karen," Colter said. He turned his face to the wall.

The two women were so shocked that they stood staring at the still figure on the bed, unable to think of anything to say.

The duty nurse came into the room and announced, "Time's up. Come away, now. He needs his rest."

Karen and Mrs. Schanley moved into the hall, and the hospital administrator put a comforting hand on Karen's arm.

"He's just upset to have you seeing him so weak and ill, is all," Mrs. Schanley said soothingly. "You know how men are. They always want us to think they're as indestructible as the Rock of Cashel."

Karen, who hadn't yet recovered, said nothing.

"Maybe we should go into the café for a bit, fix you up with a nice cup of tea," the other woman suggested.

Karen nodded, too numb to protest.

They descended to the first floor. Mrs. Schanley led the way to a small cafeteria around a bend in the corridor near her office. Karen waited until they were seated alone at one of the refectory tables before saying, "I haven't been honest with you, Mrs. Schanley. Mr. Colter isn't my fiancé."

Mrs. Schanley nodded. "I thought not."

"But I can pay his bill," Karen added hastily. "I have some money that my father left me."

"Not to worry," Mrs. Schanley said. "We'll work something out. But don't you think you'd better tell me what's going on with you and Mr. Colter? It's an unusual situation, you must admit."

Karen filled the woman in on the background of her relationship, or lack of it, with Colter. When she finished, Mrs. Schanley nodded slowly.

"I see. Well, that puts another gloss on it, I'd say."

"What?" Karen said.

"I mean, maybe you should just do as he said and go back home."

"I can't do that. I can't leave him when he's like this."

"It seems he wants you to."

Karen sighed. "Can I come back and see him tonight?"

Mrs. Schanley shrugged. "Surely. If he'll have you in the room."

"Is Miss Mandeville on this evening?"

"I believe so."

Karen stood up. "Then I'll be back." She crumpled her paper cup and threw it into the trash. "Thank you for all your help. I'll handle this from here."

Mrs. Schanley eyed Karen doubtfully as she left the cafeteria.

Young love, she thought. It was enough to shorten your life by a year.

Then she rose herself and headed back to her office.

Karen spent the day killing time with a long walk, and what she saw convinced her that she should remain in the hotel.

Belfast was like an armed camp. British soldiers in camouflage uniforms, wearing jackboots and flak vests, patrolled with their weapons at the ready, alert to every sound. Teenagers, and even small children, shouted at them constantly, hurling insults and tossing stones and bottles, stirring up enough mischief to make their presence keenly felt, but stopping just short of conduct that would demand retaliation.

The city itself looked like photographs Karen had seen of bombed-out Berlin after the war: shells of buildings surrounded by rubble, abandoned warehouses with the windows blown out, glass and broken bricks littering the streets. Armored cars and tanks glided slowly through the narrow thoroughfares. Graffiti covered all available surfaces— storefronts, walls, even the playbills and advertisements plastered on the city signs. "Up the IRA," "Bobby Fallon Lives," "Brits Out of Eire," "Remember the Hunger Strikers." The slogans were scrawled with white paint, chalk, even what looked like—and might have been—lipstick. Like everyone else, Karen had seen the magazine photos and the newsreels, but the reality was unnerving, a glimpse into another country's nightmare. She returned to the Arms in the late afternoon and took a hot shower, warming herself from the chilled air and the even chillier scenery. Then she ate and went across to the hospital, checking in with Miss Mandeville and entering Colter's room quietly.

His eyes opened when she stood next to his bed.

"You still here?" he said.

"That's right," she said firmly. "And I'm staying."

"Karen..." he began.

"We'll argue about it when you feel better. Go back to sleep."

She slipped out of the room before he could answer.

For the next five days Karen kept up the pattern of visiting once in the morning and once in the evening, never staying long enough for Colter to work himself up about her decision to remain. Each day he improved, but Karen bided her time. She bought terrible paperbacks in the pharmacy, or "chemist's," down the street from the hospital and brought them back to her room. It continued to rain while she read the novels and wrote long letters home, manufacturing tales for Grace about sight-seeing and Colter's recuperation. The hotel staff thought she was peculiar at best, but as she wasn't causing any trouble, they left her alone.

On the sixth day, Colter was moved from intensive care to a private room, and Karen decided that a showdown was in order. She waited until the evening, when Miss Mandeville was on rounds, and then asked for some privacy during the visiting hour. When she let herself into his room, he was sitting up, his back propped against several pillows. He was watching a British marathon on the portable television set that had somehow found its way into his hands.

"Do you run?" Karen asked brightly as she entered.

"Only when chased," he replied.

Karen pulled a chair next to his bed and said, "How are you feeling?"

"Like I took a bullet a week ago." He reached for the remote control and shut off the set.

"You look much better," Karen observed.

"You say that every day."

"And every day it's true."

Colter sighed heavily and ran the hand on his good side through his hair. The bottles and tubes were gone, the only remaining vestige of his injury the dressing on his bare torso.

The gauze bandage had shrunk in thickness and size, but its presence was a grim reminder of how close he had come to death. His blue eyes, clear now that the haze of drugs had lifted, met Karen's as she leaned forward to face him.

"Why are you hanging around?" he asked. "Isn't it obvious by now that I'm not kicking the bucket?"

"Why are you so determined to drive me away?" she countered.

"Because this is no place for you. You can't do anything to change what's happened, and you're just wasting your time here."

"May I ask you a question?" Karen said.

He studied her for a moment before replying. He had shaved that day for the first time since he was hospitalized, and she noticed a small crust of blood on his upper lip where he'd cut himself.

"Go ahead," he finally said.

"Why did you mention me when you were brought in here?"

He looked away, not answering.

"I'm waiting," Karen said.

"A momentary aberration, temporary insanity," he said.

"I think it was because you were scared."

His head whipped around, his eyes flashing. "What are you talking about?" he demanded.

"You knew you were hurt badly, thought you might die. And there was no one to care. Suddenly being alone didn't seem so wonderful anymore, and you wanted contact with someone who would remember you and mourn your passing. Me."

He stared at her, then shook his head. "You flatter yourself. You weren't that important to me," he said cruelly.

"Then why did my name come up when you found yourself in a hospital?" Karen asked calmly.

"I was probably delirious."

Karen stood and faced him at the foot of the bed. "You're not going to admit it, are you? You can't admit that you need me."

"I don't."

"Then what am I doing here?"

"That's what I've been asking you."

Karen had resolved before entering the room that she would keep her temper, but the task was becoming more difficult.

"Miss Mandeville says you can be discharged in a few days," she informed him.

"Great."

"She also says that your recovery has been nothing short of miraculous, but you still have to take it very easy for a while."

"So?"

"So she told me about her cousin who has a cottage in the Republic, down south by the Kinsale coastline. We can rent it for a month or so until you get back on your feet."

His eyes widened, and he sat up straighter. "'We?'" he said in a strong voice.

"Yes. I'm making the arrangements with her tomorrow."

"No, you're not," he said firmly. "You're going back where you came from as fast as I can manage it."

"You can't manage anything just yet. So why don't you let me handle this and take a little vacation on the Irish Sea?"

His jaw hardened, and she saw that he was getting really angry. "Look," he said harshly. "I have tried every way I know of to get rid of you, and nothing has worked. I'm sorry I ever told that nurse to send you my stuff; it was the worst mistake I ever made. I don't need anybody to take care of me, and I don't want you here. I don't even like you. You're always fussing around, making me nervous, taking charge like a top sergeant or something. I'm not the man of your dreams, and I'm lousy husband material. So give up, go home and set your trap for some other sucker."

Karen stared at him, tears welling up in her eyes. She couldn't speak for several moments, and then she cleared her throat.

"Fine," she said quietly. "I'm going. But there's one thing I want you to understand first. I didn't come here to set a trap for you; I came because I thought you were alone and injured and needed help. And as far as I can see that is still the case. For your information, I should be home right now, looking out for myself, instead of standing here taking this abuse from you. I don't care how sick you are; there's no excuse for treating anybody the way you've treated me from the moment I arrived. No wonder nobody cares that you're hurt. You don't know the first thing about relating to another human being. I feel sorry for you." She turned her back on him and strode out the door.

She was almost to the nurse's station, blinking rapidly to clear her blurring vision, when the duty nurse came running down the hall after her.

"Miss, please come back. Mr. Colter is trying to get out of bed and follow you, and he can't be up yet at all."

Alarmed by the woman's concern, Karen hurried back to Colter's room. He was sitting on the edge of the bed with his feet on the floor, pushing himself up with his good arm.

"For heaven's sake, Steven, are you trying to kill yourself?" Karen said, dropping her purse on the chair. She and the nurse got on either side of him and levered him back into the bed.

"Can I speak to Miss Walsh alone, please?" Colter said pointedly.

"If you give me your promise we won't be having any more of these antics," the nurse replied severely.

"I promise," Colter said grudgingly. "And don't tell Mandeville."

"You've a deal," the nurse replied.

"Afraid of Miss Mandeville, are we?" Karen said archly when the woman had left.

"I see her in my dreams," Colter replied grimly. " 'This won't hurt a bit, Mr. Colter,' " he chirped, in a close approximation of Miss Mandeville's chipper brogue. " 'Just give over and let me tidy up your dressing there, Mr. Colter. Not eating our praties, today, Mr. Colter? Mustn't miss out on all that niacin.' " He tilted his head back against the wall behind the bed. "And she took all my cigarettes, too."

"Good for her," Karen said crisply. "I can't imagine how you got them."

"Bribed an orderly," Colter said with satisfaction.

"Did you tell him that less than a week ago you were on oxygen?" Karen asked pointedly.

"He didn't take my medical history, just my money," Colter replied. He folded his arms. "I was trying to come after you just now," he announced, eyeing her warily.

"So I gathered."

He shifted uncomfortably. "I guess there was something in what you said," he admitted grudgingly.

Karen waited.

"I'll go with you on one condition," he said.

"Don't do me any favors," Karen replied flatly, still smarting from his acid commentary.

"Look, do you want me to do this, or not?" he asked testily.

"All right," Karen replied, putting his health before her pride. "What's the condition?"

"That we remain just . . . friends. I mean, nothing more, okay?"

"What makes you think I'm your friend? Friends aren't shown the door when all they've done is express legitimate concern."

He shook his head and looked out the window at the foggy, drizzly evening.

"Boy, you aren't easy, are you?"

"I'm glad you're finding that out."

He turned his head and met her gaze again. "So? What do you say?"

"About the condition?"

"Yeah."

Karen looked him over carefully, and he had the good grace to flush. She understood the workings of his mind better than he thought. To him, sex was fine as long as it remained a sport to be shared with casual acquaintances, but he didn't want to risk sleeping with someone who might actually care about him. Karen's recent interest in his welfare had proved that she fell into the latter category, and mak-

ing love to her now posed a risk of personal involvement he
wouldn't take.

"I promise not to ravish you," she finally said dryly.

He stared back at her, his color deepening.

"Of course, it may be difficult, but I think I'll be able to
restrain myself," she added consideringly.

"Very funny," he observed darkly, looking away.

"I'll tell Miss Mandeville we'll take the cottage," Karen
said, turning to go.

"Karen?" he called after her.

"Why are you doing this for me?" Colter asked. He
seemed genuinely puzzled.

She faced him squarely. "Because whether you'll admit
it or not, right now you need someone, and I seem to be the
only candidate for the job." She headed for the door, calling back to him, "I'll be in to see you in the morning."

He followed her departure with his eyes, aware that he
was getting involved with a woman unlike any he'd met before.

Colter lay awake long after Karen had left him. Night
quiet descended on the hospital corridor, and the lights were
dimmed, leaving only the old-fashioned hall lanterns burning. He could hear the now-familiar nocturnal sounds
punctuating the stillness: the padding of rubber-soled shoes
on the tiled floor, the swish and click of a nursing sister's
beads, the rattle of ice in the metal water carafes as an aide
refilled them. The coughing man across the hall was still
coughing, and the moaner in the room adjacent to his was
still moaning. It was a typical night on the third floor, and
he, typically, couldn't sleep.

But this time, it wasn't the pain from his wound that kept
him awake. That had subsided to a dull, throbbing ache and
had become so much a part of him that he hardly noticed it
anymore. It was the subject of Karen that occupied his mind
as he stared at the rain streaming down his windowpane,
Karen's presence in Belfast that he couldn't forget.

When he first awoke after his shooting and saw her
standing at his beside, he'd thought he was dreaming. But

when he looked again and she was still there, he realized that the hospital administration had summoned her. Then all he could think about was getting her to leave, an effort that had met with a spectacular lack of success. He soon discovered that she was as stubborn as he was and as tenacious as poverty. She wasn't going home.

Which left him with a significant problem: how to deal with a woman who wanted to give more than she was getting, whether that was a night of pleasure in his bed or the rescue of a comrade. Colter was accustomed to thinking of relationships in terms of barter, a trade of one commodity for another. Karen Walsh didn't fit into this set picture, and that fact made him very nervous.

Colter stirred and settled his injured side more comfortably against the pillows at his back. His left arm was becoming more mobile as the torn muscles along his side knitted and healed. The bullet had carved its path of destruction very neatly, exiting out his back. He remembered clearly the moment of impact when it had ripped into him, and he'd said to himself, I'm hit. He'd been shot before, and he always reacted calmly, but it took him only seconds to realize that this time the injury was far worse than his previous surface wounds. Blood poured from his chest, and his legs refused to function; he'd felt as if he were walking, dreamlike, through a sea of molasses. For the first time in his life he'd felt faint as the red river of life flowed out of his veins, leaving him staggered and dizzy. He'd been dimly aware of the stretcher, the ambulance, the scared young intern who didn't know quite what to do for him during the trip to the hospital. But it wasn't until he reached the emergency room and saw the grave expression on the attendants there that he had felt the flash of panic and knew he might die. And in that instant, he'd remembered Karen's face, a pale oval surrounded by a cloud of dark hair, and the touch of her lips on his. Who would care if he bought the farm right there? He'd known, somehow, that she would, and his momentary weakness then had led to his present predicament.

The rain increased in volume, drumming on the ancient slate roof above him, and he closed his eyes, listening to it. It wasn't that he didn't want Karen; he wanted her too much. But she posed a threat to the aloof, uninvolved existence he'd come to call his own, and he didn't want to change it. He was too old to take that kind of a chance.

His subconscious, however, refused to be instructed along those lines. Ever since the night when she'd melted into his arms on that Caracas beach, he'd been tormented by erotic dreams in which he'd imagined, alternatively, her helpless submission or her aggressive pursuit. In some scenarios she was ardent, clinging, shuddering under him with complete abandon; in others she was wild, tearing at his clothes, as eager and passionate as he was. But now, confronted by her reality and the possibility of fulfilling these imaginings, he felt like running for the nearest exit.

His courage, he found, was the physical variety, confined to combat. He couldn't accept the challenge of joining his life to another person's. He saw the prospect of a close relationship as yet another opportunity to be abandoned, and so it had never held much charm for him.

But what really scared him more than anything else was that Karen seemed different. He found himself wanting to go for broke with her, and so his defensive reaction was to tell her to get lost. But she wasn't listening, and he had an uneasy feeling he'd finally met his match.

A crack of thunder split the hush of the hospital night, and Colter jumped, wishing he had a cigarette. He looked at the clock on the wall, urging time to pass faster.

Karen would be back the next day and he couldn't wait to see her.

When Karen returned in the morning, she announced that she'd made the arrangements to rent the cottage.

"You'll have to go to the bank for me," Colter said gruffly in response, obviously uncomfortable. He didn't like asking her to run the errand for him. "It's the Belfast Maritime on the corner of Merchant Street. I'll fill out the withdrawal slip and call them so you can take it in for me."

"You have a bank account here?" Karen asked, surprised.

"I've got them all over," he said shortly. "It's more convenient than having to wire Florida every time I need some spare change."

"You keep your money in different countries?" Karen said, intrigued with the idea.

"Several."

"But how do you decide where?"

He fixed her with a gimlet eye. "Are you taking a survey?"

"I'm just interested," she said, mildly offended.

He sighed. "I opened accounts where I've spent the most time, where I'm more likely to . . ."

"Get shot and be laid up?" Karen suggested.

"Need money," he finished calmly. "Now can we get back to the original topic? I want to pay for this place you're renting, and I also have to settle my bill here. I asked Mrs. Schanley to come and see me later."

Karen was silent.

"Is there some problem with that?" he asked, reading her face.

"I already paid it," Karen said in a small voice, thinking that it would be better for him to receive this bulletin from her than from the hospital administrator.

"What?" he said tersely, certain that he'd misunderstood.

"You heard me."

Colter stared at her with the stony expression that she knew concealed a white-hot anger he was unwilling to show.

"You were unconscious," Karen said defensively, "and Mrs. Schanley was making noises about your not being on the National Health . . ."

"Fine," he interjected sharply, cutting her off. "Then I'll authorize two drafts, and you make one to the *exact amount* you paid. Do you understand me?"

"Of course I understand," she snapped. "Are you speaking Hindi?"

Colter sat staring out the window, shaking his head in silence.

"Anyone would think I had robbed you instead of done you a favor," Karen said resentfully.

"I don't want any favors!" Colter responded savagely.

"Good!" Karen flared back at him. "Then somebody else can go to the bank!"

He turned his head and met her eyes, holding them steadily for a count of ten, and then his lips twitched.

"All right," he sighed. "I'm sorry. I'm just not used to having people do things for me."

"I'm not surprised, if this is a sample of the gracious reception they get."

"Haven't we had this conversation before?" he inquired archly.

"I must admit that it does have a familiar ring," Karen responded dryly.

He waited a moment, and then said, "Truce?"

"I didn't start the war."

He grinned impishly and said, "As a goodwill gesture, will you buy me a pack of cigarettes while you're out?"

Karen glared at him in amazement. "I hope that was a joke."

He subsided, not replying.

"What are you going to do for clothes when you get out of here?" Karen asked, deliberately changing the subject.

He glanced at her sharply, then looked away. "Can you pick some up for me?" he said.

Something in his attitude alerted her. "But where are your things?" she asked.

"What things?"

"Your personal effects—you know—shoes, shirts, belts, like that."

"Oh, forget that junk, it's not worth retrieving," he said offhandedly, still not looking at her.

"You don't want your stuff?"

No answer.

"Okay, Steven, where is it?"

"I told you to forget it," he said harshly.

"You don't want me to go there?" Karen asked gently.

He looked at her then, his blue eyes appearing gray in the bright morning light, his blond hair mussed and too long, splashing onto his forehead.

"It's no place for you," he said shortly.

"Well, what is it?"

"A bar. Sort of."

"I've been in bars before, Steven."

"Not like this, you haven't."

"Is it in a bad area?"

"The waterfront."

"I can find it. I came into Belfast on a boat."

"It's not a question of finding it, Karen. More of what the place is like."

"So?" she said impatiently, tiring of his evasiveness.

"It has upstairs rooms," he said uncomfortably.

"And?"

"They're used for business."

"What kind of business?" she said quickly, beginning to get his drift. Then, without waiting for an answer, "Steven, are you sending me to a whorehouse?"

"I'm not sending you anywhere," he muttered. "I've been trying to tell you not to go."

"What's the name of this place?"

"Sailor's Haven."

"And is it a . . ."

"Yes," he said abruptly.

"And why were you staying at Sailor's Haven?" she asked steadily.

"I have a friend who works there."

"And is she a . . ."

"Yes."

"Did you . . ."

"No. Never."

"Then why were you staying with her?"

"They're people, too, Karen. They have friends."

"How did you meet this friend?" Karen demanded. She could see that he resented the inquisition, but wasn't about to back down on it. She was only beginning to realize how little she knew about him.

"She bailed me out of a tight spot once."

"I see. And you became acquainted with such a person when you weren't patronizing her establishment?"

"I patronized the bar," he said shortly. "That's all you have to know."

Karen gazed at his set expression and realized that he'd told her all he was going to. A tense silence lasted for about half a minute.

"You can stop looking down your fine patrician nose at me," Colter finally said wearily. "This is just more evidence of what I've been trying to tell you all along: we're too different. You work in an office and live with your sister. I work in war zones and room with prostitutes. And that's the least of it. Believe me, you're just not up for the rest, and you'd better get out while you can."

"You think I'm too 'delicate' to deal with the vicissitudes of your life?" Karen asked him.

"If I knew what a 'vicissitude' was, I might be able to tell you."

"Changes, problems, ups and downs," Karen translated.

"Then why didn't you say that?"

"You're dodging the issue, Steven."

"I forget what the issue was, Karen."

Karen put her hands on her hips and narrowed her eyes. "The issue was my ability to deal with your, er, life-style."

"Are you trying to tell me you weren't shocked?" he countered.

"About Sailor's Haven?"

"No, Karen, about the drop in pork futures on the commodities market," he said sarcastically.

"It just took me a few moments to adjust," Karen replied stiffly. "You have to admit it's an unusual situation."

"Not for me," he said simply.

"You mean you always take up residence in whorehouses?" Karen asked incredulously, forgetting to be blasé. Now she *was* shocked.

"I mean I don't associate with the nice professional people you do. I don't sit behind a desk with neatly arranged papers on it, and I don't have lunch with my colleagues and plan Christmas parties."

"What a picture you have of my life," Karen said. "You make me sound like one of those plastic people in a TV situation comedy, the ones who go to bed in display window negligees and wake up the next morning in full makeup."

"What do you go to bed in?" he asked lazily, momentarily distracted.

"Old football jerseys," Karen responded tartly. "Now are you going to tell me this woman's name, or am I going to wander around Sailor's Haven knocking on doors?"

"Mary Lafferty," he said with resignation. "You'll find her on the second floor at the back. My bags are in her room."

"What's the address?"

"12-15 Water Street. You'll see the sign out front." He hesitated. "I really wish you wouldn't insist on doing this."

"I'm going," she said flatly. She needed to show him she wasn't the hothouse flower he thought she was, and she also wanted a glimpse of his milieu. This mission afforded her an opportunity to accomplish both goals at once.

"Then tell the cabbie to wait for you," Colter said anxiously. "And go straight up; don't stop to talk to anybody downstairs."

She realized that he was really worried about her.

"Steven," she said briskly, "if I survived being held hostage in Almeria, I can survive one trip to a waterfront dive."

"I'm sorry I let you worm that out of me. I still don't know how you did it," he said darkly.

"It's my fatal charm," Karen observed airily, grinning. "You can refuse me nothing."

"We'll see," he replied, with a slight smile.

"Come on, don't worry. I'll be all right. Besides, you need your bankbook, don't you?"

"People have lost them before, Karen, and civilization survived."

"Well, you know what a terrible time they give you when you try to make a withdrawal without one; you have to sign all those papers and things. One trip to Water Street and I'll have it for you."

"You're just dying to get down there and see how the other half lives, aren't you?" he said dryly.

"I want to see how you live," she replied honestly.

"Just be careful. You're not as tough as you think you are."

"Neither are you," she said pointedly.

At this juncture a nurse entered the room to check Colter's dressing. She retaped the gauze tightly and said, "I don't know why you're not dead, Mr. Colter, but apparently you're going to survive to harass us a few days longer."

"When can I get up again?" he asked impatiently.

"Hold on there, Mr. C., this is only your first day out of bed. I told you before, doctor says a walk twice a day. And that's a walk, mind you, not jogging down the passage as I saw this morning."

"Twice is two times," Colter said briskly. "I've only been up once." He swung his legs over the side of the bed.

"Once in the morning and once in the afternoon," the nurse said.

"Oh, come on," Colter said, displaying his most engaging smile. "I'm going crazy planted on that mattress."

The nurse shook her head, sighed, then supported Colter's shoulders as he stood.

"This one could charm the devil into going to church," she confided to Karen.

"I think Miss Walsh would disagree with you," Colter said in an aside to the nurse. "She's finding me somewhat lacking in charm this morning."

"All right, Mr. C., there you go," the nurse said as Colter got his bearings and she moved away from him. "Not too much exercise, now; I'll be looking after you."

"You know I always do everything you ladies tell me to," Colter responded innocently.

"I'll believe you," the nurse observed skeptically, "thousands wouldn't. Mind how you go, the floors are slick in those paper shoes."

Karen's eyes were drawn to Colter's bare torso as the nurse left and he turned toward her. He was wearing pajama bottoms with an elasticized waist, and nothing else. He looked a little thinner from his ordeal, but the weight loss only emphasized the well-defined musculature of his upper arms and abdomen. She'd never seen him without a shirt, and the view was riveting.

A thatch of brown hair, several shades darker than that on his head, spread between his pectorals and down to his navel, ending in a line below it that disappeared into his pants. His shoulders were broad, the skin across them tanned and silky, with a sprinkling of toasty freckles. Even the bulky bandage, startlingly white against his dusky skin, could not detract from the hard beauty of his body.

Karen suddenly realized she was staring and tore her gaze away.

"Trying to keep me tied down like some kind of invalid," he grumbled, shoving his feet into the flimsy slippers the hospital provided. But for all his talk, Karen noticed that he was a little unsteady on his feet, and when he wavered as he moved for the door, she ran to support him.

In her anxiety, she overdid it. The combination of her excessive energy and his forward impetus resulted in a wrestling match that almost tumbled them to the floor. They ended up with Karen pinned to the wall and Colter leaning heavily against her, both of them breathing harshly. It was several seconds before Karen raised her head and looked into the ice-blue eyes a few inches above hers.

Colter's expression was tense, waiting, and when she didn't pull away, it became lambent, communicating a desire so intense she caught her breath. He slipped one long arm around Karen's waist, drawing her to him, and bent to bury his face in the fragrant mass of dark hair spread against her neck.

Karen clung to him, pressing her cheek to his warm bare shoulder, and felt his lips tracing a line of fire through the fine screen of her hair. She ran her hands down his back, delighting in the response of his muscles as her fingers touched them lightly. Highly sensitized, he reacted to her slightest movement, pulling her closer as she caressed him. When he moved his mouth inside the collar of her blouse and she tilted her head back, sighing, yielding up to him a creamy expanse of velvety skin, he groaned aloud.

"I thought of you so often after Caracas," he whispered. "I could feel you in my arms, just like this, and I had to stop myself from going after you."

"Why did you?" she murmured. "Oh, Steven, why did you stop?"

For an answer, he crushed her mouth with his.

Karen forgot that he'd been ill, that they were in a hospital room, and everything else. She opened her lips, and when his tongue touched hers, his sigh of satisfaction was so deep and heartfelt that she realized what it had cost him, this time, to send her away.

Colter moved his lips across her cheek and then bent his head, mouthing her breasts through her blouse. She felt the heat of his lips through two layers of clothing as if she were naked. She moaned helplessly, and he tightened his grip, trapping her between his lower body and the wall. She felt him hard against her, full and ready. She surged against him, unable to control her primitive response, and he almost lifted her off the floor. His strength was amazing, his injury forgotten, and Karen thought wildly that he might take her right then, right there.

Karen's head dropped to his shoulder, and the scent of him, hospital soap combined with the sweat of desire and heated male flesh, overwhelmed her. Impatient with their clothes, he pushed at her skirt, trying to raise it above her thighs. She melted into him, slipping her hands inside the waistband of his pants, and he gasped, turning his head to seek her mouth with his again.

"I'll be right back, Mr. Murphy," the nurse said in the hall. "I'll get that for you right away."

Her voice was so loud that it sounded as if it might be in the same room with them.

They sprang apart guiltily, and Colter fell back against the wall. His deep flush spread from his face down his neck and across his chest, and his torso heaved with the force of his breathing. He closed his eyes, and Karen watched his right hand clench into a tight fist.

"Best to think about getting back to bed, Mr. Colter," the nurse said, sticking her head into the room. "You've been up long enough—don't want to tire yourself out."

Colter turned his head and stared at her as if she were mad.

The nurse took one look at him, and at Karen, immobilized in the center of the room, and bustled to her patient's side.

"Good heavens, Mr. Colter, you're all flushed and your heart is beating like a coinin's. I told you not to overdo, and you just turned a deaf ear by the look of you." She seized Colter and ushered him back to the bed while Karen hovered in the background, wondering if she'd caused a relapse.

"Now stay just as you are while I go fetch a thermometer," the nurse instructed, heading for the door. "I'm talking to myself around here, and no mistake," she added under her breath as she scuttled into the hall. They listened to the starched whisper of her uniform fade into the distance.

"That can't happen again," Colter finally said, not looking at Karen.

She didn't answer, unable to think of an appropriate response.

"Did you hear me?" he asked, turning toward her.

"I heard you."

"And you have nothing to say?"

"You seem to be making the rules," Karen said wearily.

"Do you realize how close I...we..." He stopped, stymied.

"I realize it. Do we have to talk about it?"

"Yes, we have to talk about it!" he replied vehemently.

The nurse entered, shaking down a silver-and-white thermometer. She swabbed the tip of it with a cotton ball and jammed it firmly between Colter's teeth.

"That will be all for you today, my man," she instructed Colter. "This young lady will have to leave, and you're not to move from that bed until you're told otherwise."

Colter tried to speak around the object in his mouth, and the nurse shushed him.

"I can't imagine what Miss Mandeville will say if she comes on duty this evening and finds you in this condition."

Colter rolled his eyes expressively.

"You may well make faces," the woman said. "Ten-year-olds can take direction better, and you at death's door only days ago. I never saw the like in my life."

Her commentary didn't improve Karen's already shaky state of mind. A few minutes earlier she had been climbing all over a hospital case, and she was thoroughly ashamed of herself. By the time the nurse finally took Colter's temperature and left, Karen could barely meet his eyes.

"I'll go and get your things," she said quietly.

Colter, who did indeed look tired, evidently decided not to pursue the conversation the nurse had interrupted.

"Be careful down there," he said.

"I will," Karen said and fled. She didn't stop walking until she reached the third-floor lounge, a few paces past the nurses' station, and there she sank into a chair.

She hadn't realized until that very afternoon that she was in love with Colter. Before then she had used other terms for it in her mind: she was concerned about him; he was alone and needed a friend; she was attracted to him; he was hurt and couldn't be abandoned. But there was no denying the violent rush of feeling that had coursed through her body during the few brief seconds when he'd made love to her in his room. She told herself that it was all crazy and she hardly knew him and all the sensible things that a woman in her position should tell herself, but the bare fact remained un-

changed. She was as in love with him as much as it was possible to be, and she was terrified.

After about ten minutes of reflection, she got up and
headed for the elevator, starting out for Water Street.

Chapter 5

Karen found Sailor's Haven with little trouble. The cabbie knew where it was, and though he expressed some surprise at Karen's wish to go there, he didn't offer any further comment until they had pulled up in front of the bar.

It was a ramshackle, weathered two-story structure hugging the edge of the wharf. It seemed to be listing to one side and looked about ready to pitch into the sea at any moment. The sign out front hung from a metal crossbar and swung in the ocean breeze, creaking as it moved. It depicted a thirsty sailor downing a pint of "stout," or ale, and the painted logo beneath the picture had been so beaten by the elements that it was now almost illegible. Electric signs advertising Guinness beer and Silk Cut cigarettes flashed on and off in the streaked windows, and the front door hung askew on its hinges, its brasswork tarnished green by the salt spray. Karen and her driver stared at it in silence until the man said, "Are you certain this is the place you wanted, miss?"

"Yes, I think so," Karen said, with more assurance than she felt.

"I don't know as I'd go in there alone, miss," the cabbie said, understandably concerned.

"I'll be all right. I'm just running an errand for a friend. After all, it's only eleven o'clock in the morning."

"They're drinking in there all day long, miss, and don't take no notice of the time," the driver said.

"Oh. Don't the bars stay closed until four in the afternoon or something like that?"

"Not in Belfast," he said dryly. "Do you want me to wait for you?"

"Yes, thank you. I'll just see if the person I'm looking for is there," Karen said, opening the rear door.

"If it's one of the girls, you'd best give a loud knock; she might be sleeping," he said wisely. "They work late, you know."

Karen nodded, getting out of the car. Her nerve almost failed her as she neared the door, but she squared her shoulders, determined to find out what she could about Colter's life.

The interior was a cavern of darkness, and Karen blinked rapidly, waiting for her eyes to adjust to the dim light. It was several seconds before she could make out the figures sitting on the stools to her left, a group of customers, all of them hunched over a shot glass or a pint of beer. Behind the bar a big bear of a man in a stained apron was wiping glasses. At his back a huge fly-spotted mirror reflected the whole room, and shelves of multicolored bottles climbed almost to the ceiling on either side of it.

Everyone in the place was staring at her.

Karen crossed the aged warped floorboards in her low-heeled sensible shoes, feeling as out of place as a Junior Leaguer at a strip show. The bartender eyed her as she approached him, and he put down his rag, leaning on his meaty forearms when she stopped in front of him.

"What can I do for you, miss?" he asked in a pronounced cockney accent.

"Do you know where Mary Lafferty is?" Karen replied.

"Who wants to see her?" he asked. His crafty brown eyes surveyed her as he asked the question, and he lifted one hand to stroke his wild sandy beard, the same color as his wild sandy hair.

"Steve Colter sent me," Karen said, thinking that his name would have more impact than hers.

She was right.

"Colter? That the Yank, big blond bloke, drifts in a couple times a year on a job?"

"That's him," Karen replied, nodding vigorously. "He left his things with Mary, and I've come to get them."

"She know you?" the bartender asked warily.

"No, we've never met. Colter just asked me to come here and see her."

The bartender glanced at his companions with a "this ought to be good" expression, then gestured to a flight of stairs at the rear of the room.

"Second floor at the back, the door on your left," he said. "She wakes up cranky, so watch yourself."

Karen followed his direction, and she heard the group of men burst into laughter as she climbed the rickety stairwell into the dusty crib at the top of it. She could well imagine that she presented an amusing picture, but was too intent on her mission to mind what they were saying about her.

The second floor was nothing more than a large window-less attic divided into four rooms by rudely constructed walls, with an alley of a hallway down the middle. She picked her way past a single electric bulb left burning in the ceiling and knocked at the indicated door.

She heard nothing but silence until the third knock.

"What is it?" The voice was muffled, querulous, and very young.

"My name is Karen Walsh. I'd like to speak to you about Steve Colter," Karen answered.

She heard a thud, muttered oaths, and then the door swung inward. She could see one large green eye streaked with the previous night's mascara and a shock of black hair.

"What's that about Steve?" the girl asked.

"He sent me to pick up his clothes," Karen explained.

She could see the green eye roving over her, taking in the navy skirt, crisp striped blouse and conservative shoes.

"Who are you?" the girl asked.

"A friend of his."

"You don't look like no friend of his to me," the girl observed adroitly.

"Look, have I come to the right door?" Karen asked. "Are you Mary Lafferty?"

"Yeah, that's me. How do you know Steve?"

"Well, we met a little over a month ago, and he's in the hospital here in Belfast...."

"The hospital!" Mary said, alarmed. She yanked open the door to reveal a tiny room crammed with every kind of clothing draped on doorknobs, bedposts, and window frames, and an assortment of mismatched furniture.

"You'd best come in and tell me," she added, stepping aside.

Karen entered the apartment, making her way through the clutter to an overstuffed armchair in the corner. Mary swept a pile of gossamer underwear off the back of it and said, "Sit yourself down. Would you like a cup of tea?"

Karen saw that she was indicating a hot plate on a counter and nodded mutely. She got her first good look at Mary as the girl bustled to fill a kettle at a cracked porcelain sink affixed to the same wall.

She was all of about twenty, and would have been beautiful with her face washed clean of the excess of makeup disfiguring it. Tall, slim and barefoot, she was wearing a flowered cotton robe belted at the waist with a man's necktie. Her black hair hung down her back past her shoulder blades and fell into her eyes as she moved. She kept pushing it back behind her ears impatiently while she talked.

"What's up with Colter, then?" she said to Karen, turning to face her. "Is he ill?" She yawned, then covered her mouth contritely.

"He was shot recently, and he's recovering at Mercy Hospital."

"Is he going to be all right?"

"Yes, I think so. He'll be discharged soon."

Mary nodded. "And how do you figure in all of this?"

"He asked for me when he was brought to the emergency room, and the hospital administrator called me."

"He asked for you?" Mary said, arching her brows.

"Yes."

"And you came all the way from the States?"

Karen nodded.

"But you've not known him long?"

"Not very long, no."

Mary folded her arms. "Then I'd say he must have changed. The Colter I know would take on the devil with his own pitchfork and never look behind him."

Karen wasn't sure of the exact meaning of that statement, but understood that Mary was surprised Colter had asked for anybody, much less the prim specimen she saw before her.

"He was hurt badly," Karen said quietly. "I don't think he wanted to be alone."

Mary digested that for a moment, then said, "He got shot up in the trouble?"

"Yes."

"That post office job?"

Karen nodded.

Mary sighed. "They couldn't pay me enough to get involved with those hooligans, but you know Steve." She shook her head.

"How do *you* know him?" Karen asked pointedly.

Mary stared at her for a second and then laughed lightly. "Oh, you're not thinking there was anything between Steve and me?" she said, waving her hand dismissively. "No fear, no fear. Not that I would have turned him away, mind you, but Steve is real picky that way. Particular, you might say. Never saw him with any woman, and I thought for a while he might be kinda funny, you know. Some of those real good-looking ones are." She eyed Karen shrewdly. "I'll warrant you know better."

"I can vouch for the fact that he's straight," Karen said, blushing.

"I wasn't worried," Mary said, laughing again. "But I figured out right quick I wasn't to his taste. He slept here on that couch," she added, pointing to a sofa obscured by several pounds of laundry, "for three nights running and never touched me." She leaned in closer to Karen confidentially. "Not even when I let him know I was interested, if you take my meaning."

"He told me that you got him out of a tight spot once," Karen said, diverting the conversation to less sensitive territory.

The water began to boil, and Mary went to unplug the hot plate. "Oh, that," she said. "Not much at all to tell. There was a fight in the bar, and I took Steve and one of those soldier friends of his up here to give the slip to the coppers." Mary looked back at her. "That's how I met him. He reminded me of a boy I knew back in Antrim."

"Is that home?" Karen asked.

Mary nodded. "Just north of here."

"Why did you leave?"

"No work there." She shrugged philosophically. "No work here for the likes of me, either, except flat on my back."

Karen was silent as Mary brewed a pot of tea. She set it out for the two of them with little china cups and a jug of cream from a half-sized refrigerator under the sink.

"So you're after him, are you?" Mary asked suddenly, in a friendly tone.

"I . . . excuse me?" Karen stammered. She didn't know what to say.

"Don't get all lathered up about it. I just wondered. You'll have a tough row to hoe if you are, I'll say that. He wants taming, to be sure, but you'll need a buggy whip for the job."

Karen took a sip of her drink, not replying.

"You're not thinking you'll set up housekeeping with him in one of those condominiums, are you?" Mary asked slyly. "And he'll be trimming the hedges and painting the garage?"

"I wasn't thinking any further than getting him well," Karen replied coolly.

"You poor thing," Mary said sympathetically. "You've got it bad for him, haven't you?"

"I don't know what you mean," Karen said, not looking at her.

"Sure you do, darlin', sure you do. And are you going to sit home and say your prayers while he takes off to fight his wars?"

Karen set her cup down with a sharp click. "I think I'd better be going. I have a cabbie waiting for me downstairs."

She got up, and Mary followed her to the door. "There's his duds. Do you want me to help you get them down?" she said, pointing to two duffel bags in a corner of the room.

"No, I can manage."

"I can call Kevin, the bartender," Mary volunteered.

"It's all right." Karen picked up the bags and slung them over her shoulder, eager to be gone.

"You mind what I said, now," Mary advised as Karen stepped through the door.

"Thank you for the tea," Karen said.

"Tell Steve I hope he's fit again soon, and to stop in anytime."

"I will," Karen murmured. She walked down the dark hall as Mary shut the door behind her and then staggered down the steps with her burdens.

The bartender came running when he saw her carrying the bags.

"I'll take those for you, miss," he said. "Have you a car outside?"

"There's a cab at the door," she said.

He assisted her outside and then waved her off as the cabbie headed back downtown on her instructions.

"You were inside a good bit of time, miss," the driver observed. "Did you get what you came for?"

"Yes, I did," Karen replied thoughtfully.

"I'm glad the trip wasn't wasted," he said.

"So am I." Karen sat back against the seat and watched the waterfront go by, thinking that it had been a very profitable morning.

Karen spent the rest of the day straightening out Colter's affairs and arranging for his discharge the next morning. She rented a car and arrived in his room that evening dangling the keys in front of him.

"What are those?" he asked warily, watching the movement of her hand.

"Exactly what they look like. Car keys."

"You're driving?"

"Well, let's put it this way. You're not."

"How did you make out with Mary?"

"We had a very interesting visit. I think she has a crush on you."

"Give me a break."

"I got your stuff and went to the bank."

"Did you take back the money you spent on me?" he demanded.

"Yes, yes. You can relax. You don't owe me a farthing."

Miss Mandeville arrived and tucked Colter's sheet in around his middle. She patted his abdomen with satisfaction and left without saying a word.

"I can't wait to get out of that woman's clutches," Colter said, closing his eyes.

Karen smiled to herself. "You'll probably miss her."

"I doubt that very seriously," he replied, without opening his eyes.

"You look tired," Karen observed, going to sit on the side of his bed.

"I'm all right," he said, his lashes lifting.

"Did I wear you out this afternoon?" Karen asked sheepishly.

He grinned. "I'd like to see you try."

"Mary Lafferty said she used to be worried that you were gay."

He looked so thunderstruck that she laughed.

"Why in hell would she think that?" he asked incredulously.

"Something about your not responding to a sweet invitation from her," Karen said innocently.

He shook his head. "That kid thinks she's irresistible."

"She is very pretty."

"Yeah," he said thoughtfully. "I tried to get her a job once, but I think she's just used to that life now."

"It's a shame. She's so young."

"So I guess she convinced you that we were just pals, huh?" he asked, shooting her a sidelong glance.

"Yup. Just pals. Just like you and me."

He smiled in exasperation, picking up her hand and toying with her fingers. "You really are a pain in the neck, you know that?"

"I know it."

"But I want you to understand that I do appreciate all you've done for me."

"I'll try to remember that the next time you're yelling at me."

"How do you know there will be a next time?"

"With you there's always a next time."

"Then why do you stick around?" he asked. He tried to sustain the light bantering tone of their previous exchange, but a listening look in his eyes told her his mood had altered.

"Because I think, deep down, you really want me to," she answered honestly.

He looked up at her for a long moment and then said, "Clever girl." He glanced at the clock. "How much time have we got before Miss Manhandler throws you out?"

"Ten minutes."

"Then come here," he said, reaching out to pull her down to his shoulder. Karen half lay against him, snuggling into his good side, and curled her free arm across his chest.

"I'm not hurting you, am I?" she asked.

He made a contented sound to indicate that she wasn't.

"Where are we going tomorrow?" he asked drowsily.

"I told you. Kinsale, in the Republic."

"I've never been to the Republic."

"No?"

"All the action takes place up here."

"The town is apparently very pretty, a little boating resort on the water."

He snorted. "According to who—Mandeville? I wouldn't trust anything she says. I think she's a robot in a dress."

"Everybody says Kinsale is nice, even the man who rented me the car today."

He grunted. "The place will be full of crazy Irishmen."

"You're talking to one of them right now, bud. Besides, the cottage is supposed to be secluded, so we don't have to see anybody if we don't want to. The idea is for you to rest."

He didn't answer, and she thought from the even quality of his breathing that he was asleep. But when she moved to get up his grip tightened.

"Don't go," he said huskily.

"Miss Mandeville will be in here in a minute."

"The hell with her," he replied. "Stay with me."

Karen couldn't resist such an invitation. As she relaxed against him, she felt his lips moving in her hair, and tears sprang to her eyes. He *did* care about her; she could feel it. Why did he fight it so stubbornly?

"Karen?"

"Mmm?" she responded, clearing her throat.

"What about your job?"

"I don't have a job."

"That's what I mean. Don't you have to look for one?"

"It can wait until you're well."

She could tell he didn't like the sound of that. "I feel like I'm taking advantage of you," he said.

"Will you stop worrying about it and go to sleep?" Karen said.

He did. By the time the nurse came in to say that visiting hours were over, he was unaware of her entrance.

"Look at that, now," Miss Mandeville said as Karen stood and straightened her clothes. "Just like a little boy."

Karen glanced back at Colter and saw that the other woman was right. He was sleeping with his head turned to one side, his lips parted, the arm that had encircled Karen still curved in a protective circle.

"You'd never believe he was such a hell-raiser," the nurse added.

"Are you sure he's well enough to be discharged?" Karen asked anxiously.

Miss Mandeville shrugged. "There's little more we can do for him. Mostly what he needs is to take it easy, and I've an idea he'll listen better to you than he will to me."

"What about his medication?" Karen said.

"I'll have it all ready for you in the morning," the nurse said soothingly. "Doctor will write a prescription, and you can have it renewed when the bottle runs out. It's just an antibiotic you can get anywhere."

"Okay."

"Don't fret yourself," Miss Mandeville said, patting her arm. "He'll be fine."

"I hope so."

"Well, he has you to take care of him, doesn't he?" the nurse said confidently. "Now be off with you, get some sleep, and tomorrow he's all yours."

If only that were true, Karen thought. But she left nonetheless and went back to her rented room to wait for morning.

Colter's discharge went more smoothly than she had anticipated. As good as her word, Miss Mandeville had done all the paperwork, and when Karen showed up at nine o'clock, the patient was all set to leave.

Colter was sitting in the chair in his room, dressed in jeans and a plaid shirt from one of the bags Karen had delivered. He was wearing sunglasses and an impatient expression.

"Let's blow this pop stand," he said when he saw Karen.

"Not so fast. The nurse is getting your wheelchair."

"Wheelchair?" he said.

"Hospital policy."

"Forget it."

The nurse chose this inopportune moment to push the offending item through the door.

"I'm not leaving in that thing," Colter said firmly.

"Then you're not leaving at all," Karen replied. "Now will you stop behaving like a spoiled child and sit in it?"

He complied, grumbling. He didn't say a word until they had descended in the elevator and the nurse had waved goodbye on the front steps, taking the wheelchair back inside with her.

"I hope I never have to see that place again," he muttered, leaning against the side of the rented Renault as Karen fished in her purse for the keys.

"I hope so, too, although those people in there undoubtedly saved your life," Karen said.

"Let them save somebody else's."

Karen got in the little car and started the motor as Colter climbed in beside her. He folded his long legs under the dash and put his head back against the rest.

"I have the seat pushed back as far as it will go," Karen said to him. "I know it's a little tight, but they don't rent Cadillacs in Ireland."

"It's okay," he said. "I'm used to European cars. Anything is better than that hospital bed. Let's go."

"At least the sun came out in honor of your discharge," Karen said cheerfully.

"I almost forgot it was there."

"It's a good omen."

He turned his head to look at her and smiled slightly. "What an optimist."

"The map is in the glove compartment. The man at the rental place said we'd cross into the south at a town called Crossmaglen. Do you see it there?"

He looked for a moment and then said, "Yup."

"Good. Keep the passports right there. They'll be checked at the border. Then we just drive south until we hit Kinsale, which should be late tonight."

"Do you have directions to this cottage?" he asked.

"In my purse. There's supposed to be a crossroads in town, and one of the streets leads to the Mandeville place."

"Just as long as Miss Mandeville isn't there," he said darkly.

Karen chuckled, pulling out into a lane of traffic. "I don't know why you don't like her. She's very fond of you."

"She's very fond of pushing people around," he answered.

"Look at it from her point of view. I don't think you were the most cooperative patient she ever had."

He grunted.

"I heard the nurses were all going to wear black armbands after you left. They're mourning the loss of the opportunity to view your manly form."

He glanced at her as if to gauge her expression. She had noticed before that he didn't respond well to such teasing, but she couldn't resist.

"I guess you think all this is pretty funny," he said flatly.

Karen downshifted and then looked at him. "What do you mean?"

"Me winding up in a hospital, stuck with tubes and needles, at the mercy of that old battle-ax."

"Steven, everybody gets sick sometime. Not everybody gets shot, I'll grant you, but illness is something we all have to tolerate."

"Not me. I hate it. I'll bust loose and take my chances if I ever wind up in a place like that again."

She realized with a feeling of alarm that he was perfectly serious. "But surely you've been in a hospital before, the other times you were hurt."

"Nope. Doctors just patched me up and let me go."

She absorbed that for a moment, then said softly, "You can't bear the helplessness of it. Being hospitalized, I mean."

"Lying there, trussed up like turkey, can't even smoke a damn cigarette, everybody issuing orders and moving you around like you were paralyzed or something," he said bitterly. "Once I woke up, I thought about taking off but..."

"But?" Karen said.

He shrugged one shoulder, not looking at her. "You were there, and you wanted me to stay."

Karen didn't comment, trying to swallow past the lump in her throat. It was the closest he had come so far to an admission of feeling for her.

"Why don't you try to take a nap?" she finally asked him when she could talk.

"I've been taking more naps than a toddler lately," he observed grimly.

"Yes, I know, but it's a long drive and you should conserve your strength."

He muttered something under his breath, and she didn't ask him to repeat it.

"Is there anybody you want to contact?" Karen asked as she headed for the highway leading out of Belfast.

"Contact?"

"You know, write or call. We can stop if you want to send a telegram or make a call."

"No."

"Isn't there anyone who'll be wondering where you are?" she asked.

"Bill collectors," he said curtly.

Karen couldn't believe that anyone was as alone as he seemed to be. "What about your place in Florida. Don't you have a landlord or something?"

"He doesn't care if I'm on the moon as long as the rent is paid."

Karen dropped the subject. No amount of probing would bring forth information he didn't want her to have.

Colter fell asleep as she drove south, and she crossed over into the Republic at midmorning. She had worried that there might be some trouble at the border, but the guard merely checked their passports, glanced at her sleeping companion, and waved them through, saying, "Welcome to Eire." Deciding that he had pegged them for a couple of tourists, Karen smiled brightly and gunned the motor. She'd had some vague idea that Colter might be recognized and was relieved to find he wasn't as famous as she thought.

Karen picked up the coastal road at Dundalk and had passed through Drogheda and the Republican capital of Dublin before Colter awoke as they approached the Wicklow mountains. It was afternoon and Karen was starving, but she hadn't wanted to wake him by stopping the car.

"Time is it?" he said, sitting up and looking around. She'd observed before that he came awake very quickly, alert at once.

"About two."

"Where are we?"

"Wicklow."

"That's a big help."

"About halfway there."

"Oh, okay." He stared out his window for a while before saying, "Pretty country."

"Yes. It's just as green as it looks in all the travel posters."

"I always suspected they touched them up," he said, grinning. He glanced over at her. "You must be tired. Why don't you let me drive for a while?"

"No, thanks. I want to survive this journey."

"What is that supposed to mean? I'm not going to pass out at the wheel or anything."

"How do you know?"

"I feel fine."

"Which is the reason you just slept for five hours."

"You know something? You're a..."

"Pain in the neck. Yes, you've told me. Look, there's a place to stop and get something to eat. I'm famished." She pulled the little car into the gravel lot of a low barn-sided structure advertising Lunch, Snacks, Sandwiches. Behind them Lugnaquillia, the chief peak in the coastal range, soared to a height of 3,000 feet, looming into a gray mist that still swirled about the summit even at midday. Ahead of them the road stretched away into the distance, with rolling fields on either side.

"Why don't you wait here, and I'll bring you something?" Karen suggested.

"I'm coming in," he said firmly, and she decided not to argue with him. The walk wasn't far, and he probably wanted to stretch his legs.

As soon as they got inside, Karen wished that he had stayed behind. She had passed some road construction about five minutes earlier, and what looked like the entire work crew was in the pub having lunch. The air was thick with cigarette smoke and the pungent smell of the strong beer being served up liberally from taps behind the bar. An overworked barmaid and an overworked waitress were trying to deal with the capacity crowd, and they were not happy to see two new arrivals come through the door.

"What'll it be?" the waitress barked to Colter as they pushed their way to the counter.

"Do you have a menu?"

She pointed to a blackboard, on which was scrawled a choice of soups and sandwiches.

"Out of beef and barley," she said. "You'll have to make do with the leek."

"Leek?" Colter said, looking at Karen.

"That'll be fine," Karen said hastily. "And we'll take two egg-and-bacon sandwiches also."

The woman nodded.

"Is there a place to sit?" Colter asked.

"Just what you see," the waitress said, gesturing expansively. "Will you have a drop, too?" she asked.

"Ice water?" Karen said.

The waitress lifted an eyebrow, but went to fill the order.

"Nice quiet place you found, kid," Colter said to Karen, raising his voice above the babble. "What the hell is leek?"

"They're related to onions. I've had the soup, it's good."

He leaned against the wall, and Karen wished she could find a place for him to sit. He would never admit to fatigue, but he had to be feeling the effects of his first day out of bed.

Just then two of the workers vacated a booth near the door, and Karen grabbed Colter's hand, leading him to it. He had just settled down gratefully when one of the men returned with a fresh glass of stout in his hand.

"You've taken my spot," he said to Karen, smiling thinly.

"Oh, I'm sorry, we thought you'd left," she said, rising.

Colter put his hand on her arm. "Haven't you ever heard that you should let a lady have your seat?" he said quietly.

"Depends upon if there's a lady present, Yank. I'm thinking that anything sitting with the likes of you would be no lady."

Colter stood, and Karen jumped in front of him. "We don't want any trouble," she said hastily to their antagonist, who looked as though he outweighed Colter by about fifty pounds. "This was just a mistake. We'll go."

"Your woman makes a pretty speech," the workman said. "Does she always fight your battles for you?"

Colter lunged for him, and Karen seized the stranger's hand in desperation.

"Please," she wailed, "he just got out of the hospital this morning." She turned, and before Colter realized what she was doing, she had pulled open his shirt to reveal the gauze dressing on his chest.

The workman's expression changed. "I'm no bully to beat up on an injured man," he muttered and pushed his way past them, losing himself in the crowd.

Colter was white with anger. Looking straight ahead, he walked carefully around Karen and threaded his way through the crush to the door.

Karen followed him, and as she passed the counter, the waitress called, "Here's your food, miss."

Karen kept going, running out the door. She circled the building until she found Colter sitting on a picnic bench set up outside in view of the mountains.

"Don't you ever do that to me again," he said tightly when he looked up and saw her.

"What was I supposed to do, let you get into a brawl with that blockhead when you can barely stand? What is wrong with you, Steven, do you have a death wish? You just finished telling me how much you hated the hospital, and now you're trying to land yourself back there."

"I wasn't going to let that clown push me around."

Karen stared at him. "I don't understand you. All you want to do is fight. It's your profession, your hobby, your life. Everybody's your enemy, and you're going to show them all. Why are you so angry all the time?" Then, to her horror, she burst into tears.

He stood immediately, trying to embrace her. She fought him off until he pinned her arms, and then she fell against him, sobbing.

"All right, all right, I'm sorry," he murmured, stroking her hair. "Don't cry, please don't cry."

"I was so afraid he was going to hurt you," she whimpered. "Did you see the size of him?"

"Ah, the big ones just bleed more, that's all," he said deprecatingly, lifting her hair off her neck and planting a kiss on her nape.

"Don't cosset me," she said, stiffening. "Why would you do something so foolish?"

"I don't know," he said wearily. "I won't anymore, I promise, if you'll just stop crying."

"I'm not crying," Karen said, pulling away from him and wiping her eyes with the back of her hand.

"Oh," he replied, suppressing a smile and putting his hands behind his back. "I see."

"Good. Now I want you to sit right there on that bench while I go back inside and get our order. Wait for me, don't move, and don't get into any more trouble."

He sat and folded his hands on the table before him, bowing his head. "Okay, teach," he said meekly.

Karen returned shortly with the food, and noticed that Colter's shirt was stained with perspiration under his arms and in the middle of his back. It was a cool autumn day, and she was wearing a sweater. He was overexerting himself.

"Are you hungry?" she asked as she sat across from him, handing him a paper cup of soup.

He nodded. "Pretty much."

"I hope your appetite has picked up from the hospital; you weren't eating very much."

He took out a sandwich, opened it, then closed it again like a book he didn't wish to read. "Nobody could eat that food," he said darkly. "Most of it was unidentified." He jerked his thumb at the sandwich. "Bacon and eggs. That's breakfast."

"I've seen it on lunch menus all the time since I've been here."

He shrugged, picked it up and took a bite. "Not bad," he said, brightening.

"I'm so glad. Now finish it; you have to regain your strength."

He shook his head, chewing. "You sound just like one of the nuns at the school. 'Eat this, finish that,'" he mimicked. "'The starving children in Asia would love to have that broccoli.' I always told them to send it to the starving children in Asia because I didn't want it."

"And how did they respond to that?"

"Stood me in a corner when I was little, set me to washing floors and painting walls when I was bigger," he answered.

"Were you a discipline problem?"

He shrugged. "I guess so. I sure wasn't the star pupil."

"Didn't you learn anything while you were there?" Karen asked, putting down her sandwich.

"How to get by."

"And not to trust anyone or rely on anybody but yourself," she supplied for him.

He looked up from his last bite and said, "That's a good enough education for me."

"I don't agree," Karen said softly. "If that's what the people at the orphanage taught you, they did you a disservice."

He looked away from her into the distance where the mountain melted into the drifting clouds. "It wasn't their fault," he said evenly. "All they had time for was food and clothing, supplying the necessities. There were just too many kids."

"And no time to love them," Karen said.

He didn't answer. He picked up the empty wrappers and rolled the paper into a ball, tossing the wad into a rusted garbage can standing nearby.

"Let's hit the road," he said. "I don't think we'd better hang around for any more of the locals to drop by."

Karen silently concurred, and once they were back in the car, she tried to pick up speed a little and make better time. The Irish roads were narrow and winding, single lane for the most part, a challenge to her ability to drive a standard transmission car. They were descending once more toward the sea; she could hear it murmuring in the background and smell the salt in the damp breeze. Colter fell asleep again, and she passed through the larger towns of Wexford and Waterford, hitting the latter at rush hour and sitting in traffic for fifteen minutes. Karen almost woke her passenger for the breathtaking beauty of Youghal Bay, where *Moby Dick* had been filmed. But she decided to drive back later when he was feeling better and could appreciate it, and continued southward, hitting Cork at dusk.

Colter stirred as she crossed one of the bridges over the River Lee and skirted the harbor, picking up a side road marked for Kinsale in English and Gaelic.

"Sorry I keep passing out like that," he mumbled, rubbing the back of his head. "It's that happy juice they're giving me. I'm not taking any more of those pills."

"You certainly are," Karen said firmly. "I'm getting the prescription filled first thing in the morning."

"God, you are a tyrant," he complained. "I think you want to keep me in a coma."

"That's right. At least I know you're resting then. And your being unconscious offers the added benefit of my not having to listen to any more of your lip."

She looked over at him and saw that he was laughing silently.

"What's so funny?"

"To think when I met you I was convinced you were such a nice girl."

"I am," she said defensively, peering at the road sign that directed her down a cobbled street. "What does that say?" she asked him.

"Cobh," he answered. "Where do they get these names?"

"That's 'Cork' in Gaelic. We're going the wrong way."

"Great." He glanced around at the warren of tiny streets and alleys leading down to the river. "How could you get lost?"

She turned to stare at him in outrage. "I like that coming from the man who snored during this entire trip," she said archly. "I think I've done very well so far." She pulled up to a stoplight and examined the array of signs fixed to the lamppost. "Oh, I see. I was supposed to turn left here." She

NOW THAT THE DOOR IS OPEN . . .
Peel off the bouquet and send it on the postpaid order card to receive:

4 FREE BOOKS
from

Silhouette Intimate Moments®

An attractive burgundy umbrella FREE! And a mystery gift as an EXTRA BONUS!
PLUS

MONEY-SAVING HOME DELIVERY!
Once you receive your 4 FREE books and gifts, you'll be able to open your door to more great romance reading month after month. Enjoy the convenience of previewing 4 brand-new books every month delivered right to your home months before they appear in stores. Each book is yours for only $2.49—.26¢ less than the retail price, with no additional charges for home delivery.

SPECIAL EXTRAS—FREE!
You'll also receive the Silhouette Books Newsletter FREE with every book shipment. Every issue is filled with interviews, news about upcoming books and more! And as a valued reader, we'll be sending you additional free gifts from time to time—as a token of our appreciation.

NO-RISK GUARANTEE!
— There's no obligation to buy—and the free books and gifts are yours to keep forever.
— You pay the lowest price possible and receive books months before they appear in stores.
— You may end your subscription anytime—just write and let us know.

RETURN THE POSTPAID ORDER CARD TODAY AND OPEN YOUR DOOR TO THESE 4 EXCITING LOVE-FILLED NOVELS. THEY ARE YOURS ABSOLUTELY FREE ALONG WITH YOUR FOLDING UMBRELLA AND MYSTERY GIFT.

Take this beautiful
FOLDING
UMBRELLA
with your 4 FREE BOOKS
PLUS A MYSTERY GIFT

If offer card is missing, write to: Silhouette Books,
901 Fuhrmann Blvd., P.O. Box 9013, Buffalo, NY 14240-9013.

retraced her route, saying, "I can't tell which way south is anymore since the sun went down."

"If you go far enough south, we're going to be swimming," he observed crossly. He closed his eyes and folded his arms across his chest. "What am I doing here?" he asked. "How did I let you talk me into this?"

"Oh, shut up," Karen muttered, gunning the engine. "I'm doing the best I can."

They hit Kinsale about twenty minutes later, and Karen followed the directions from the center of town to an unpaved road leading in the direction of the water.

"This must be it," she said, turning onto it. "I wonder what that says," she added, pointing to a hand-lettered sign in Gaelic fixed to a tree.

"Let's just hope it doesn't say 'Cliff, ten feet ahead,'" Colter muttered.

"Do you see anything?" Karen inquired.

"Trees."

"Where do you think we are?"

"Tree City?"

Karen stopped driving and turned to face him. "Will you please cooperate?" she said. "I'm tired and hungry, and the last thing I need right now is your sarcasm."

"All right," he said, chastised. "Why don't we get out and look?"

Karen complied, and they left the car behind, walking down the road about a thousand feet. They rounded a curve and were suddenly confronted by a vista that brought them both to a halt.

A cottage stood alone in a clearing on the edge of a bluff. Below it they could hear the pounding of the surf, and above it stretched a limitless night sky, spangled with an infinity of stars.

"Isn't it beautiful?" Karen whispered.

"It sure is," Colter answered, putting his arm around her. "And well worth the trip."

"What?" she said, turning to look up at him. "May I have that in writing, please?"

He bent his head and kissed her lightly on the lips. Before she had a moment to react, it was over. It was as if he wasn't giving her a chance to make it into anything more.

"You're a wonder," he said.

"It wasn't my idea," Karen said honestly. "Miss Mandeville suggested it."

"Do you mind if we don't give her the credit for it?" Colter said, taking Karen's hand. "I expect to find her waiting for me inside with a ten-inch needle."

"I'll protect you," Karen said valiantly.

"I believe you would," he answered softly. Then he took a step back toward the car, tugging her after him. "Come on, I want to see the inside. You have the key?"

"Right in my pocket—assuming this is the place."

"It has to be."

"It better be, or whoever owns it is going to be having guests for the evening. I can't push that glorified tin can another foot tonight."

They got back in the car, and Karen drove it almost to the front door, where a paved turnaround provided a parking space.

"Where's the water?" Karen asked as she unlocked the door. "I can hear it."

"I think there's a sheer drop to the ocean on the other side of the house," Colter said. "I suggest we don't do any exploring until tomorrow when we can see where the hell we're going."

"Good idea."

Inside Karen found a switch on the wall near the door and flicked it. Nothing happened.

"Uh-oh," she said.

"Don't worry. There's probably a generator here somewhere. We just have to find it. I didn't see any power lines, so this place must have its own source."

"I feel like an explorer," Karen whispered.

He went ahead, stumbling around in the dark until he found a box of candles and lit one. In its glow they could both see a large paneled room with heavy oak furniture and a massive fireplace along one wall.

"There it is," Colter said, pointing to a tanklike affair in one corner. He went to it and fiddled around for a while, then hit the wall switch again.

The room was flooded with light.

They were quiet for a minute, looking around. There were actually two rooms, the one they were in, a combination living room and kitchen, and another one beyond, obviously a bedroom. The place looked fairly new; the appliances in the kitchenette were modern, the rag rugs and print curtains bright and cheerful.

"Who owns this place again?" Colter asked.

"Miss Mandeville's cousin. He's a teacher on sabbatical."

There was a sofa bed against one wall near the fireplace, and Colter walked over to it immediately and sat down. Karen glanced at him anxiously. There were dark rings under his eyes, and his shirt was again stained with sweat.

"Stretch out there, and I'll see if there's a pillow in the other room," she said to him. "You look beat. I'm afraid we shouldn't have attempted this long drive so soon."

"I'm all right," he said, but he didn't sound it.

"You should have stayed in the hospital a few more days," Karen called to him from the bedroom, which contained a large brass bed and a matched set of bleached oak chests. A tiny bathroom opened off it to the right. Karen pulled back the quilted patchwork comforter on the bed and grabbed a pillow from the top of it.

"Karen, I was not going to spend another night in that hospital, even if I had to burn the place down," he answered as she returned and put the pillow under his head. His hair was damp, and his skin felt clammy.

"We'd better change your shirt," she said to him. "Where's your bag?"

"Still out in the car," he said, struggling to a sitting position. "I'll get it."

"Stay right where you are," she replied in a strong voice.

He fell back on the couch, watching her go out.

Karen fetched their things and found a clean shirt for him. She sat on the edge of the sofa and helped him take off the plaid one, slipping it carefully down the arm on his injured side.

"Does this still hurt?" she asked softly, touching the bandage lightly.

"Not much," he replied huskily, his light eyes flickering, holding hers intently.

"You liar," she whispered. "I'll bet it's killing you."

"Karen?"

"Mmm?"

"Thanks for arranging all of this," he said quietly. "I know I've been grousing about it, but sometimes I have a little trouble saying what I mean."

"Sometimes?" she said, teasing. "A *little* trouble?"

"Okay," he said, smiling slightly. "I always have a lot of trouble, but I do feel things. I just can't..." He broke off, leaving the sentence unfinished.

"It's all right," she said soothingly. "I understand. I really do."

The shirt he'd taken off was on the floor, and she still held the clean one in her hand. He was naked to the waist, and inches away. She fancied she could feel the body heat emanating from him, enveloping her in a cozy glow that would warm her forever.

"You'd better put this on," she said to him briskly, and he shouldered into it obediently, leaving it unbuttoned.

"It's gotten quite chilly. I think I'll start a fire," she announced, standing and going to the mantel for the matches.

"I think I saw some wood by the door as we came in," he said, "but you'd better make sure the flue is open first."

Karen made a nest of some old newspapers she found and put twigs on top of it for kindling. Colter looked on as she brought in the logs he had mentioned.

"Let me get those," he said, swinging his legs to the floor.

"Please, Steven, I can do it," Karen said hastily. "Will you kindly stay still? You're making me very nervous."

He grumbled under his breath but complied. She soon had the fire going and went rummaging in the kitchenette for something to eat.

"Should have stopped for supplies in town; the cupboard's bare," she reported to him. "This refrigerator contains a bottle of tonic water and two limes."

"Where's the gin? The guy must be a drinker."

In one of the cabinets she found a jar of peanut butter and got two spoons from a drawer.

"We're roughing it this evening," she said as she sat next to him again. "I'll go to the store in the morning."

"Funny-tasting peanut butter," Colter commented as he licked his spoon. "Kind of gummy."

"It's a European brand," Karen answered, looking at the label. "Maybe their peanuts are different."

He smiled. "You're being a very good sport about this. It can't be much fun for you."

Karen looked at him. Was that what he really thought? Didn't he know yet how she felt about him?

"What do you mean?" she said casually. "I like peanut butter."

They finished off the jar and then split the tonic water between them.

"Is the tap water on?" he asked. "I want to use the john."

Karen went to the sink and turned on one of the spigots. The water came out muddy at first but soon cleared up.

"It looks all right," she said to him. "There must be a well. These appliances are of British manufacture and seem a little quirky. The taps turn backward."

He rose unsteadily, supporting himself with one hand on the wall. She ran to help him, and they walked together to the bedroom.

"I don't know what's the matter with me," he said as he leaned on her heavily. "I was all right earlier."

"You're just done in," Karen replied, opening the door to the bathroom in front of him. "You have to give yourself a chance to recover."

"But how long is it going to take?" he asked irritably.

"Longer than you've given it," Karen answered dryly. "I'll wait right here, okay?"

He nodded and went in. Karen explored the bedroom while he was occupied, checking out the prints on the wall and the books in a case under the window. She looked up as Colter emerged, his hair wet, rubbing the stubble on his chin.

"God, I look like hell," he said to her. "Have I looked this bad all along? I'm surprised you didn't feed me to the fish."

"Didn't they have mirrors in the hospital?" she asked, grinning.

"Yeah, I avoided them. Now I know why."

"Why don't you sit on the bed and rest while I open up that sofa in the other room?"

He looked at her.

"I think you're better off in there with the fire, and I'll sleep in here."

He waited for a long moment, then said, "Okay."

He was being remarkably agreeable. Karen ascribed it to his exhaustion and told herself to enjoy it while it lasted, which surely couldn't be long.

She found linens in a hall closet and made up his bed. The fire was burning steadily, and the living room was warm and pleasant. The flames cast dancing shadows on the walls, filling the cottage with an amber radiance.

When she turned to go back for him, she saw that he was standing in the doorway between the two rooms, leaning against the jamb, watching her.

"You're working very hard at this," he said in a low tone.

"Will you stop getting up and walking around?" Karen said grimly. "I feel like I should tie you to a chair. Don't you know enough to lie down when you're sick?"

"I guess not," he replied. "I'll probably die standing up, like a horse."

"Very funny." She led him to the newly made bed, and there was no mistaking his sigh of gratification when he sank down on it. He turned his head on the pillow and reached up to take her hand. He put it to his lips and kissed it.

"Good night, Florence Nightingale," he said softly.

"Good night, tough guy," she answered.

She went to add another log to the fire, and when she looked at him again, he was asleep.

Colter woke in the middle of the night. His mouth was dry from the peanut butter, and the room was stiflingly hot. Karen had built up the fire before she retired, and it was only now burning low.

He felt much better after his long nap and got up to get a drink. On his return to bed he stripped off his clothes and left them on the floor. He always slept raw, anyway, and the fire had made him warm.

Actually, the fire wasn't the only thing that had raised his temperature. He'd been dreaming about Karen. Again. She kept telling him how sick he was. He might have warned her that he wasn't quite as ill as she thought. Not too ill, for example, to contemplate certain activities with her that were guaranteed to keep him sleepless for the rest of the night.

He put one arm behind his head and pulled the sheet over him, staring at the shadow play on the ceiling cast by the dwindling flames. She was so close, right in the next room, and he couldn't forget it.

He wondered what would happen if he just went in there and got into her bed. He closed his eyes and sighed heavily. She would doubtless remind him that he'd said he wanted them to remain friends, give him two aspirin, and pat him on the head. He gritted his teeth. He was waging a war within himself, and he was losing. He wanted her so badly now that he was finding it difficult to remind himself of the possible consequences of their involvement.

He just didn't care anymore.

Suddenly the door to the bedroom opened, and Colter shut his eyes, feigning sleep. He heard the padding of bare feet, and then the shifting of the logs as Karen moved them. She was stoking the fire.

He slitted his eyes and looked at her through his lashes. What he saw froze him, and he hardly dared to breathe.

Karen was wearing a floor-length batiste nightgown, but as she stood in front of the fire, the light shone through it, making it seem almost transparent. Her body was clearly outlined against it, and he could see her as well as if she were naked. His gaze moved over her greedily, taking in the full breasts, their taut nipples stiffened by the night chill, and the line of her back down to her narrow waist. The slight swell of her abdomen curved into a dark triangle of hair at the apex of her legs. Colter swallowed hard. He was so aroused he almost groaned aloud and had to bite his lip to stifle the sound.

Karen finished with the fire and turned, stopping when she noticed the puddle of his clothes on the floor. Her eyes moved upward to his face, and she gave a visible start when she saw that he was awake.

Colter propped himself up on one arm and extended his hand to her.

"Come here," he said huskily.

Chapter 6

Karen stared at him. The firelight was turning his hair to molten gold and dancing along the planes of his face, making his cheekbones more prominent. The pale hairs on his tanned arm glinted in the darkened room, and the hand he held out to her was curved upward in supplication.

It was an invitation she couldn't resist.

She hardly felt the rug beneath her feet as she crossed the floor. She bent toward him, and before she was able to sit, he had pulled her into his arms.

Karen knew as soon as she felt his body next to hers that he was naked beneath the sheet. She drew back slightly, but he held her fast, nuzzling her neck.

"Don't go," he whispered.

"Steven, I . . ." Karen began, but he silenced her with a kiss.

His mouth was hot, urgent, and she remembered the way he always kissed her: as if he would consume her, as if she were the most desirable woman he had ever touched. She felt the stubble of his beard graze her cheek as he turned his head, and his lips left hers to travel a path along the line of her neck to the collar of her gown. He paused there, fumbling with the buttons at the yoke.

Karen stayed his hand. "Steven, you're sick," she murmured.

He looked up and met her eyes. "If you say that to me once more, I am going to have it tattooed on your forehead," he answered grimly.

"But you weren't feeling well earlier," she persisted.

He sat back and took her hand, moving it to his chest where she could feel the runaway beating of his heart. "Do I seem sick?" he muttered. "Incapacitated?" He guided her hand down his body to his thigh. She could feel him, stallion-ready, through the thin barrier of the sheet.

"Incapable?" he said huskily.

Karen's fingers closed around him, her head falling forward to his shoulder. "You said you just wanted to be friends," she whispered desperately.

"I know what I said," he replied impatiently, pulling away. "Forget what I said. I didn't know what I was talking about."

"You knew," Karen said. "You had a reason for saying it, and I can't forget that."

He seized her shoulders and drew her up to face him. "Can you deny that you feel what I do?" he asked, almost angrily.

"No." The word came out like a sigh.

"Then what are we yammering about?"

His fingers were digging into her flesh, and when she tried to move, he held her still.

"But you've felt it with lots of women," Karen protested softly.

"What?" he said alertly, watching her face.

"Desire," she murmured.

He released her suddenly and covered his face with his hands. "You are going to drive me crazy," he said, between his teeth. "Didn't you just tell me today Mary Lafferty said I *wouldn't* sleep with her?"

"Yes, but that was different. You had a different reason."

He threw up his hands in mystification. "Okay, I'll bite. What are you talking about?"

"I can't treat this as casually as you can."

"What makes you think I'm treating it casually?" he asked, his eyes locked with hers.

Karen shook her head sadly. "Steven, I may not be the most experienced woman in he world, but I even I can see what's happening. Your first instinct was right. You resisted getting involved with me because you knew I would want more than you were prepared to give. But tonight you're feeling grateful because I helped you, and we're alone here together, and you're saying to yourself, What the hell. Then tomorrow, or the next day, or maybe not then but sometime, you'll be sorry and wonder what you've gotten yourself into. Isn't that right?"

He stared at her for several seconds, then looked away. He didn't say anything for so long that she was about to speak again when he turned his head. There was an expression on his face she'd never seen before.

"You don't understand anything about me, do you?" he muttered. He blinked, and she saw the rise and fall of his chest as he took a deep breath.

"What?" Karen whispered, leaning forward and touching his bare shoulder. "What is it, Steven? You can tell me."

"I didn't want to get involved because I know a girl like you would never stay," he said hoarsely. "Not for the long haul. Right now I'm unusual, a new experience, and attractive for that reason. But that will wear off—it always does—and you'll be left with me, Steve Colter. And Steve Colter doesn't have a promising career; he doesn't even have a steady job. He's not the type of person you could introduce to your sister and be proud." He bent his head. "I know what I am Karen, and I'm no bargain for any woman." He looked up again and held her gaze. "Are you sure you're the only one who's taking a chance?"

Karen couldn't reply. So this was what lay behind the smokescreen of his hurtful words at the hospital.

She reached out and touched his cheek gently. "But you take chances every day," she finally managed to say. "You put yourself in danger all the time."

He shook his head, not looking at her. "That's not the same. It's only possible to die once, and then the pain is over. But if you became necessary to me, then you left . . ." He broke off and shrugged. "I don't want to miss you all my life."

Karen leaned forward, putting her face against his shoulder. "Oh, Steven," she whispered, "you're just like everyone else, after all."

"What do you mean?"

"You're afraid of being hurt."

He made no reply.

"I didn't think you were afraid of anything," Karen murmured. She looked up at him, and his blue gaze met hers.

"I guess we're both taking a chance," she added softly.

He slipped his hand under her hair, inside the collar of her gown. He stroked the nape of her neck, and she shivered with anticipation.

"Karen, I need you," he murmured. "Make love with me tonight."

Her fears forgotten, Karen turned willingly into his arms.

Colter held her quietly for a long moment, and Karen explored his torso with light, caressing fingers, taking care to avoid the bandage he still wore. He gasped as she traced the line of hair that bisected his middle, then sighed, disappointed, when she stopped at the sheet folded at his waist.

Colter pulled her into his lap, kissing her, and Karen wound her arms around his neck, giving herself to the experience. He smelled wonderful, warm and musky, his skin fragrant with a unique scent she clearly recalled, masculine and definitely his. He ran his hands down her flanks, seeking the hem of her gown, and Karen stiffened.

"Hey," he said into her ear, half laughing, "this has to come off."

"I know," she replied, hugging him to cover her embarrassment. "But I'm a little nervous; it's been so long."

He pulled back and lifted her chin with his hand, searching her face. "How long?"

Karen dropped her eyes. "Two years."

He stared at her. "Two *years*?"

"Since my divorce. And even before that we didn't...I mean, not very often, and he wasn't..." She stopped, mortified.

"Okay, okay," Colter said soothingly, patting her back with circular motions, as if burping a baby. "I get the picture. I'll try to take it slow and easy, all right?"

"All right," she whispered.

"Now, first things first." He tugged at the nightgown again. Karen sat back, lifting it to her thighs and then crossing her arms and pulling it over her head. She held one arm behind her back and let it drift to the floor.

Colter's eyes moved over her, drinking in her beauty. She was next to him on the couch, sitting on her haunches in the firelight. Dark hair cascaded over her shoulders, contrasting vividly with her ivory skin. Her body was half in shadow, but he could make out the swell of rose-tipped breasts and the slim curve of her hips. He reached out to touch a smooth pale thigh, and Karen caught her breath.

"You are so lovely," he whispered.

He put his arm around her middle and pulled her toward him, kissing the petal-soft skin at the juncture of her breasts. Karen held his head against her and arched her back, thrusting forward to seek his mouth.

Colter moved and took a nipple between his lips, sucking gently. Karen moaned and then looked down, watching him as a wave of longing engulfed her. He was flushed, as if with fever, and his eyes were closed, the better to lose himself in the luxurious sensation. His thick sandy lashes lay on his cheeks, and his hair fell in careless strands across his forehead. She felt his large hands encircle her waist and hold her steady as he increased the pressure of his mouth. She bent like a willow, ever closer to him, gasping as his teeth grazed her, heightening her sensitivity almost to the point of pain.

He pulled back abruptly, and she whimpered, following after him. He caught her and eased her downward until her back touched the mattress, and then loomed over her, tracing the line of her breasts with his hand. His touch was deliberately light, drifting, and she yearned toward him, unconsciously asking for more. He caressed her lower body, sculpting the long muscles of her thighs, and her legs fell apart in response. Making a low sound deep in his throat, he bent and pressed his cheek to her abdomen, and Karen started at the contact with his fiery skin.

"Relax," he murmured. "Just let go, and let me love you." He was finding it difficult to hold back, but he paused until he could feel the tension lessen in her body as he held her.

"That's good," he whispered. "That's fine." He dragged his lips slowly over the satiny surface of her belly. "You're like silk, all over." He put his tongue into her navel, and she bit back a cry, covering her mouth with her hand. Then it fell away in abandonment as his mouth created a heated path that cooled the instant he moved on, making her writhe in frustration.

"What?" he muttered. "What do you want?"

"I don't know," she moaned.

"I do," he said hoarsely. He slipped his hands beneath her hips and lifted her to his mouth.

The sensation was so exquisite that Karen couldn't make a sound. She held her breath as he caressed her, curling one hand in the sheet that lay twisted under them, digging the fingers of the other into his hair. He drove her to a mounting frenzy and then lifted his head when she clawed at his shoulder, trying to pull him up to her.

"You want me?" he said softly, kissing the smooth surface of her left hip.

Karen nodded wordlessly.

He moved over her for the first time and embraced her fully, twining his fingers with hers and pinning her arms above her head.

"You sure?" he whispered, lifting himself on his elbows and gazing down into her eyes.

Karen turned her head. "You tease me," she whispered.

"No, baby," he replied huskily, kissing her lightly on the mouth. "Waiting makes the pleasure sweeter."

"Enough," she gasped as he relaxed and she felt the length of his body pressed to hers. "Take me now." She shifted her legs restlessly, trying to force him into position.

He remained immobile, watching her with an intensity that bespoke his true feelings.

Karen put her head down against the pillow and gazed up at him, at the pale eyes that seemed to fill the world. His skin was misted with a fine dew of perspiration, and her fingers glided across the slick muscular surface of his back as she urged him closer. Acting purely on instinct, Karen reached down and enclosed him with her hand, feeling his pulse of life respond to her caress.

He gasped and shut her eyes. "You win," he said hoarsely. He molded her to him, and Karen surged against him. The movement thrust her shoulder into the wound on his chest.

Colter grunted and stiffened, rolling off her. Karen clasped both hands to her mouth in horror, staring at him. The silence was awful. Beads of sweat formed on his forehead, and he bit his lip with the effort of not crying out.

"My God, Steven, are you all right?" Karen wailed, when she had found her voice. She felt like crying. "We shouldn't have done this. I told you it was too soon."

She moved to rise, and his hand shot out, grasping her wrist in an iron grip that belied his injury.

"No," he said fiercely. "Don't stop now."

"But we can't," she protested.

"Come on to me," he said urgently, drawing her toward him. "Come on." She realized that he wanted her to take charge, make love to him.

"Please," he rasped.

Karen crawled back into his arms, careful not to touch his chest. "I'm afraid I'm going to hurt you again," she whispered.

He ran his hands down her back, pulling her across his thighs. She felt his muscles tense to receive her and the friction of his leg hair against her bare skin.

"You won't," he answered, drawing her closer. He put his face against her breasts and held her tightly, then slipped his hands beneath her, guiding her onto him. An involuntary sound escaped his lips as she enclosed him, and he threw his head back, exhaling sharply. Karen fell forward onto his shoulder, and neither of them stirred for a long moment, lost in the intense pleasure of their union.

"You can't imagine how you feel to me," Colter finally murmured, lifting her damp hair and kissing her neck tenderly. "No matter what happens, I'll never forget this night."

Karen's eyes misted, blurring her vision. He always talked as if all they could share was memories.

"I'm not going to move," she whispered. "I want to stay like this forever."

"Move, please," he groaned, gripping her hips and lifting her. "I'm dying."

Karen put her hands on his upper arms to steady herself, and they were rigid, tensed powerfully, expectantly. He held her gaze with his and guided her in a pace that soon had her breathless, frantic. Suddenly he held her still and arched her backward. Karen trembled as he thrust upward, and she felt him move more deeply inside her.

He pulled her down to him and kissed her wildly, tangling his fingers in her disordered hair. For the first time he seemed to be out of control, and Karen was exhilarated by her effect on him. She pulled back, and he let her go reluctantly, watching with intoxicated eyes as she sat astride him, taking his face in her hands.

"Has it ever been like this for you before?" she asked, running her thumbs over his lips, his bearded cheeks.

He closed his eyes. "No." The word was barely audible, an admission.

She bent and kissed him again, gently. "I understand, Steven. You don't have to say anything more."

He lay back and allowed her to continue, but they were both too carried away by their mutual ardor to last much longer. Impelled by Colter's forceful hands on her hips,

Karen drove to a frenzied completion, and then collapsed against him, spent.

There was no sound in the room for a long while except their breathing, gradually returning to normal, and the hiss and crackle of the fire.

"Hmm," Colter finally said drowsily, "did I underestimate you."

"I hope that's a compliment."

"It certainly is. When you told me two years, I thought I was really in trouble...."

She jabbed him in the ribs.

"But you did very well."

"I surprised myself. With Ian, it was, well, a lot different."

"Your husband, you mean?"

"Mm-hmm."

"No fire, huh?" he said.

"No. No fire."

"Well, we may have our problems, but that's not one of them," he said quietly, kissing her temple. Then he asked, "Were you with anyone else, before your husband?"

"Never."

"So you were disappointed with him?" Colter persisted.

Karen shrugged within the confines of his arms. "I had no basis of comparison. I'm not sure that I felt I lacked anything, but I always wondered if there wasn't something..."

"More?" he suggested.

"Yes, that's right. More."

"And now you know," he said. There was a long pause, and then he added, "The only problem is that sometimes you can strike sparks with the wrong person."

"Steven Colter, if you start that now I swear I will do something violent. I'm too happy for that lecture tonight," Karen said firmly.

He fell silent. Karen listened to the rustle of the fire for a while, then said, "I didn't mean that you couldn't talk at all."

He sighed. "What would you like to hear?"

"Something that won't spoil the mood."

"Fairy tales?"

She twisted around to look at him. "That isn't funny."

He kissed her brow. "I'm sorry."

She studied him until he said, "What are you thinking?"

"I was remembering the first time I saw you, in Almeria."

He grunted. "Not exactly like meeting at a garden party, was it?"

"I was afraid of you."

"I guess that's not too surprising," he conceded, "considering the circumstances."

"I thought for a minute that you were with them, the rebels."

He snorted mirthlessly. "Not much real difference between us, when you get right down to it. Which side you're on doesn't matter a whole lot in the end."

Karen sat up, and he reached for her as she left his embrace.

"Where are you going?" he asked.

"To put some more fuel on the fire," she replied. Retrieving her nightgown from the floor, she pulled it over her head and padded barefoot to the fireplace to add several logs to the dwindling blaze. It smoked, then shot up, and she waited until it was burning steadily before returning to him and sitting on the edge of the bed.

"What is it?" he asked quietly, touching her shoulder. "Something's wrong."

Karen shook her head.

"Come on. Tell Uncle Steven all about it."

"Why did you say that you were a gun for hire," she blurted, "working for anyone who would pay you?"

His hand fell away, and he turned his head. "Because it's the truth."

"No, it's not. Linda told me that you're a rescue expert, brought in to break up hostage situations, like you were in Almeria."

He didn't answer for a moment, then said, "Who's Linda?"

"My friend from Government House; she worked there with me."

"Oh, the British gal."

"Yes."

"And how does she know so much?"

"She has her sources. Was she correct?"

He shrugged negligently. "It's all in the way you look at it. I'm still hiring myself out, right?"

Karen folded her arms in annoyance. "Why do you persist in describing your life in the worst possible terms? It's like you're attempting to drive me away, or something."

"Could I?" he asked, watching her carefully.

"You didn't answer my question," Karen said patiently. "Why didn't you tell me the whole story?"

"Because you're trying to make me out to be something I'm not!" he replied angrily, rolling away from her. "You don't want to face the fact that you're sleeping with a mercenary, so you're changing everything around in your mind to fit a prettier picture. I'm not Lancelot rescuing Guinevere from the stake or St. George slaying the dragon. I'm a man who takes money to do a job, and that's all. The Lone Ranger rode off into the TV sunset a long time ago, Karen; there are no more white hats."

She was silent for several seconds, then said softly, "I don't want to fight."

He rolled over onto his back and looked up at her, reaching out and running a strand of her hair through his fingers. "Neither do I."

"I want us to be close."

"We are," he answered quietly. "You don't get any closer than we just were."

Karen shook her head. "No, I mean emotionally. Like friends."

He dropped his hand. "I guess I don't know how to do that."

She smiled slightly. "It's easy."

"Not for me."

"I'll show you."

He had to smile, too. "Okay, show me."

She leaned forward eagerly, moving the sheet aside and taking his big hand in both of hers. "Well, the first thing is to share confidences. You tell me things, and I tell you."

He was looking very suspicious, but he said, "All right. What do you want to know?"

"Tell me what it's like to be shot."

His brow furrowed. "Why do you want to know that?"

"I've never been shot."

"You haven't missed anything."

"Steven."

"Okay. Well, it's kind of like a bee sting."

She stared at him. "A bee sting?"

"Yeah, you know, that sharp, hot jolt, so sudden, but magnified about a hundred times."

"Is it very painful?"

"Not at first. It's just a shock, like—wow, what hit me? The pain sets in later, after you realize what happened."

"How many times have you been shot?"

"Three. No, four. This makes four."

"Is this a scar from one of the bullets?" Karen asked, touching an irregular lump of pinkish flesh on his upper arm.

He glanced down at himself. "Nah. That one's from a knife fight in the army. Did three weeks in the brig that time."

"Oh. What were you fighting about?"

"A girl," he said levelly.

"I hope she was worth it."

"I don't remember."

Karen made a face.

"What do you want?" he said wearily. "I was eighteen. I would have fought over the weather report."

"It doesn't appear to me that you've changed very much."

"Yeah, I have," he replied. "I've gotten more selective about the fights. I want to be paid for them now." He cast her a sidelong glance. "How'm I doing at this friendship stuff?"

"Not bad."

"Isn't it your turn to tell me something now?"

"Yes."

"I'm waiting."

"I'm falling in love with you, Steven."

He looked at her for a long moment, then dropped his eyes. She could still see a circle of blue iris through the screen of his lashes, focused on nothing. He was motionless, as still as a portrait.

"I must say you don't seem overjoyed to hear the news," Karen observed nervously. Her heart was beating so hard she thought he should be able to hear it.

"It's not news," he said softly.

"Oh, you knew?"

"Yeah."

"And here I thought I was making a dramatic declaration," she said, striving for lightness. If he didn't say something significant soon, she was going to get very upset.

"I figured a girl like you wouldn't go away with me unless you'd made a commitment," he said. "I mean, you could have come over here when I was hurt because you felt sorry for me, but you didn't have to stay and do this, too."

"You thought I felt sorry for you?" Karen asked him wonderingly.

"The idea did occur to me," he said tightly.

"Why?"

"Well, you're so tenderhearted. When you heard that I was alone and in the hospital, it wasn't hard to guess your motivation."

"I'm not that 'tenderhearted,' as you put it. I came because I care about you."

He lifted her hand and placed a kiss in its palm. "I believe that now."

"But you're still not happy about it."

He gestured helplessly. "I just don't think this has much of a chance to work out in the long run."

"Because we're too different?"

"That's one reason."

"What are the others?"

He hesitated. "Karen, I've done things that I'm not proud of, things that would make you run from this room and from this relationship, if I told you about them."

"Then don't tell me," she said evenly.

"Don't you care?" he said hopelessly.

"I care that you're with me now, and that's all."

"But my life was all wrong from the beginning. How can it match up with yours at this late date?"

"What do you mean, 'all wrong'? How can anybody's life be wrong? Is there a set of rules? You're talking nonsense, Steven."

"No, I'm not," he said stubbornly.

"What are you saying? Because we didn't go to high school together we can't have anything now?"

"I didn't go to high school, Karen," he said dully. "I got an equivalency diploma in the service."

Karen sighed, cursing herself for reminding him of yet another disparity in their backgrounds.

"But don't you want someone to love forever, someone who'll be yours alone?"

"More than anything," he said quietly, his head bowed.

"Then why are you so certain she isn't me?" she whispered.

He wouldn't look at her. "Because I'm not destined for that kind of an existence. I've known it from the beginning. Life isn't fair, Karen. Some people just don't fit the happy pattern of wife and kids and a house with a dog. I'm one of them. I'm on the outside, a square peg in a universe of round holes. I always have been and I always will be."

She was amazed at how convinced he sounded, as if this were a conclusion he had reached a long time ago and never found reason to doubt.

He finally met her eyes, reaching up to touch her cheek. "I just don't want to make promises I can't keep," he said softly.

Karen put her arms around him and snuggled into his good side. "We'll just take it one day at a time, okay?" she whispered.

"Okay," he responded, just as quietly.

They lay together for a long while with no need of further conversation. Then Karen felt him stir and pull her closer.

"Are you cold?" Karen asked him, pulling the sheet up to cover them both. "There's a heavier blanket in one of the chests."

"No," he answered. "You feel like a little bonfire right here in bed with me."

"I wonder," Karen said teasingly, "what happened to that clever little plan calling for me to sleep in the other room?"

He chuckled. "Don't remind me. I got one look at you in that transparent nightie, and all bets were off."

"Transparent!" Karen said, shocked. "I beg your pardon. I do not wear transparent negligees."

"I don't care what it's supposed to be; when you stood in front of the fire, I could see right through it."

"Oh," she said, chastened. "I didn't think about that."

"But I did," he said, rolling her under him. "I thought about it quite a bit, especially while you were posing five feet away from me, as good as naked."

"I was not posing," she protested. "I didn't think you could see me."

"Oh, no?"

"I thought you were asleep."

"A likely story," he murmured, kissing the tip of her nose, then her lips. "And while we're on the subject of this lousy nightgown, why the hell are you wearing it again?" He took the collar between his teeth and dragged it away from her neck, then dipped his tongue into the exposed hollow at the base of her throat.

"It was chilly when I got up to tend the fire," Karen said breathlessly, "and..."

"It's not chilly now, is it?" he interrupted. "In fact, aren't you feeling a little... warm?"

"Yes," she sighed as he bent his head and mouthed her breasts through the cloth. Her nipples rose at his touch, straining the sheer cotton so that he could feel them, defined like pebbles, with his tongue. She turned sensuously beneath him, almost wanton in her unspoken demand. He moved to kiss her again, passionately this time, communicating his intention clearly.

"Wait," Karen began, attempting to take the gown off.

"Just lift it," he said urgently, shoving the folds up her thighs with eager, impatient hands. She could feel him hard against her, and when he'd pushed the nightgown out of the way, he entered her in almost the same motion.

This time it was swift and silent. They moved as one, unthinking, uncaring, and when it was over, they slept.

When Karen woke again, it was morning, and she was alone in the sofa bed. Colter had drawn the quilt up to her chin, but the fire had gone out and the cabin was cold.

She got up and found her watch in the other room. It was nine-thirty and Colter was gone.

Karen didn't know whether to be worried or furious. He was in no shape to be out and running around, but she blamed herself for oversleeping. He would always do too much if he weren't watched, and she hadn't been watching.

She was opening her suitcase to get a change of clothes when the cottage door opened and Colter came through it, carrying two paper sacks of groceries. He was wearing a green sweatshirt with a pair of tan chinos, and his bright hair looked soft and freshly shampooed. The stubble of his beard was gone.

He held up his hand as she entered the living room and he saw her expression.

"Don't yell at me," he said, depositing his burdens on the kitchenette counter. "I've been feeling very guilty with you waiting on me hand and foot, and I wanted to do something for you."

"And that was?" Karen asked.

"Get breakfast," he said. "Which turned out to be much more of a project than I had anticipated."

"Really?" she said, smiling slightly. "How so?"

"Well," he said, leaning back against the wall and crossing his legs at the ankle, "first I had to buy the groceries. No easy task. I soon discovered that nothing opens until ten o'clock. Apparently these people aren't as concerned as our countrymen with making money."

"It looks like you found something."

"'Something' is right. I took that roller skate you call a car down into Kinsale, and remind me to award you a Purple Heart for driving that thing all the way from Belfast yesterday. Anyhow, I found this little one-room place down an alley off Cork Road. An old guy was sitting outside drinking a mug of tea when I pulled up and asked him if he was open. He took about ten minutes to think about it before he answered that it 'might be getting near the time' and took me inside to this incredible junk pile. Every conceivable space was covered with shelves and boxes filled with stuff I haven't seen in years. Coke in the hourglass bottles, Band-Aids in the metal tins, cocoa in those old square boxes. It was amazing. I felt like I was in a time warp. And look at what he sold me."

Karen went to his side, smiling, as he revealed his purchases.

"I'm not even sure it's safe to eat the stuff," he said. "This, for example, is supposed to be bacon."

He unwrapped a side of meat, and they both stared at it.

"Looks like pork chops cured like ham, doesn't it?" he said, clearly puzzled.

"It's all right," Karen said, laughing. "That's what they call bacon around here. I've had it and I assure you it's edible."

"And what about this?" he asked. He indicated a brick of butter. "Did you ever see butter that color? It looks anemic or something. It's called Kerry Gold, but there's nothing gold about it."

"They don't add any food coloring," Karen said. "I'm sure it's actually better for you."

"Hmm," he said doubtfully. "And this bread," he went on, holding up an unsliced loaf, "is gray. How the hell do they manage to achieve gray bread?"

"It's stone ground or stone milled—I forget—but the process doesn't remove the husk from the wheat. Very nutritious."

"Brown eggs," he said, opening a box and pointing.

"Oh, come on, Steven, don't be such a chauvinist. You've seen them at home."

"And the milk," he said, looking at her out of the corner of his eye, "comes in those glass bottles they used to deliver in the forties, with the cream in a layer on top. I haven't seen one of them since the last Bowery Boys movie on the late show."

"As far as I know," Karen said dryly, "no one ever died from drinking bottled milk. They just don't homogenize it, like we do now."

"How do you know so much about the food?" Colter asked suspiciously.

"I was buying it in the stores the whole time you were in the hospital, remember? I couldn't afford to eat every meal in the hotel dining room."

"Oh, yeah," he said. "Well, since you're still alive, and I survived the Mandeville meal plan, I guess it's okay to proceed with my next move."

"Which is?"

"Cooking you a Colter home-style breakfast."

"You can cook?"

"Of course. When you've lived alone as long as I have, it's either learn or starve." He began to unpack the rest of his purchases, inspecting each item as he picked it up.

Karen watched him until he said, "What are you doing still standing there?"

"Waiting for my orders."

"Very funny. Weren't you going to take a shower when I came in?"

"Yes."

"Then go ahead. I'll build up the fire and have this ready when you come out. But first let me tell you about the shower."

"Uh-oh."

"Yeah. It's one of those hand-held jobs, you know, with the little wand?"

"I see."

"And it has a hook that you're supposed to hang the wand on, except when you do it falls through and crashes to the floor."

"Oh."

"And if you try to hold the wand with one hand you can't adjust both of the water taps."

"I know I shouldn't ask this, but why do you *have* to adjust both of the water taps?"

"Because the temperature keeps changing while you're showering. I think it has to do with pressure problems in the tank, but the end result is that you need both hands free to fool around with the spigots when it runs too hot or too cold." He raised his eyebrows at her as he unwrapped the bread and began to slice it.

"Maybe I should just dump a pail of cold water over my head," Karen said gloomily.

"Maybe I should hold the wand for you while you shower," he suggested, grinning wickedly.

"Never mind," Karen said airily. "Just get cooking. I'll be right back."

It was the quickest shower of Karen's life. Colter was right about the temperature control; it went from the hot of a Mojave Desert summer to the cold of an Arctic snow pit with no notice at all. She leaped out after about two minutes of it and ran, streaming and wrapped in a towel, into the living room. The cook burst out laughing at the sight of her.

"Oh, poor baby," he said, with mock sympathy. "Are we uncomfortable?"

"I admit it. I'm a spoiled American," she said, hurrying to the fire he'd restored and holding out her hands. "I like hot showers and hot coffee, cold lemonade and cold beer. I can't help it."

"You never drank beer in your life," he said, grabbing a blanket from the bed and draping it over her shoulders. He stood behind her and crossed his arms over her waist, enfolding her in it.

"Figure of speech," she replied, leaning back against him. He put his lips to the side of her neck and closed his eyes. "You smell scrumptious."

"Steven," she said warningly.

"Hmm?" He curled one hand inside the blanket, dislodged the towel beneath it and enclosed her breast.

"Steven, weren't you doing something?"

"Yup. Making love to you." He bent and slipped one arm beneath her knees, straightening and scooping her up in his arms. She squealed as he strode to the bed and tossed her on it, dropping beside her and peeling the blanket away from her body. Karen put her arms around his neck, subsiding as he kissed her deeply. But when his mouth moved to her cheek, she began to sniff.

"Steven?"

"Give me a break. I'm concentrating." He traced the shell of her ear with his tongue.

"The eggs are burning."

"Let them burn."

"But I'm famished."

He sat up and looked at her, incredulous. "Are you telling me you want to eat brown eggs at a moment like this?"

"So did you until you started . . . you know."

"Food, food, food," he grumbled, getting up and going to the stove. "All you think about is food."

"And all you think about is . . ." She stopped.

He chuckled as he scooped the omelet from the pan. "Go ahead, Miss Priss. You can say it. I was the guy in bed with you, remember?"

"You love to embarrass me," she muttered, yanking the blanket around her in irritation and standing up.

"That's because you turn such a peachy shade of pink," he replied, examining the toaster. "This thing looks like a waffle iron," he observed.

Karen padded over to the counter in her bare feet and stood behind him. "No, it opens up like a book, and you put the slices inside, see?" she said, showing him.

He turned and kissed the top of her head. "You're such a smart cookie. Why don't you go in and get dressed while I dish this stuff up? I don't want you to catch cold."

"I've got a better idea," Karen said firmly, taking the spatula from his hand and pointing to the sofa. "Why don't you go and sit down before you fall down? I'll handle this."

To her surprise, he obeyed, confirming her suspicion that his early morning errand was catching up with him. He sank onto the pile of rumpled sheets and sat with his back propped against the wall, watching her.

"All this looks pretty good," Karen observed as she fixed the plates. "I guess you weren't lying."

"About what?" he said, taking his platter from her hand.

"Being able to cook." She sat next to him and dug into hers with relish.

"What do you think?" he asked, around a mouthful of toast.

"Delicious," she pronounced. "Especially on the heels of that peanut butter orgy last night. But where's the coffee?"

"Instant," he replied. "The kettle's on the electric burner."

There was silence for a while as they consumed the meal in indecent haste. Karen got up to turn off the water when it boiled, bringing their empty plates to the sink.

"No dishwasher, huh?" she said to Colter, looking around.

"Nope. Got to wash them by hand, just like those courageous pioneers. You can draw the water from the well while I boil the tallow for the soap."

Karen had to laugh. "I really wish you would stop making fun of me," she said, spooning the coffee into two mugs and adding hot water.

"I'm not making fun of you, sweetie, and I really wish I had a cigarette."

"Wouldn't this be a good time to quit?" Karen suggested brightly, searching the cabinets for dishwashing liquid.

"It's never a good time to quit," he replied darkly, sighing. "That old fool in the grocery didn't carry cigarettes.

Can you believe it? What kind of a 'convenience' store is that?''

"One that believes in promoting the health of its customers?" Karen said.

"There isn't a store like that in the world."

She closed the last cabinet and said, "The dishes will have to wait. No detergent."

"I should have picked some up while I was out," Colter replied. "I guess old lady Mandeville's cousin likes dirt."

"Dirty dishes, anyway. Oh, well, maybe he eats out a lot."

"I would, too, if I had a set of appliances like those."

"I'm sure the Irish can figure them out; they're used to them." She joined him on the sofa, bringing the mugs with her. "Black?" she said, handing him the cup.

He nodded, taking a large swallow of the steaming liquid. Then he set his cup on the floor and took her hand.

"I bet I can make you put that down," he said softly.

"No bet," she answered.

"Why not?"

"I know you too well. I'd lose."

He removed the mug from her hand and placed it next to his on the rug. "Do I have that much power, Karen?" he asked seriously, dropping the teasing tone.

"You know you do."

"Just can't resist me, huh?" he whispered, pulling her into his arms.

"No," she answered softly, closing her eyes. "Sometimes I wish I could."

"Don't wish that," he murmured. "People live out their whole lives and never have that magic with anyone."

He drew her down beside him, and Karen submitted once more to the lure of his embrace.

Chapter 7

For the next three weeks Karen and Colter stayed at the cottage above the sea in Kinsale. It was a period suspended in time for both of them. They shared almost every moment, waking and sleeping, and grew so intimate that they could each guess what the other was thinking from a comment or a glance. Colter mended rapidly, since, as he began to trust Karen more, he listened to her, took it easy and let her help him without fighting it. After two visits to the local doctor that Miss Mandeville had recommended, he was pronounced recovered and dismissed from medical care.

During the day the two of them explored the Irish countryside in the comfortable Peugeot Colter had procured in exchange for the "roller skate." They saw the old Norse forts that had become the coastal towns of Wexford, Waterford, Cork and Kinsale, the staggering beauty of Youghal Bay, the lakes and medieval castles of the Ring of Kerry to the west. And in the evening they would go out to dinner, then return to the cabin to make love in front of the fire. Each night they fell asleep entwined, like amatory gods on a temple frieze.

Karen had never been happier in her life. Although they were both careful not to mention the future, or even when their current idyll would end, she couldn't imagine that Colter would part with her after what they had found together.

She discovered him to be much more than an ardent lover. He was a fascinating companion, as well. He knew so much about the world from direct experience and could talk about things she'd never heard of and issues she'd never considered. He became a changed man from the hostile, guarded stranger who'd awakened in Mercy Hospital and told her to go home. Relaxed, and in her loving company, he was witty, intelligent and fun, intensely aware of almost everything around him, a man of simple tastes but complex emotional makeup. Why did he hide this wonderful person from the rest of the world? Karen wondered. It was so difficult for him to open up, and when he did, he revealed a man whom she knew few people ever saw.

Colter insisted on paying for everything, and when she saw how important this was to him, she agreed to let him do it. He seemed to have plenty of money, and never mentioned taking another assignment, though she was afraid every day that he would bring up the subject. He acted, in short, as though their current circumstances would continue forever. And Karen went along with the game, hoping that in the end he would be as in love with her as she was with him and unable to let her go.

One evening as they were dressing to go to a restaurant in Cork, Colter came into the bedroom and examined the clothes she had put out to wear, looking over her things like a drill instructor inspecting a recruit.

"Where is that killer dress you wore on our date in Caracas?" he asked.

"I left it at home, Steven," Karen replied. "I didn't think I'd have much use for it while tending the wounded."

"The wounded being me?" he asked.

"You got it."

"Wounded no longer," he said, grabbing her arm as she walked by and whirling her into his arms.

"Oh, no," she said. "You've kept us late for dinner three times this week already. Why do you make the reservations if you intend to pull this all the time?"

"I guess I'm just disorganized," he sighed, peeling the strap of her slip down one arm and kissing her shoulder.

"Out," she said firmly.

"Oh, all right," he answered, pretending to pout. He went through the door and then stuck his head back into the room.

"You'll pay for it tonight," he hissed in an exaggerated stage whisper.

"Goodbye, Steven," she sang.

He slammed the door.

When she emerged into the living room ten minutes later, he was reading. He had picked up a book on Irish history someplace and found it captivating. He was fond of quoting from its pages.

"Listen to this," he said as she went to get her shoes. "'During the reign of the Celtic tribes in Ireland, a female slave, or cumal, was worth a fixed price of three cows.'"

"Charming," Karen observed.

"What an unfair system," he said, closing the book.

Karen waited. She could tell by the tone of his voice that something else was coming.

"I would say," he went on, "that most women should have been worth at least four cows, and you, for example, possibly even five."

Karen threw her left shoe at him.

He ducked it, laughing.

"What did it say about the men?" she asked him pointedly.

"Oh, quite a few things. They achieved reputation and status by staging cattle raids on one another's herds, and the guy who wound up with the most beef at the end was the leader."

"Your time is out of joint, my friend," Karen told him dryly as he picked up her shoe and handed it to her. "It sounds like you would have fit right in."

"I beg your pardon," he said, smiling slightly. "Such larcenous escapades were celebrated in song and story. One of the most famous poems from that period is called 'The Cattle Raid of Cooley.'"

"Cooley was the chief thief?"

"I guess so."

"Well, you have to admit it must have been easy. No fooling around with ballot boxes or electoral colleges, just count the cows."

"What's amazing," he said, warming to the subject, "is that all of this barbarism was going on at the same time that one of the most sophisticated cultures in Western Civilization was developing right beside it. And both completely separate from the Roman Empire, by the way. The Romans never conquered Ireland, though they did think about it. Tacitus says they hoped one legion would be enough to subdue the island, but they never got around to making the trip across the water from continental Europe."

"History intrigues you, doesn't it?" Karen asked as she looked around for her purse.

He glanced at her sharply. "Why do you ask?"

Karen stared at him. "Steven, you've been reciting that book to me, chapter and verse, as if it were the Bible, and you've dragged me to see every mound and megalith and relic within a fifty-mile radius of this house. If there's a Viking shield or a Celtic ax head that we missed, it isn't your fault."

The tips of his ears were turning red, and he put the book down. Karen realized that he was embarrassed.

"What's the matter?" she asked softly.

"Nothing." He shook his head.

"I wasn't making fun of you."

"I know."

"But you're sensitive about a perfectly natural intellectual curiosity. Why?"

"It's not natural," he answered, "not for somebody like me. It's ridiculous."

"Why is it ridiculous for you?" she persisted, moving closer to him. His thought processes intrigued her. Every day she discovered something new about him.

He shrugged. "What's it going to get me? It doesn't help to lose yourself in other times, other places, and dream…" He stopped.

"What do you mean?" Karen faced him, ready to pry it out of him if she had to do so. It was so rare that he volunteered information like this that she meant to capitalize on the opportunity.

"I never got very far in school," he said obliquely.

"So? That means you can't be a history buff?" What was he talking about?

He gestured helplessly. "I get restless sometimes, when I read and see things. I know there's a whole other world out there, just beyond my reach, and I want to touch it, but I feel I'm not suited, or ready, or something." He snorted and made a face. "You probably think I'm nuts."

Karen put her arms around his waist and rubbed her cheek against his shoulder. He stiffened for a moment, then embraced her.

"I don't think you're nuts," she said softly. "My father was a Chaucerian scholar; he spent his whole life in the Middle Ages. I'm sure the pilgrims in *The Canterbury Tales* were more real to him than his own children. It's not crazy to have an imagination and feel an inarticulate longing for something else, something better. That's part of being human."

"That's what you are," he said, so quietly that she almost didn't hear him.

"What?" She raised her head and looked at him.

"You're the 'something better,' for me."

Karen held her breath. Was he going to say more, indicate that they would continue beyond this magical month? But he released her suddenly, as if afraid to give away too much, and said, "Come on, we're going to be late."

Karen was quiet during the drive to the city, thinking over what Colter had said. What might he have done with his life if he'd been afforded the opportunities she'd seen some of her contemporaries throw away? But then he would have been a different person, and it wasn't possible for her to imagine him other than he was. She loved what he was and didn't want him to change.

Colter drove to a restaurant on the south channel of the River Lee, just across from the impressive limestone structure of "new" city hall, rebuilt after it was burned down by British auxiliary forces in 1920. The Ivernian Garden had been recommended to them for the atmosphere as well as the food, and as they were ushered inside, Karen could see why.

All the tables were white wrought iron with glass tops, laid with linen napery. The lighting was subdued, and greenery abounded, giving the impression of a country garden on a "soft" evening. The walls were hung with shields depicting the coats of arms of the various clans famous in Irish history. The establishment itself was named for the Ivernii, the chief tribe in Ireland during the second century, and scrolls embellished with their runic writing adorned the oak panels of the entry hall.

"I knew you'd enjoy this place," Karen said to Colter as the maître d' seated them.

"These people love their past," Colter agreed, more interested in the decorative hangings than the menu. "Who else would even think of opening a restaurant with this theme?"

"Oh, I don't know if it's that unusual," Karen said. "Don't Italian restaurants at home have place mats with the map of Italy on them, things like that?"

"We're not talking place mats here," Colter replied. "The management of this outfit has gone all out, and with good reason. The Ivernii were something else. Did you know that they would paint their faces blue before a battle and then go into the fighting naked, to show that they weren't afraid?"

"Who were they fighting?"

"Everyone, apparently. I wouldn't want to encounter one of them in a dark alley. The Romans considered them such a formidable obstacle that they postponed their invasion plans indefinitely."

"Maybe you're descended from them," Karen observed impulsively, encouraged by his obvious admiration for the ancient Celts. Then she realized it was the wrong thing to say.

He shrugged noncommittally.

She was silent for a moment, then said, "Don't you know anything about your parents?"

He shook his head.

"The nuns wouldn't tell you?"

"The nuns didn't know. They were as much in the dark as I was."

"Do you still wonder about it?"

"Not so much anymore. I did when I was a kid. I felt cut off, without a past. But now I guess I've accepted it."

The waiter came and they ordered, and Colter asked the steward for a bottle of wine. Music drifted in from another room where there was dancing. They listened for a while, then Karen began to hum along with the tune.

"What is that?" he asked.

"'Aileen Aroon,'" she said. "It's very old, I think. My father used to sing it when I was little."

"What does it mean?"

"Beloved Eileen."

He reached over and took her hand. "Were your parents happy together?"

"I think so. I remember things like the singing and laughing, and I know I felt secure and loved. My sister and I were devastated when they died."

"And then you went to live with your aunt?"

"Yes, and she was very different. She was a good person, but she'd had no children and didn't have much patience with a couple of 'silly girls.' She had all these rules and timetables, and it was..."

"What?" he coached.

"Oppressive."

"So to escape you got married."

"I guess so," Karen sighed. "I didn't see it that way at the time, but in retrospect I think that was true."

"And your husband was older?"

"Yes."

"Kind of fatherly?"

"I suppose so. Steven, why are you asking me about this now? You never showed any interest before. In fact you seemed to avoid the subject of my life before I met you."

"I don't know," he answered. "I guess I want it to be just us, with no outside connections, but that's not realistic, is it?"

"No," she murmured as the wine arrived and the steward filled their glasses.

"May I ask you a question now?" she said, watching his pale eyes find hers when she spoke.

"Go ahead."

"What did you do when you ran away from the orphanage? You were just a kid; how did you live?"

"Odd jobs, stealing, anything that came my way. The army saved me, really, gave me a place to sleep and regular food, trained me, taught me to grow up. You learn fast that you fall into line or wind up in the brig."

"Where you landed a few times."

He lifted one shoulder negligently. "Only a few."

"Did you hate it, all that regimentation, I mean?"

He smiled slightly, taking a sip of his drink. "No, actually I didn't. It reminded me of the home, in a way, all the bunks in one room, the lights out, the communal meals, the regulations. Once you learned the system you were fine."

"Would you go back to it?"

He eyed her levelly across the table. "I never left it, Karen," he said.

She realized he was right.

Their appetizers came, and Karen played with her shellfish, distracted. She wondered how long they could possibly go on like this, acting as if the rest of the world didn't exist and would never intrude upon them.

Colter sensed her mood and didn't press for conversation. When they'd finished the main course, he led her by the hand to the next room and they joined the dancers.

The music was slow and mournful. The male singer, the requisite tenor, segued from one sad ballad to another until

Colter said in Karen's ear, "I can't take much more of this. If that guy doesn't liven it up soon, I'm going to jump on the stage and start belting out 'Oh, Susannah.'"

Karen smiled. "You know what G. I. Chesterton said."

He sighed. "No, I don't, but I have a feeling you're going to tell me."

"'The great Gaels of Ireland are the men that God made mad; For all their wars are merry, and all their songs are sad.'"

He chuckled. "Very true. But for tonight I've had enough of this musical funeral. What do you say we blow this pop stand?"

Karen tilted her head back and looked into his eyes. "I'm with you."

Colter paid the bill, and they emerged into a thick, chilly mist that enshrouded Patric Street and surrounded the street lamps with a pearlized, otherworldly glow.

"It's raining," Karen said, pulling up the hood of her polo coat.

"What a surprise," Colter commented dryly.

"Come on," Karen said, hugging him as they walked. "Don't be such a grump. You know how cozy it is inside the cottage in weather like this. We'll build a fire and cuddle up and . . ."

"And?" he prompted, smiling down at her.

"Have a good time," she finished lamely.

He laughed. "Oh, I intend to have a very good time." He stopped walking and turned her to look at him, pushing the hood back from her face and tilting her chin up with his hand.

"Are you happy?" he asked.

"Very," Karen whispered.

"I haven't disappointed you?"

"How could you disappoint me?"

His hand fell away. "By turning out to be someone different than you thought," he answered flatly.

"You are different. You're more interesting and challenging and varied than I ever anticipated. Every day with you is an adventure. I wouldn't have missed this for any-thing,'' Karen answered.

He put his hands into his pockets and stared down at the damp pavement, and she realized after a moment that he was too emotional to speak. She waited until he cleared his throat and said, "You make me hope for..."

"What?" she asked breathlessly.

He hesitated, then shook his head. "Never mind. It doesn't matter. Let's get back before this turns into fog and we're stuck here."

That was the second time in a few hours he'd done that, cut off the conversation when it seemed they might discuss their situation, get something resolved. It was difficult not to pursue the subject, but Karen had learned that pressing him got her nowhere. She fell into step beside him, and they returned to the car.

It was raining hard by the time they got back to the cot-tage, and Karen went into the bedroom to change while Colter built up the fire. When she emerged, dressed in her robe, he was piling logs on the hearth and about to set a match to them.

"I don't know why Miss Mandeville's cousin built this place without central heating," Karen said, shivering.

"Maybe her insanity is familial, and he's just as crazy as she is," Colter replied.

Karen giggled. "That's a terrible thing to say. That woman helped save your life and found us this place. Why haven't you got a good word to say about her?"

"Probably because she was jamming syringes into my butt every time I opened my eyes." He rose from his knees, dusting his palms on his pants.

"That was her job, Steven."

"She enjoys her work a little too much."

"Well, you do have a very nice butt," Karen said coyly.

"Huh. She's a sadist."

Karen went to him and put her arms around his neck. "I don't think you give her enough credit. She understood about us, you know."

He looked down at her. "What do you mean?"

"When I first arrived at the hospital, I told her that we'd really only met once, but that I felt I had to come when you called for me. And she understood. No questions asked, she just accepted it. As if something like that had happened in her life, and she knew how it was."

He was silent for a long moment, then said, "Maybe you're right. She was young once, too, I guess."

Karen nodded, reaching up to brush his hair from his forehead. "And maybe in her youth she met a tall dashing blonde who'd made such an impression in one evening that she would have followed him halfway around the world."

"Dashing?" he murmured, bending to kiss her.

"Very dashing," she replied softly as his lips met hers.

He kissed her thoroughly, then set her aside for a moment while he pulled a blanket from the sofa bed and spread it on the rug before the fire. Karen sat on it, then opened her arms to receive him when he joined her.

He rolled onto his side and pulled her with him, cushioning her body against his. She still avoided his injured side out of habit, but it no longer bothered him.

"Better now?" he asked.

"Perfect," she sighed.

He stared over her head into the flames, his expression pensive.

"What's on your mind, Mr. Colter?" Karen finally said.

He blinked. "I was just thinking that I never knew what a woman was like before."

"Before me?"

"Yeah."

"Why?"

"I never lived with one, never saw her every day. I used to wonder about that, how it was to get along, be close with somebody." His embrace tightened. "And now I know."

"How do you feel about it?" she asked tentatively.

"Like I was blind before, and now I can see."

Karen bit her lip. He said the most touching things without even trying, like a child. At such times she forgot how maddening he could be and forgave him everything.

She reached for the top button of his shirt.

"I don't think we need this, do we?" she said.

He let her unfasten the shirt and then shrugged out of it. Karen ran her hand over the smooth surface of his shoulders, then dragged her nails through the thicket of brown hair on his chest. He sucked in his breath.

Her fingers stopped at the angry ridge of tissue that covered his recent wound. The skin had knit unevenly and was still reddened, slightly swollen. One day it would be a thick pink-white scar.

"Steven, you never told me how this happened," she said. "Who shot you?"

"One of the local cops."

"By mistake?"

"Yeah. He was trying to help me break it up, and in all the smoke and confusion he hit the wrong man."

"I hope that doesn't happen often," Karen said, shuddering. She traced the line of his ribs thoughtfully with a delicate forefinger.

He made a disgusted sound. "More often than you think, a lot more often than it should. Those scenes are always chaotic, all kinds of noise, screaming and shouting and running feet, and everybody involved is so charged up, so scared."

"You, too?"

"Me, too."

"Do you know why that gang took over the post office?" she asked, circling a flat, dark nipple with her thumb.

He shrugged expressively. "I don't think *they* know. Some British dignitary was visiting, or something, but any excuse will do. These people have been at each other's throats for a thousand years, and it just goes on endlessly. I sometimes wonder if they could tell you what they're fighting for, if they even remember why and how it started."

"You're involved in these situations all the time, aren't you? Civil wars, rebellions."

He nodded wordlessly.

"Doesn't it get to you?"

He sighed. "I don't know how to answer that. Human nature being what it is, somebody's always fighting. It's a contentious planet." He chuckled humorlessly. "I'll never be out of work."

Karen took her hand away from him, and he caught it in his own.

"Don't stop," he said huskily.

"Oh, Steven," Karen burst out, sitting up to face him. "What's going to become of you?"

"Hey," he said gently, smiling, "take it easy. I'll survive. I always do."

"No," she said sadly. "One of these times all the near misses will catch up with you."

"Not me," he said, taking her by the shoulders and lowering her to the floor. "I'm a cat with nine lives, and I've only used up about three of them."

Karen began to protest, but he silenced her with his mouth. He moved over he eagerly, and she slid her arms around his neck.

He undid the belt of her robe and pulled the lapels apart roughly, so anxious to discard it that he almost ripped the cloth. Holding her up with one arm, he pulled the robe off with the other and tossed it aside, and then they dropped back together, his body enveloping hers.

He kissed her again, and her response was so abandoned that it excited him further, driving him to lift his head and look at her. He loved to see her in the grip of passion; her expression became transformed, hungry, fixated solely on him as the object of her desire. Now her eyes were heavy lidded, agate-dark and glowing, her mouth wet from the contact with his. He could just see the edge of her teeth, set against her lower lip, and she gasped with pleasure when he slid his hands beneath her buttocks and lifted her against him. Her eyes closed luxuriously, and she pulled his head down, sinking her fingers into the wealth of hair at the nape of his neck.

He caressed one soft, pliant nipple, and it rose at his touch as he pressed lingering kisses into the soft skin at the base of her throat. His fingertips were rough and calloused, and the contrast with her tender flesh was unbelievably erotic, making her long for the wet heat of his mouth to replace it. She tugged on his hair and yearned upward, sighing with gratification as he took a swollen bud between his lips and sucked hard. She held still for long, breathless seconds, accepting, and then became impatient, reaching for the waistband of his pants.

He moved back, unbuckling his belt. Karen watched with greedy eyes as he stood and took off his pants, then she grabbed his hand as he knelt beside her.

"I feel," she whispered, holding his hard brown fingers to her cheek, "I feel so much that I don't know how to say it all."

"I know," he murmured, "I know." He tried to pull her down with him again, but she resisted.

"Let me," she said. She embraced him and kissed the taut muscles of his stomach, letting her lips run down to the tops of his thighs. He closed his eyes, trembling as she made love to him, too enraptured to move. Finally the tension became unbearable, and with a guttural sound he seized her and put her on her back, pinning her beneath him. He thrust into her wildly, but she was his match, wrapping her legs around his hips and surging to meet him. He sensed that she wanted to let go as much as he did, and he raced to a headlong conclusion that left them both drained, crumpled like rag dolls before the lowering fire.

Colter fell asleep, but Karen remained awake, listening to the rain falling on the roof and the soft counterpart of her lover's breathing. He was sprawled across her, his sweat drying on her skin, and when she moved him to get up, his fingers closed around her ankle.

"Where you going?" he murmured, his eyes still closed.

"Just to take a shower."

"Good luck," he muttered, referring to their erratic plumbing, and drifted into slumber again.

Karen retrieved her robe and belted it around her, checking to see that there was enough wood on the fire before she left him. She was no Camp Fire Girl, and when the blaze went out, she had a tough time getting it going once more. There were several stout logs just beginning to burn, however, so she went into the bedroom and got a pair of jeans and a sweater, leaving them on the bed. It was only nine o'clock and too chilly to run around in a nightgown. Then she got ready to do battle with the shower.

She had devised an intricate system of controlling the fluctuations in temperature, and this time she only got doused with cold water once. She dried off and dressed, thinking that by the time she mastered the fine art of taking an Irish shower, she would be home again.

Home. She wasn't sure where that was anymore. The word's meaning had altered for her. She thought of the cottage, with Colter, as her home now, even though she knew the arrangement was only temporary. She ran her brush through her hair and went into the living room.

It was empty. Colter had a habit of disappearing that she found disconcerting. For long years he'd never been answerable to anyone but himself, and now he didn't seem able to change. Karen opened the front door and looked through the curtain of falling rain. The car was still there, so he couldn't have gone far.

Karen went back inside and got her coat, then walked around to the back of the cottage where the land dropped off into the sea.

Colter was sitting under the roof's overhang, protected from the rain, wearing the eggshell Aran sweater they had bought for him in Cork. He stared down at the pounding surf barely visible below, his hair darkened with moisture and his hands jammed into his pockets. Phosphorescence glowed on the crest of the waves, but otherwise the sea was as dark as the night, blending into the inky sky above it so that the line of the land was lost.

Karen wrapped her arms around her torso and picked her way through the wet grass to his side.

"What are you doing out here?" she asked, sitting next to him on the bench he occupied.

"Hiding from you," he answered. He raised his right hand, which had been concealed at his side, to show her the glowing cigarette wedged between his fingers.

"You don't have to hide," Karen said softly. "I promise I won't nag."

"Thanks." He took a deep drag and exhaled slowly, savoring the smoke.

"I think you'd better come inside before you catch a chill," Karen said.

"I'm okay," he replied. He laughed softly. "I have an eerie feeling I may be adjusting to this climate."

"Oh, dear."

"Yeah, I'm a little worried about it myself." He finished the cigarette and tossed it away, turning to look at her.

"You know that old Jim Croce song, 'Time in a Bottle'?" he asked suddenly, brushing his mist-dampened hair out of his eyes.

"Yes, I remember it."

"That's what I'd like to do with this past month I've spent with you—save all the memories in a bottle, so I could take them out and look at them when things got . . . bad."

Moved, Karen asked, "Why do things have to get bad, Steven?"

"They always do," he replied remotely.

"So happiness is a gift you can have only for a little while, not something you can count on to remain?" she said to him.

He shrugged. "You're asking the wrong person. I don't know. Do most people seem permanently happy to you?"

Karen thought about it. "My sister seems happy," she finally said.

He nodded slowly. "She's married to Joe College—perfect husband and father. Right?"

"That's not the reason," Karen replied cautiously. "She would love her husband even if he weren't doing so well. They get along; they're compatible. That's all that matters."

"I wish it were," he said dully.

"Steven, what are you thinking?" Karen asked, alarmed. "Can't you tell me?"

He shook his head, then gestured dismissively. "Just a mood. It'll pass."

Karen didn't like the sound of it and stood up. "I'm going inside to make some tea. Are you coming?"

"I'll be along in a minute," he replied. "You go on."

Karen went inside, and Colter lit another cigarette, inhaling until the tip of it glowed redly in the rain-swept darkness.

The weather was an accurate reflection of his spirits. This time with Karen should have been the best period of his life. In one way it was, but the subliminal uneasiness was always with him, eating away at the core of his contentment like a burrowing worm. She had completed him in a fashion he'd never thought possible, but he was now faced with a choice he found intolerable. Though she had said nothing and made no demands on him, he felt the pressure from within to forge ties with her, to ask her to share his life in the future.

Colter sat back against the shingled outer wall of the house and closed his eyes, the cigarette burning away between his fingers. But what could he ask her to share? The danger, chaos and constant turmoil that were his daily lot? It wasn't fair to demand that of any woman, especially not one who had transformed his existence from an abyss of loneliness to a haven of intense, quiet joy. He didn't want to turn her into a camp follower, waiting anxiously for him to return from each mission, but the thought of living without her now was insupportable.

So what was the alternative? Could he change? He wanted to; God only knew how much he wanted to become the middle class man of her dreams. He longed to transubstantiate miraculously into the good provider, to be like the brother-in-law he had never met, but who haunted him, the specter of everything Karen's mate should be. It was a fantasy as far away from him, as unreachable, as travel to the stars.

Ash fell on his hand, and he shook it off, raising the cigarette to his lips once more. It was too late, Colter felt, too late for him to try for that elusive life with her. Ten years earlier, maybe, before he had seen too much and grown too little, but now the chance was gone, like an unused ticket on a flight that had left him stranded and alone. It wasn't that he didn't trust her; he didn't trust himself. His track record

was awful, and no one knew it better than he did. He could
be faithful because he loved her, of that he was certain, but
he had no confidence in his ability to provide the kind of life
she deserved. Wasn't it better for him to bow out now and
let her move on to someone else who would be capable of
doing that? She would be unhappy for a short while, because he did believe she truly cared for him, but better off
in the end. Love sometimes expressed itself in sacrifice, and
maybe the best thing would be for him to sacrifice his own
needs for Karen's ultimate welfare.

The thing now was to tell her. The thought of breaking it
off with her was so painful that each day he put the task off
until the next, hoping that soon he would have the guts to do
what had to be done. But the man who could face machine
guns and mortars and the madness of a continual, unre-
lenting state of war could not tell one slim girl that they
shouldn't see each other any more. She would only accept
it if he made her believe that their time together had been
wonderful, but he didn't want her on a permanent basis,
and that wasn't true. There were all kinds of courage, and
he simply didn't have the nerve to tell her that lie.

He sat up and dropped the cigarette on the ground,
crushing it under his heel. Then he stood and went back into
the house.

Karen was sitting on the sofa next to the fire, sipping tea
and leafing through a magazine she'd bought. She looked
up as he came in and said, "The tea's on the stove. Take off
that sweater, Steven. It's wet."

Obediently he pulled the sweater over his head and spread
it on the back of a chair to dry. Then he joined her, sitting
on the floor at her feet and putting his head back against her
knee.

"All through thinking?" she asked him, a light, teasing
note in her voice.

"Yeah."

"'He thinks too much; Such men are dangerous,'" she
recited, bending forward to kiss the top of his head. "Did
you come to any conclusions?"

"The same one I always come to, but I don't like it."

"Oh. Can I help?"

"Yes, you can."

He turned and tumbled her gently from the seat into his lap, cradling her as she protested that he'd crushed her magazine.

"I'll buy you another one," he murmured, kissing her cheeks, then her mouth. Karen responded, as she always did, with that instantaneous ardor that was like touching a light to a pile of kindling.

Colter made love to her then, slowly, gently, in contrast to the fierce, exhausting unions of the past, as if she were precious and fragile and liable to break. And when they fell asleep afterward, there were no bad dreams to trouble them.

Karen awoke in the middle of the night when she heard a noise outside the cabin. She sat up, alert, and glanced at Colter, who was still sleeping on his side, one leg carelessly entwined with hers. Not alarmed enough to wake him, she disengaged herself carefully, standing up and glancing around in the semidarkness for her clothes. She settled instead for Colter's shirt, pulling it on and buttoning it in front as its tails fell to her hips.

She was just walking toward the door when it suddenly crashed inward, splintering the frame. She gasped, terrified, as three armed men burst into the room, holding their weapons at the ready and staring at her.

"Colter," the first one said, in accented English. "Where is he?"

Chapter 8

Karen backed away, too frightened to speak, as Colter leapt up and took her by the shoulders, shoving her behind him, placing his body between her and the intruders. He barked something harshly in a language she couldn't understand.

The first man, obviously the leader, replied angrily, and Colter shouted in response, clearly ordering the men out of the house. They exchanged glances, debating what to do, and then the leader gestured roughly at the door, indicating that the others should follow him through it. Karen didn't move until they were gone, then she whirled on Colter.

"What is it?" she demanded fearfully as he buckled his belt. "Who are they? What do they want?"

He grabbed her hand and pulled her forcefully toward the bedroom.

"Get in there and wait for me," he said shortly. "Don't come out—do you understand? I'll deal with them."

"But why are they here? What's going on?"

He looked at her white face, the stark panic mirrored in her features, and put both his hands on her upper arms, holding her steady.

"Karen, do you trust me?"

"Yes," she said in a small voice, swallowing.

"Then do as I say. Go into the bedroom and stay there. I'll come in to you when I'm done. All right?"

Karen stared up at him, at the pale hair backlit by the fire, at the eyes the color of an Indian summer sky, at the mouth that had clung to hers as if fitted to it by a master craftsman. She nodded. She would do as he said.

"Good girl." He ushered her inside and shut the door. Seconds later she heard him talking to the men, speaking in the same language he'd used when they arrived. They replied in angry voices. The heated exchanges seemed to go on forever while she sat on the edge of the bed, unable to think of anything but what might be happening in the next room. Finally the voices fell silent, and Colter came through the door.

Karen stood, searching his face. When he put his arm around her, she hid her face for a second against his shoulder.

"You okay?" he asked.

"I think so."

He sighed. "God, I would have done anything rather than drag you into this," he said resignedly.

"Drag me into what?" she asked anxiously. "What are we in?"

He sat her back down on the bed and moved next to her, taking her hands.

"Those men are from a separatist group in their country, an underground movement trying to overthrow the government."

Karen nodded impatiently. She didn't know enough to discuss the subject, and she didn't care. Her only concern was the threat they posed to Colter.

"Well," he went on, "I did a job for them a couple of years ago, and I botched it. It was especially hazardous work, and I insisted on payment in advance. When the job went wrong, I offered to return part of the payment, but they didn't want it. All they wanted was my promise to step in sometime when they needed me." He paused. "They've come to collect."

"They tracked you here?" Karen said incredulously.

"I had no doubt they'd find me anywhere," he said bluntly.

"You didn't know they were coming?"

He stared at her. "Of course not. Do you think I would have come here with you if I thought they'd follow?"

"I thought maybe that's why you tried to get rid of me at the hospital," she said.

He shook his head. "I just figured something would happen," he said dully. "And I was right."

"But you don't have to go with them, do you?" she asked. "Can't you send them away, tell them you'll join them later?"

"No."

"Why not?" she asked desperately. "We can run for it, get away. Surely there's someplace we can go where they can't find us."

Colter stood and paced the room, shoving his hair back with his fingers. "First of all, you're up to that 'we' stuff again. This is my problem and I'll solve it. You're getting out of this as soon as I can arrange it."

"Wait a minute..."

He held up his hand, and she stopped short.

"Second," he went on, "there's no place in the world where you can hide from a group like this. Believe me, I know. I've seen others try. All I can do is pay my debt and hope I get out of it with my skin intact."

"But who are they? Where are they from?"

"It's better you don't know."

Karen shook her head. "Steven, why do you know such terrible people?" she whispered despairingly.

"I tried to tell you," he said quietly, not meeting her eyes. She looked away. He had.

"I've gotten them to agree to let me take you to a safe place," he said flatly. "But they're coming along."

"Why?" she said, startled.

"They don't trust me," he replied grimly.

"Oh, no," she murmured, as the full implication of what he was saying hit her. "Isn't there any way out, anything we can do?"

He sat down again and made her look at him. "Karen, listen to me. You have to understand. They've seen you now. They know who you are. If I don't do what they want, they'll hurt you."

Karen froze. "What do you mean?"

He closed his eyes in pain. "Do I have to draw you a picture? You're a hostage. They'll let me take you to a safe place, but only if I go with them afterward. If I renege on this, you'll pay the price."

Karen didn't know what to say. He looked so miserable that she took refuge in a nonjudgmental silence.

"I'm sorry, Karen," he finally said. His voice broke on her name.

"It's all right," she replied, pulling herself together. "I'll be fine. Where am I supposed to go?"

He shrugged hopelessly. "I don't know."

"To my sister's house? They'd find out about the rest of my family."

"Your people would be in no danger, but that's out," he said flatly. "These guys can't get into the U.S."

Karen looked at him inquiringly.

"Revoked visas," he explained.

She glanced away. "I can see where they might not be desirable visitors," she commented softly.

He said nothing.

"What about Linda?" Karen asked suddenly.

He looked at her. "In England?"

"Yes. She's asked me several times to come and visit. Maybe I could go there. Would that be all right?"

He thought about it. "These guys can travel in Europe, I know. That shouldn't be a problem. She's in London?"

"I'm not sure. Her family has two houses. I'd have to find out."

She could see that he was considering it.

"Steven?"

"Yeah?"

"Are you sure they wouldn't hurt her?"

He shook his head. "No. There's no reason." He smiled humorlessly. "They're very practical," he added dryly. "Their violence is always methodical, goal directed. It would be you they'd want, to get to me."

Karen tried not to show the effect of that statement. She touched his arms, and he turned to her.

"Couldn't I just stay here?" she asked quietly. "Stay here and wait for you to come back?"

He took her hand. "I want you to be with someone else, a friend, with other people around."

Karen tightened her grip on him. "Steven, how do they know to use me as leverage? I mean, why are they sure I'm not just someone you picked up for the night?"

He looked down at their intertwined fingers. "They tracked me through the hospital, and they found out you were there. They know we've been together all this time, that you're important to me."

Karen didn't answer. He'd said what she wanted to hear, but now it might be too late.

They heard a sound in the next room, and both of them started.

"So what happens now?" Karen asked.

"You dress and pack your things. We'll get in touch with Linda and see if you can go there. Then we'll catch the next plane to London."

"And they'll go with us?" Karen said unhappily.

He was silent for a moment, then said, "Karen, if it were just me, I'd tell them to go to hell and take my chances. But I'm not fooling around with your safety. I'm going to do what they say."

"I wish I weren't such a problem for you," Karen said quietly.

He caressed her hair. "You're not the problem, sweetie, I am. This is just my past catching up with me, and I knew it would. I should never have stayed with you, taken the chance on something like this happening. But ..."

"But?" Karen prompted.

"I wanted to be with you," he said simply.

She reached up to touch his face, but he disengaged himself and stood.

"Selfish," he said savagely. "I've been so selfish."

Karen stared at him, bewildered. "But how?"

He shook his head dismissively. "You don't understand."

"I understand that the past month was worth anything," Karen said firmly. "I don't regret a moment of it—do you?"

He glanced back at her, and his expression softened. "No, baby. Not a moment." He looked toward the door and reached down to pull her up. "Come on. They're not going to wait forever. You'd better get packed."

Karen nodded.

"I'll go out there and keep them at bay," Colter said. "Are you sure you're okay?"

"I'm all right. Go on."

Colter left her to go into the other room, and Karen got her things together hurriedly, tossing items into her two suitcases in random fashion and exchanging Colter's shirt for slacks and a sweater. She put on her coat, picked up her bags and joined the men in the living room.

The rebels didn't even look at her. All their attention was focused on Colter, as if he might explode into resistance at any moment. Karen got her first inkling of how dangerous he might be in such a situation by the cautious, watchful way they treated him.

They left immediately, disregarding the fact that it was the middle of the night, and drove north to Dublin. The leader sat in the back seat of Karen's car with her as Colter drove, and when the man moved, she caught sight of a shoulder holster under his jacket. She was certain he would use the gun if Colter gave any sign of departing from the arranged plan, but they stuck to the main road and reached the capitol hours after the sun rose. A second car with the other two rebels in it followed them the whole time and pulled into a space next to theirs at the airport when they arrived.

Colter put the car in park and said something to their companion. The man grunted and got out, waiting for Karen to do the same.

"What did you say to him?" Karen asked.

"I told him we were going inside to call your friend in London. He's going with us."

What a surprise, Karen thought sourly. She clung to Colter's arm as they threaded their way through the airport crowd to a bank of phones near the Aer Lingus ticket desk. Karen wondered if any of the people hurrying past them could guess at the human drama taking place before their eyes. She knew they looked like three casual companions strolling through the concourse at a leisurely pace, but she thought there must be some way her fear and anxiety would show. No one glanced at her twice, however, and when she looked longingly at a security guard they passed, their companion eyed her meaningfully, opening his jacket. Karen bit her lip and kept on walking.

When they reached the phones, Karen placed the call to Linda, using Colter's credit card. At another time she might have been amused that he had such a thing, it being the hallmark of staid businessmen, but she was in no mood to appreciate the irony. She could see that it would be useful to him, considering the amount of traveling he did. As she gave the number to the operator, she wondered what they were going to do if Linda couldn't be reached.

The connection was made, and a second later she heard the shrill one-two European ring on the other end. It rang twice, and then was answered by a servant, who said that "Miss Linda" had guests and couldn't be disturbed. He would take a message.

"I must speak with her now," Karen insisted, trying to keep the rising note of hysteria out of her voice. "This is Miss Walsh from America. I worked with Linda in Almeria, and I have to talk to her right away."

The rebel was watching her impassively. She didn't know how much English he spoke, but he seemed very alert to nuances and was aware of her every move.

"I received very strict instructions from madam..." the servant began.

"It's an emergency," Karen interjected hastily.

The rebel took a step forward, and Colter blocked his path.

"Take it easy," Colter said to him in English. "Keep your hands off the lady, or your troubles at home are going to seem mild by comparison with what I'll do to you."

The man stared at Colter defiantly for a moment, then subsided. On the other end of the phone, the butler, or the footman, or whatever he was, was still trying to decide whether to disobey his orders and summon his mistress.

"I'll take full responsibility," Karen said desperately. "Please, she'll be very upset if she misses me."

The man, convinced now that he would be in worse trouble for not calling Linda to the phone than for disregarding instructions, said, "Hold the line please, madam. I'll see if Miss Linda will take your call."

The trunk line crackled emptily for what seemed like days, and then, miraculously, Linda said, "Karen, is that you? I gave you up for dead."

"Linda," Karen sighed, closing her eyes in relief. She opened them to find Colter nodding at her encouragingly.

"I've been writing letters until my poor hand was turning blue. Have you vanished into the wilds of New Jersey?" Linda asked.

"No, I've just been, uh, busy," Karen answered lamely. "I'm sorry to disturb you, but I didn't think that man was going to get you."

"Oh, Field is useless. He's about a hundred and ten, and my father keeps him on because he was born in the barn or something. He's quite deaf and probably didn't even know what you were saying."

"He called you 'Miss Linda.' I always knew you had slaves," Karen said, laughing nervously.

"Don't be such an American," Linda replied tartly.

Colter gestured for her to hurry it up.

"I hope I didn't interrupt what you were doing," Karen said.

"You didn't interrupt anything. It was just a tiresome brunch with my stepmother's tiresome friends. Any excuse to escape them is welcome."

"I was wondering if I could take you up on that offer you made for me to visit."

"Darling," Linda said delightedly. "But of course! When can you come?"

"Right now?" Karen said weakly.

"You mean today?"

"Yes."

"How wonderful. Just tell me the airline and your flight number, and I'll send a car to pick you up at Heathrow."

"I haven't booked the flight yet, but I'll be coming in from Dublin sometime later this afternoon."

There was a slight pause. Then, Linda repeated doubtfully, "Dublin?"

"That's right."

"Darling, it may be presumptuous of me to ask, but what on earth are you doing in Dublin, of all places?"

"I'll explain it all when I get there, Linda."

"Karen, does this have anything to do with that man who rescued us? That blonde you lusted for—what was his name, Mustang or Pony or something like that?"

"Colter," Karen said. Both men looked at her alertly when she said the name.

"That's right, Colter. Well, does it?"

"Yes, but I can't go into details just now. I'll tell you all about it when I get there, okay?"

Linda, who was only slightly less clever than the average CIA agent, was beginning to smell a rat.

"Karen, are you in some kind of trouble?" she asked seriously.

"I'm fine," Karen answered loudly, directing it at their armed companion, who was stirring restlessly. "I'll call you when I land, and you can send the car for me then, all right?"

"All right," Linda echoed. "But you're going to give me every last scrap of information about this when you arrive, do you hear?"

"I promise I will. Thanks a lot, I'll see you tonight."

"See you then."

"And Linda?"

"Yes?"

"You're a lifesaver." Karen hung up before her friend could react, and Colter took her arm.

"All set?" he asked in an undertone.

"Yes. You heard; it's all arranged."

"She suspected something, didn't she?"

Karen darted a glance at the rebel, who was listening.

"She just asked me if it had anything to do with you, and I told her I'd explain when I got there," Karen replied casually.

Both men seemed satisfied with her answer, and they went to get their tickets.

They were on the plane in an hour; a regular shuttle ran from Dublin to London, and flights were frequent. Their guard, or so Karen thought of him, sat behind her and Colter, and a few minutes into the trip he fell asleep.

"Looks like bullyboy is taking a nap," she whispered to Colter, who was staring out the window.

"Why not? Where the hell can we go to get away?" Colter replied.

Karen leaned closer to him and put her lips against his ear. "What did he do with his gun? He got through the metal check with no problem."

"He ditched it before we boarded," Colter replied.

"I didn't see that."

"You weren't meant to."

"But then he's unarmed," Karen pointed out.

"Don't worry," Colter said, aware of what she was thinking. "They'll have somebody meet the plane at the other end. They do this all the time, and have quite a little system worked out."

"Steven?" she said, in a tone that made him turn and look at her.

"Yeah?"

"What do they want you to do for them?"

He hesitated for a moment, then answered, "One of their comrades is being held in a government jail. He's going on trial soon, and he'll be convicted, sentenced to death. They want me to break him out."

"Can you?" Karen asked in a subdued tone.

He lifted one shoulder. "I've done it before."

"Was he arrested fairly? I mean, had he really done anything wrong?"

"As it happens, no."

"Then you agree with their cause."

"In this case, yes, but not always with their methods."

"They seem like such...ruffians," she said, shuddering.

"They're desperate men," Colter answered flatly. "Their situation doesn't leave a lot of room to worry about civilized behavior."

"You speak their language," Karen observed.

"Well enough to get by. I spent a good deal of time in their country."

"How many languages do you speak?" she asked, thinking again that she really knew so little about him.

"I don't know," he answered, shrugging. "Never counted."

The plane hit an air pocket, and Karen clutched her stomach.

"Uh. I hate that feeling," she moaned, waiting for the falling sensation to diminish. The plane leveled off, and she put her head on Colter's shoulder, closing her eyes.

"Karen, there's something I have to say to you. We probably won't have time alone later, so I'd better say it now."

Karen sat up and looked at him. There was a tone of finality in his voice that she didn't like, but she was ready to listen.

"I want you to know that I'll never forget you," he said. "The time we spent together was the best thing that ever happened in my life, and you'll always be with me, even if we never see each other again."

"What do you mean?" she asked, frightened. "You're coming back from this. You're coming back to me."

"I want to, yes, but it's a very tricky job, and I just don't know how it will go. I wish I could promise you that everything will work out all right, but I've never lied to you and I don't plan to start now."

"Don't go," she whispered, clutching his hand.

He looked away. "I have no choice."

Karen fell silent, tears of frustration welling up in her eyes. She had never felt so trapped.

They landed a few minutes later and passed through customs uneventfully. Karen tried to get a look at the guard's passport, to see where he was from, but then realized it didn't matter, anyway. If Colter didn't return, she wouldn't care where he went, and if he did, it was immaterial.

A second man joined them just outside of the arrival area, and Karen realized he was meeting the plane, just as Colter had said. He conversed briefly with their guard in close quarters, and then took off in another direction.

Karen called Linda from the airport and was told where to wait for the car. She clutched Colter's hand like a child as they walked toward the double glass doors, and a feeling of unreality came over her as she accepted the fact that she would soon be parted from him, perhaps permanently.

They stood in silence on the central pickup island, looking for the black limousine Linda had described. There was so much Karen wanted to say, but the words dried up in her mouth, inadequate and wrong. When the Bentley glided to the curb almost at their feet, and the uniformed driver got out and asked if she were Miss Walsh, Karen felt like bolting back through the crowd, leaving the nightmare far behind her.

"Go on now," Colter said. "Don't keep him waiting."

Karen looked up at him, trying to memorize his bold, even features, the slight cleft in his chin, the way his sandy lashes shaded from light brown to gold at the tips. She wanted to imprint his face on her memory so indelibly that it would remain there, clear and unaltered, forever.

"You have Linda's address," she asked shakily.

He nodded. "Give me a hug?" he said quietly.

Karen flew into his embrace, and his arms came around her so tightly that she knew what he was doing: trying to retain the feel of her, for the time when her touch would be only a memory.

"I love you," she said against his chest.

"I know," he murmured, smoothing her tangled hair. "I know."

"Come back," she pleaded again. "Come back to me."

He disengaged her arms from his neck and held her off, searching her face.

"Don't cry," he said. "Forget what I said. I'll be all right."

She nodded, biting back a sob. She was not convinced. Only a full appreciation of what he was up against could have made him admit what he had.

"I mean it," he added reassuringly. "It'll take more than this mangy group to do me in."

She nodded once more, unable to talk.

"Goodbye, sweetheart," he said, touching her cheek. Then he turned and walked off, his rebel guard at his side.

Karen barely looked at the driver as he held the door for her while she climbed into the rear seat of the car. She watched Colter go back into the terminal as the limo pulled away.

The green English countryside rolled past her window, as gorgeous as she recalled, but this time she saw everything through a blur of tears. The driver took the direct route to London, and after a short tour of the autumn glory of the suburbs, they were threading through the busy streets. Karen noticed the red "underground" entrances, the yellow double-decker buses, the signs directing traffic to "Give Way" rather than "Yield," but this time they held no charm for her. As if in reaction to controlling herself during the difficult parting from Colter, she could not seem to stop crying. If the chauffeur thought it was unusual to have his passenger sobbing and snuffling in the back seat, wiping her streaming eyes and nose ineffectually with a ragged tissue, he kept his distinguished British reserve and gave no indication of it.

Karen drew a shaky breath and glanced in the rearview mirror accidentally, then froze when she saw the man who'd met her plane driving the car behind them. She realized she was being followed and closed her eyes. Of course. They would have to keep an eye on their insurance policy while Colter was gone. It was the perfect ending to her horrendous journey, and she let her head fall back against the seat, her whole body slumping with despair.

The driver turned on a quiet tree-shaded street. It was graced by widely spaced Georgian homes with lush front gardens enclosed by black wrought-iron gates. He entered the drive of the most elaborate mansion on the avenue, a two-story white stucco Colonial with wide marble steps. The red door had a polished Regency knocker and brass kick-plate, with a carved oak lintel. Lustrous dark emerald ivy trailed down the sides of the long, shuttered windows, and twin carved lions flanked the Greek revival portico, which was supported by four Ionic columns. A row of etched-glass lanterns mounted on hanging posts lined their way as they drove up the circular gravel path, and the car glided to a stop at the foot of the entry stairs.

Karen got out when the driver held the door for her, and he bowed slightly as she hurried past him and ran up the steps. As if by magic, the red door was opened by another uniformed servant, and behind him stood Linda.

Her friend took one look at Karen's reddened eyes and tear-stained face and grabbed her arm, ushering her into a side room. Linda dismissed the servant and yanked the door closed behind them. Karen hardly got a look at the high, vaulted ceiling of the entry hall, the Baccarat chandelier or the antique furniture, before she found herself confronted by an angry, exasperated Linda.

"I knew it!" she said. "I knew something nasty was afoot, and you wouldn't tell me. You just present yourself on my doorstep in this condition. I mean to say!"

Karen fell into a brocaded Louis XIV armchair that was probably worth more than her entire life's earnings and sighed heavily.

"Don't holler at me, Linda; I don't think I can take any more today," she said wearily and blew her nose.

"Oh, give me that," Linda said imperiously, snatching the disintegrating tissue and shuddering delicately as she tossed it into a lacquered wastepaper basket at her feet. She went to a carved armoire in a corner and returned with a freshly laundered, scented linen handkerchief.

"Here, have this. They're supposed to be for guests, and I assume you qualify. Wipe your face properly, and then you can tell me what's been going on." She grabbed a velvet bell pull behind Karen's head, the like of which Karen had previously seen only in Sherlock Holmes films, and seconds later there was a discreet knock at the paneled door.

"Come in," Linda called.

A maid in a gray dress with a sheer ruffled apron presented herself.

"Please bring a pot of tea and some sandwiches for us, Doris," Linda said. "We'll take the tray right here in the study."

The maid disappeared as silently as she'd entered, and Linda uncaped a crystal bottle on a silver tray sitting on one of the side tables. She poured two fingers of dark amber liquid into a glass.

"Drink this," she said to Karen, handing her the tumbler.

"What is it?"

"Brandy."

Karen grimaced. "I don't want it."

Linda put her hands on her hips. "Drink that this instant. I am losing patience with you very fast. If you don't calm down, every one of the boring matrons my stepmother is entertaining down the hall will shortly be in this room. And you don't want to deal with *them*, that I can promise you."

Karen took a sip obediently and made a face as the searing warmth spread through her body.

"Tastes awful," she said.

"Good, you're not supposed to like it. Only riverboat gamblers in those dreadful historicals *like* it. Ladies drink lemonade."

"If those books were so awful, how come you read every one I gave you in a single night?"

"May we get back to the subject, please?" Linda said, arching one aristocratic eyebrow and tapping her foot. "Which was your dramatic arrival ten minutes ago in a state of semihysteria. I repeat, what happened?"

"Colter is gone," Karen said sadly.

"Well, since he isn't here, and much to my regret, I might add, I gathered that. Where is he?"

"On his way to someplace I don't know, with this group of revolutionaries, to break one of their comrades out of a government jail."

At this news Linda didn't look so well herself and sat hastily on the settee to Karen's right, her expression blank.

"I beg your pardon?" she finally managed to say.

"You heard me. They brought me here so he would go with them."

"You mean they were blackmailing him into it?"

"Sort of. It was an old debt that he owed them, and when they arrived to collect on it, I was there. So they seized the opportunity, you might say."

"And you were in Ireland?"

"Yes."

"Why?"

"Colter was injured there about a month ago, and he sent for me when he was in the hospital."

Linda sat forward, interested. "Really? He asked for you to join him?"

"Well, he thought he was hurt badly, and he was . . . scared."

"Hmph," Linda said. "I don't believe it."

"You don't know him," Karen said quietly.

"Not as well as you do, apparently," Linda replied significantly.

"No, I mean it," Karen insisted. "He's actually very emotional beneath that tough facade."

"The facade will do," Linda observed dreamily. She clasped her beringed hands together and studied Karen alertly. "So, you stayed all that time with him in Ireland? What happened?"

Karen folded her arms. "Linda, don't be obtuse. What do you think happened?"

Linda sighed. "One can only hope."

"We became quite close."

"How close?"

"Lovers."

Linda clapped softly. "Oh, goody."

"But then those men came and . . ."

"You wound up here."

"Yes."

"And you wouldn't have told me a word of this if you hadn't needed a place to hide. You would have kept it all to your selfish, niggardly self and left me waiting for the post like a jilted maiden in a Victorian romance."

Linda looked so genuinely outraged that Karen had to laugh. It felt good.

"What's so amusing?" Linda said, sniffing.

"You are. You're making all these noises about my condition and my situation, and what's really bothering you is that I didn't keep you informed on the progress of my affair."

"Well, you could have dropped me a postcard," Linda said grudgingly.

"Linda, I was busy."

"Oh, no doubt. Busy rustling under the counterpane with that gorgeous male, while I was trotting around after the dragon lady, emptying ashtrays and folding napkins for her garden parties."

Linda smiled mischievously. "You know, Linda, judging from the number of servants on the staff around here, I would have sworn you weren't killing yourself."

"A lot you know about it," Linda said crossly. "Sometimes I wish I were back on Almeria—the atmosphere in this

mausoleum is so stifling. At least in Ascension I was gain-
fully employed.''

"Can't you get another job?'' Karen asked, trying to take
the subject seriously. Linda's need for employment was
about as critical as Kuwait's need for oil.

"Not one that would suit my father. Almeria was accept-
able because it was a government house and he'd got the
position for me. But I can't exactly become a ribbon clerk
at Harrods now, can I? And the usual pastimes are so dull
and routine that I could absolutely cry.''

"What are the usual pastimes?''

"Oh, socials, teas, museum benefits, hunting in the
country, you know the sort of thing.''

Karen didn't, but she was aware that some people spent
their lives completely absorbed in such pursuits. Linda's
house looked like the type of place where they might hang
out.

"What about beaux?'' Karen asked.

Linda snorted. "Wax dummies, right out of Tussaud's ''
She turned on Karen abruptly. "I'd give my dear old mum's
star sapphire for one night with a man like Colter.''

"Not if you want to keep your sanity,'' Karen replied
darkly.

"Who says I have it?'' Linda retorted.

They both glanced up as Doris returned with a tray. Karen
was dimly aware of a sotto voce conference between the two
women before the maid left. As Linda poured the tea, Karen
looked around the room.

Furnished with antique pieces like those in the hall, it
featured a well-worn Aubusson rug in a pale pink rose pattern, with matching pink satin draperies at the leaded case-
ment windows. Twin book chests stood on either side of the
windows, filled with volumes that were obviously both old
and valuable. An escritoire that seemed to be of the same
period as the armoire occupied a nook in a bay window on
the other side of the study, and chairs and love seats were
scattered around the vast stone fireplace that covered most
of the far wall. The other three walls had been "dragged,''
treated with an eggshell paint and then rubbed with grass

cloth to give a finely streaked two-tone effect. The whole place looked, and felt, like one of those display houses opened to tourists on Sunday afternoons.

Linda brought Karen a cup of tea, served in a tiny Meissen china cup with a slice of lemon on the side.

"Just as I thought," Linda said. "The dragon lady is on the prowl, wondering what the two of us are doing in here."

"Is that what the maid said?"

"No, Doris said that Margaret's guests were missing me, which is a blatant lie if ever I heard one. I told her to send word that you were exhausted from your trip and 'indisposed.' Don't you love that word? It always conjures up images of ladies in empire gowns passing out in swooning chairs."

"'Swooning chairs'?"

"You've never seen them? There's one in the library; remind me to show it to you. It has only one arm, so you can faint on one side and support your head on the other."

"You're making that up."

Linda held up her hand as if taking an oath. "On my honor as a former Girl Guide. Do you want some cream for that tea?"

"No, this is fine."

"I must say your color is improving. You looked like death when you arrived."

"I am feeling better. This is lovely china," Karen said.

Linda nodded. "My father's mother's. It's quite precious, made from an original Dresden pattern that's been discontinued. You can't buy it any more at any price."

Karen set the cup down carefully. "Don't you have any Farberware?"

"Beg pardon?"

"My little joke."

"All right," Linda said, handing her a miniature sandwich. "You've been glossing over the details, just hitting the high points, and I want all of it, right now."

"Okay."

For the next twenty minutes Karen told her as much as she could remember of recent events, and at the end of it Linda stood, smoothing the skirt of her navy cashmere sweater dress and patting her hair.

"Just as I thought," she said crisply. "Nothing ever happens to me."

"You were kidnapped on Almeria."

"Nothing *good* ever happens to me."

"I wouldn't call being escorted out of Kinsale by a trio of thugs something good."

"At least it was different."

"It was that, all right."

"I wish something a little unusual would happen to light a fire around here, and that's a fact."

"Well," Karen said, squirming uncomfortably, "something may."

Linda looked at her.

"I think I was followed here. By one of those men."

"What men?" Linda said sharply.

"The men who came after Colter."

"One of them trailed you from the airport?"

Karen nodded. "I recognized him in the car behind me as your driver was bringing me to the house."

Linda ran to the window, which faced the street. "What did the car look like?"

"A dark blue compact."

"What's a compact?"

"A . . . mini, I think you call them."

Linda peered through the shrubbery that partially obscured the view. "He's out there," she said positively.

Karen came to stand at her shoulder. "Where?"

"Parked at the foot of the drive across the way. Do you see?"

Karen did, and her heart sank.

"Linda, I'm sorry. I didn't mean to involve you in all of this. I just had no idea what else to do. They wouldn't let me go back to the States."

Linda turned to face her. "Darling, don't be ridiculous. This is too exciting. Shall we go out and talk to him?"

Karen stared at her, aghast. "Linda, these people are dangerous."

"So is Colter; you said so yourself. Can you imagine how lonely that poor man must be, sitting out there staring at this house with nothing to do?"

Karen shook her head. "Linda, he's watching me, making sure I say here until Colter does what they want. He's not looking to make any friends."

"You always were a spoilsport," Linda said huffily. But she left the window as a light tap sounded at the door.

"Yes?" she called.

The same maid who had brought the tray came in and said, "Madam is asking for you again, Miss Linda."

Linda shot Karen a pained glance.

"Tell her I'm with my guest and will join her shortly," Linda replied and waited until the woman had left before adding, "I wondered how long it would take her to send out the second alarm."

"I guess she's not going to take no for an answer."

Linda rolled her eyes. "I imagine I had better get in there and show my teeth. You might as well come along."

Karen's eyes widened. "Linda, look at me."

Linda studied her dishabille. "Yes, I see your point. Where are your things?"

"In the car."

"Then Stock brought them in."

"Stock? His name is Stock?"

"Do you have anything suitable to wear?" Linda asked, ignoring the commentary.

"To see your stepmother? Of course not. I have wool slacks and pullovers, and you're wearing that slinky thing."

"Then we'll go upstairs and get you dressed. We can't have Margaret thinking I dragged you in off the street."

They left the study and ascended a central curved staircase to a long hall on the second floor. An Oriental runner covered the washed pine floorboards, and every five feet or so a round window set with colored panes shed streams of filtered light across the opposite wall.

"Nice little shack you got here, Lin," Karen commented dryly.

"Oh, hush," Linda said. "It's not mine, anyway, belongs to the family trust."

"I'm impressed just the same."

Linda opened a six-paneled door at the end of the passage. "We'll see if we can't find you something in here."

"Here" was an entire room that looked like one big closet.

"What is this?" Karen asked, awed at the racks of clothes, the clear plastic drawers of shoes and hose.

"My dressing room."

"And where's the bedroom?"

"Through there." She pointed to a door in one wall.

"I can't believe you left this to live in three rooms on Almeria."

"I was happier there," Linda said, in such a desolate tone that Karen knew she was telling the truth.

"I can't choose from so much," Karen said, overwhelmed.

"I'll do it. This suite was my mother's before she died," Linda said quietly. "When my father remarried, he moved into the other wing with Margaret, and I took these rooms."

"Does Margaret have children?" Karen asked.

Linda shook her head. "Which leaves all of her considerable time free to work on improving me," she said sourly. "It's her favorite hobby, next to cultivating her country house roses for the county prize and doing good works for the charity bazaars."

Karen was staring at one of the racks, obviously not listening. Linda put her arm around the other woman's shoulders.

"Don't worry about him. He's tough. He'll get through it in splendid shape."

Karen nodded.

"I'm going to keep you so busy you won't have a minute to think about it."

Karen smiled. That would be busy, indeed.

Linda found Karen something to wear and then took her to meet the formidable Margaret, a perfectly coiffed and made-up glacial blonde who looked as if she emerged, encased in plastic, from a doll box every morning. She barely tolerated Linda, although she was so exquisitely polite and deferential to the younger woman that only Linda's reaction gave her away. Karen began to see that her presence in the house would provide Linda with a welcome ally, and she felt a little better about descending on her the way she had.

Linda was as good as her word. For the next three weeks Karen joined in the whirl of social engagements that occupied Linda's days, and at the end of it she had to dispute the term "idle rich." These people were rich, but they certainly were not idle. They spent most of their time working for charities, as if in expiation for their inherited wealth, and literally exhausted themselves with luncheons and teas and auctions to raise money for everything from the Kensington Orphans' Home to the British War Veterans. Karen fell into bed at night dead tired and slept, but her first thought upon waking was always of Colter.

Karen had wired her sister Grace to let her know where she was, but as time went on, she began to feel guilty about imposing on Linda's hospitality. Linda, for her part, said that she wished the present arrangement could continue indefinitely. She had even taken to waving to the watchdog in the car across the street every time they went out. After two weeks, sheepishly, he began to wave back.

From Colter, and of him, they had heard nothing.

At 7:30 one evening they were in Linda's bedroom, dressing for a dinner party that Margaret was hosting. Linda's father was away on government business, but his wife was entertaining some of their friends in his absence. Linda was expected to put in an appearance, and Karen, as usual, had been pressed into service to accompany her.

"Linda, I don't think I look right in this dress," Karen observed, glancing at herself critically in her friend's cheval mirror.

"Don't be silly, darling. That Japanese style suits you perfectly." Linda stepped into her shoes, turning from side to side on the Kirman rug to study the effect in the glass.

"I don't know why I let you talk me into this," Karen murmured. She sat on the edge of the ice-blue quilted silk spread and began to brush her hair.

"Very intelligent of you to select it. If the English did calisthenics at lunchtime in the factories, perhaps, we, too, could make microchips and beaded kimonos."

"I'm too tall for it."

"Nonsense. You're hardly a lumberjack."

"But this is supposed to be a geisha-type outfit."

"So? You have little feet. That's all you need. Nobody wears the white makeup anymore."

Karen signed and looked away.

"You're thinking about him again," Linda said warningly.

Karen glanced back at her reflection. "The top is too bare."

"All the better to expose those lovely shoulders. Some of these undersecretaries coming tonight are decidedly libidinous, despite their scholarly appearance. They may not be able to talk about anything but the Labour Party and the Falklands War, but their instincts are still in the right place."

Karen didn't answer.

Linda's eyes met Karen's in the mirror. "I perceive that I'm not amusing you."

"I'm sorry, Lin. It's just . . . it's been three weeks."

"If you say that once more, I'm going to make you stand in a corner and face the wall. You keep announcing 'It's been three weeks' like the town crier giving the time. Along with 'I should go home' and 'I have to get a job.' It's boring, darling."

"I'm worried."

"I know, and I'm as concerned as you are. But you know very well that you're trapped here as long as Colter is on this mission. If you tried to leave, that person watching this house would have something to say about it, and we don't want to arouse his interest, do we? So you might as well relax and wait it out and try to enjoy yourself in the meantime."

"How can I enjoy myself when Colter is . . . I don't know what he is, or where."

"And that's exactly my point. Why fret about something over which you have no control?" Linda tugged at the bodice of her strapless gown. "This thing is killing me already; I'll never last the evening. Oh, well, no matter, maybe it'll give me an excuse to bow out early. I'll say my underwire is coming undone." She chuckled, turning her head to admire an earring.

"I keep thinking every day that something will happen soon," Karen said unhappily.

Linda shrugged. "Springing people out of jail takes time. He can't just march up to the gates and say, 'Release your prisoner immediately; Karen is waiting for me.'" She went to the window and peered out across the lawn. "Maybe we should ask our friend the spy to the party."

"What if something's gone wrong?" Karen asked, still pursuing the same line of conversation.

"Then our watchdog friend wouldn't still be with us," Linda replied logically. "He's waiting, too, just like we are. Right?"

"Right," Karen agreed resignedly.

"So cheer up and help me get through this. It's time we went downstairs and faced the gathering of ghouls Margaret has assembled. Wait until you meet Peter Mainwaring."

"What's his story?" Karen asked, following Linda out of the bedroom and into the hall.

"He has none. That's why I can't wait for you to meet him. The man does nothing but mumble and stare into his sherry glass like a zombie. Which he could easily be mistaken for, incidentally, except for the rise and fall of his chest, indicating breathing and forcing me to conclude that he is, in fact, alive."

"I suppose Margaret has seated you next to him."

"No, darling, she's seated *you* next to him," Linda informed her, with obvious enjoyment. "Let it be a challenge to you. I have heard that he can occasionally be drawn out on the subject of horses, but I wouldn't stake my life on it." They walked down the staircase and heard the sound of chatter floating toward them from the salon on the first floor.

"Linda, I know nothing about horses."

"That should make you a good match for him, since he knows nothing at all."

"He can't be that bad."

"Oh, I assure you, he is. This is really a choice group, a definite coup for Margaret, who has, in her time, been known to orchestrate the most deadly assemblies since the Montague boys attended the Capulet ball."

"Nobody interesting will be here?"

"Interesting? Well, George Mortimer's mother shot his father about ten years ago, if you call that interesting. Of course, no one discusses such an unfortunate incident—very bad form, you understand."

"Is that really true?" Karen asked, momentarily nonplussed.

"Certainly. There's also the matter of Lucy Forrester's insane husband, but again, don't bring it up over the savory."

"'Insane husband'?" Karen said faintly. They had paused in the front hall and were conversing in hushed tones.

"Crackers, darling, absolutely mad as a hatter. Locked up in one of those expensive loony bins lined with cotton wool and hidden behind a stand of Lombardy poplars. I hear he still thinks it's World War II, and every time a fire siren goes off, he crawls under the bed to hide during the air raid."

Karen bit her lip.

"Oh, you may well laugh at our little eccentricities. If you think that's funny, I won't tell you about Margaret's brother, the painter, who moved to Paris when he was twenty and has been painting the Louvre ever since."

"His painting is in the Louvre?"

"No, dear, just what I said. He's been painting the exterior of it, great beastly canvases filled with acrylic gobs that no one can stand to look at, much less buy."

"But how does he live?"

"On his trust fund, of course—how does anyone live? Just don't mention him to Margaret. He's a sore spot in a family that has quite a few of them, take my word for it. Her parents, who comprise another subject I won't get into, managed to raise the most amazing goblin brood you ever saw in your life. Margaret is a brick by comparison with the rest of them. Stick to the weather and the food and the shocking conditions of our British rail system. That should exhaust her mentally in no time and let you off the hook, as you Americans say."

"I don't know if I'm ready for this," Karen murmured.

"Of course you are. If I can stand it, so can you. They all *look* harmless; you'd never guess what was going on if you judged by appearances. Just make polite chat, like the well-bred young lady you are, and they'll all be wild for you." She tugged on Karen's hand and managed to hustle her along the hall.

Karen had to agree that Linda's assessment of the situation was correct. Margaret's guests were perfectly behaved and said the right things, and if Karen hadn't heard the gossip in advance she never would have guessed the truth. Peter Mainwaring *was* a bore, but all she had to do was nod enthusiastically when he made an infrequent comment in an accent she could barely decipher, and he seemed satisfied. Karen knew so little about British politics, "the Royals," or the races, which were the main topics of conversation, that she was forced into the role of agreeable dummy, seconding everything anyone said. Her jaw ached from smiling. She was taking a break, standing by the ormolu clock stand in the front hall while the after-dinner drinks were served, when Linda found her.

"Ah-ha," Linda said. "Just as I suspected. You managed to tear yourself away from Peter, you clever girl."

"Please don't make me go back in there yet. I'm ready to do a tap dance down the center of the table to give them something new to talk about."

"I take it you've already covered the trompe l'oeil Zuber wallpaper and the Turkish carpet," Linda said sarcastically.

"I can give you chapter and verse on the wallpaper. It depicts India during the sixth century, was made from the original blocks cut during the early nineteen hundreds, and was hidden in a cave during the blitz, which explains the moss stains on the seams."

"My, you have been listening. Margaret is very proud of that paper, outbid a couple of old crones from the historical society to get it, though I can't think why. It seems a moldy depiction of a child's nightmare to me. Even the bananas look wrong, like yellow balloons."

"I'll see it in my dreams tonight," Karen sighed.

"Psst, they've found us," Linda hissed dramatically as Margaret, wearing her nailed-on smile, appeared in the doorway of the dining room and gestured for them to join her.

They went back in to the party, and Karen accepted a glass of sherry, taking a sip while Linda, wearing a numbed expression, listened to a Mrs. Merriwether tell her about her daughter's special school. Karen was certain that it was a wonderful school, perfectly suited to the child's exceptional abilities, but didn't stay to hear about it. She wandered off to a corner to occupy herself by licking the top layer off a selection of petits fours. There she was joined by George Mortimer, who proceeded to inform her of the evils of refined sugar while she was wolfing down the fondant icing. She put the last confection on a tray and smiled at him weakly.

"Excuse me, I have to speak to Linda," Karen said evenly. George nodded and turned to his companion to continue his lecture.

Karen went to her friend's side and took her arm.

"May I see you for a moment?" she said between her teeth.

Linda excused herself from Mrs. Merriwether.

"The only school that dreadful brat should go to is a Borstal," Linda observed darkly, referring to her recent conversation.

"Linda, I have to get out of here," Karen said. "Tell them I went upstairs with a headache, tell them I died, anything."

"You're not going to leave me alone with this crew," Linda said, outraged. "And to think what I've done for you."

"Linda, please," Karen insisted, near tears. "I can't even concentrate on what they're saying."

"Nobody could concentrate on what these people are saying," Linda observed crossly.

"I'm going," Karen said.

"I don't think so," Linda said softly, looking over her shoulder.

"What do you mean?"

"I don't think you'll want to leave just yet," Linda went on, gesturing toward the door.

Karen turned, and her heart leapt into her throat.

Standing just inside the sliding cherry panels to the hall was Colter.

Chapter 9

Conversation in the room began to die out as more of the diners caught sight of the apparition in the doorway. Finally a stunned silence fell as Colter's eyes bypassed the others and settled on Karen, who stood transfixed, relief and joy welling up within her.

Colter was wearing a navy double-breasted pea jacket, open down the front, with the collar turned up to his chin. Under it was a royal blue Shaker sweater, paired with tight faded jeans and well-worn boots. There was a patch of gauze on his forehead, tied in place by a narrow strip of cloth, and his left hand was bandaged, wrapped in tape to his wrist. The formally attired partygoers stared at him with a mixture of fascination and disdain, but he seemed unaware of them, his attention fixed on the woman he had come to see.

"I'm sorry, madam, I tried to stop him, but he said he knew Miss Linda..." Field was saying nervously in the background to Margaret, who stood by, unsure what to do. The intruder certainly looked questionable, but if she threw him out, she risked breaking the cardinal rule of British etiquette: "Thou shalt not make a nasty fuss in front of thy guests."

Suddenly, as if on cue, Colter opened his arms, and Karen ran into them.

He embraced her so tightly that he lifted her off her feet, swinging her in an arc. The diners looked on in shock, unable to believe what they were seeing.

Margaret was appalled. Linda's American friend had really been less trouble than she'd first anticipated, but this was too much. Throwing herself at this person who'd barged into a private home and a private party, dressed like some navvy from the docks... It was unforgivable. She glanced around worriedly at her company, but they were too fascinated with the scene unfolding before them to pay much attention to her discomfiture.

Karen clung to Colter as he set her down and lifted her chin with his good hand.

"Hi," he said softly.

"Hi, yourself," Karen replied half laughing.

"You all right?" he asked, smiling into her eyes.

"I'm wonderful," she answered. "But what about you?" She reached up to touch the dressing on his head.

"I'm fine." He smoothed a tendril of hair back from her brow. "Now."

Karen closed her eyes, willing back the tears. He embraced her again, cradling her against his side, and Karen sighed, at peace for the first time since he'd left.

Linda coughed behind them, and they both turned to look at her. They had forgotten their audience.

"Hello, Colter," Linda said archly, nodding to him.

He nodded back, breaking into the grin that made him look like an errant but irresistible teenager. "Thanks for taking care of my girl," he said to her.

"It was my pleasure," Linda replied.

Margaret, beginning to recover, inched forward, and Linda stepped in front of her, taking Karen's arm and leading her a few paces away.

"Get him upstairs to your room immediately," she said in Karen's ear.

"But what about the party, your stepmother?"

"I'll handle Margaret," Linda said firmly. "Just take him out of here before one of these frustrated matrons attacks him. They haven't been in the same room with that much vigorous masculinity since the canteens during the war, and in a moment they're going to stop being stunned and start salivating."

Karen chuckled. "Linda, you're awful."

Linda patted her hair. "Yes, I know, and I find it a full-time occupation. Now go before one of these overstuffed grande dames passes out from the strain."

Karen glanced around her. "They do look terribly shaken, don't they?" she said, giggling.

"I'm surprised dear Margaret didn't lose all those expensive jackets on her teeth."

"Won't she tell you to ask Colter to leave?" Karen said with concern.

"She had better not try," Linda answered grimly. "This is still my house, and you two are my guests, and there's an end to it."

Karen wasn't going to argue the point any further. She went to Colter and took his hand.

"Linda has asked us both to stay," she said evenly, holding his glance with her own. "Do you want me to show you upstairs?"

He nodded, going along with her, and they left the dining room together, walking down the hall to the foot of the staircase. Behind them they heard the rustle of clothing and the murmur of subdued voices as the guests emerged from their trance.

"What the hell's going on?" Colter said to her as soon as they were out of earshot. "Are they calling the bobbies on me, or what?"

She threw her arms around his neck. "You're spending the night," she informed him happily.

"With you?" he said warily.

"No, silly, with the Queen Mother. Of course with me."

"Well, all right," he responded, bending his head to kiss her.

It was as if he'd never been away. The taste and feel of his mouth was the same, and the urgency of his lovemaking remained unchanged. When he pushed her back against the wall and dropped his hands to caress her bare shoulders, Karen pulled away.

"We'd better get out of here," she whispered, jerking her head toward the stairs. "Margaret's liable to come after us with a broom."

"Is that the aging Barbie doll?" he asked, as they ran up the stairs together.

Karen nodded.

"I doubt if she's ever used a broom in her life," he said sarcastically. "Except to ride on, of course," he added as an afterthought. "I think I gave her a tic when I arrived; did you see her twitching?"

Karen snickered.

He paused on the landing. "Which door?" he said in confusion. "This place looks like the White House."

Karen took him to the room where she was staying, and he closed the door behind them and locked it. He turned to her instantly, pulling her into his arms.

"God," he sighed, burying his face in the soft sweep of her hair against her neck, "you don't know how often I thought of this. It kept me going until I could get back to you." He moved his head and trailed his lips along the smooth line of her exposed shoulder. "This is some outfit," he murmured huskily.

"Do you like it on me?" she asked, drawing back and looking at him.

"I'd like it better off you," he answered and reached for the zipper at the back. He ran it down the track to her waist and then peeled the strapless bodice away from her torso, exposing her breasts. He took one shell-pink nipple in his mouth and sucked greedily until she clutched at him, weak-kneed, then he picked her up and carried her to the bed.

He had her dress off in seconds and disposed of the rest of her underthings summarily, dropping them on the floor. Then he stripped hastily, tossing his jacket and pants on a needlepoint chair that stood by the side of the Dutch tiled fireplace. He threw himself down next to her on the woven counterpane and pulled her tightly against him, gasping at the electric contact of her bare flesh with his.

Karen closed her eyes as he kissed her lightly, then opened her lips when he increased the pressure of his mouth. He ran his uninjured hand down her body, caressing her, and she arched upward, yielding eagerly to his touch. Colter tried to go slow, but they were both too hungry, and when he pulled away to turn Karen on her back, she held him, slipping her leg between his. Colter moaned, his unfulfilled need during their time apart taking over, and he pressed her into the bed, letting her feel his arousal.

Karen pulled her mouth from his and pressed her lips to his neck, past the stubble of his beard to the soft flesh at the base of his neck. She felt the pulse of life beating there, pumping wildly, an indication of the level of his excitement, which matched her own. Increasingly impatient, he bunched his fists in her hair and pushed her down, crushing her breasts against his chest. She lay mute with anticipation as he lifted himself on his hands and poised himself above her. Her eyes locked with his as she curled her legs around him, and he entered her.

Karen made a sound in her throat, a soft growl of pleasure, and dug her heels into his hips, forcing him deeper inside her. He bucked wildly, but carried her with him, and they fell back on the bed together at the end, spent and satiated.

They lay drowsily entwined for a timeless period, content just to realize they were together. Then Karen half sat and draped her arm across Colter's chest, looking down into his face.

"Do you think all those people on the first floor know what we've been doing up here?" she asked Colter, smiling slightly.

He touched the tip of her nose. "It's a sure bet they don't think we're playing backgammon," he replied dryly. "What an ossified group. I don't see how your friend Linda fits in with that bunch."

"She doesn't; that's the problem. She and Margaret don't get along, and she isn't very happy here." Karen touched the bandage on his wrist. "How did you do this?" she asked.

"It's a powder burn," he answered.

"Oh." Karen paused, and then said, "That must have been very painful."

"You can block out pain if you concentrate on something else, something good," he said, covering her fingers with his other hand. "You just have to have a positive ideal in mind, a fine thing to think about that's more powerful than the pain."

"What did you think about when you hurt your hand?"

His eyes sought hers guilelessly. "You."

Karen's face changed, and she didn't respond for a long moment. Then she spoke quietly. "Steven, that's the nicest thing you've ever said to me."

He continued to stare up at her, as if surprised. "Is it?"

She nodded seriously. "Yes."

He looked disturbed. "I don't say enough nice things to you, do I? I mean, I don't compliment you enough, make you feel special."

"You make me feel special," she said tenderly. He didn't know that he charmed without effort. His personal comments were artless but heartfelt, all the more precious for their rarity.

He shook his head. "No, that's not true. I'd like to think of the right things to say, but I'm just not good that way." He sighed, frustrated, and dropped his eyes. "I wish I were different," he said fiercely.

"I don't," Karen said, snuggling next to him and putting her head on his shoulder. "I think you're terrific just as you are."

"So many things would be better, then," he murmured, as if to himself.

"Steven," Karen said absently, shifting her weight to get comfortable, "what are you babbling about?"

"Nothing," he muttered. But his expression was still distracted, unhappy, as he pulled the side of the spread up from the floor to cover Karen.

"Steven?"

"Mmm?"

"Why were you gone so long? I was terribly worried."

"The prison had very tight security. It took a long time to plan the raid."

"Did it go off all right?"

"Like clockwork."

"You got him out?"

He smiled. "Sort of. We raided the exercise yard and quite a few of them got out."

Karen turned her head to peer up at him. "You sprang a whole bunch of them at the same time?"

"Yeah. It was unplanned, but very satisfactory." He sounded pleased with himself.

"But maybe some of them were dangerous."

"Nah. They were all political prisoners; none of them belonged inside in the first place."

"You enjoyed it, didn't you? Letting them all out."

"I didn't enjoy the fireworks," he said ruefully, lifting his injured hand.

"You must forget what it feels like not to have some sort of injury," Karen commented.

"Yeah, and every year I seem to wind up with a few more of them," he said flatly. "I think I may be getting too old for this business."

"How do you mean?"

"Losing that edge, that sharpness, you know? It's a funny sort of balance you have to strike. When you're real young you're quick and alert but inexperienced, and you make mistakes because of that. But when you're old enough to know what's going on, you're already slowing down. There's really only a couple of years when you're at your peak."

"Have you reached it?"

He glanced at her. "Maybe."

"What happens to retired mercenaries?" Karen asked lightly, aware that she should tread carefully. "Do they fade away, like old soldiers?"

"There's no such thing as a retired mercenary," Colter replied.

"Why not?" Karen asked, already knowing the answer.

"They're all dead," he said shortly. "Can we change the subject?" He sat up and got out of bed, striding naked to the window. Karen could see his lithe form partially illuminated by the lanterns on the drive.

"The guard is gone," he informed her, referring to the man in the car across the road.

"Did you know he would be sent to keep an eye on me?" Karen asked.

He nodded.

"Why didn't you tell me?"

He shrugged. "One more thing for you to worry about. I knew he wouldn't harm you as long as I fulfilled my part of the bargain."

"I think Linda has a crush on him," Karen said, amused.

Colter turned, snorting with surprised laughter. "What?"

"It's true."

"You're crazy."

"She was always talking about inviting him inside for a drink."

"Maybe you and your friend aren't as different as I thought," he said, rejoining her and stretching out on the bed. "You're both attracted to that element of danger you sense in guys like me, and him."

"Oh, you've got it all figured out, have you?" Karen asked archly, putting her arms around his neck and throwing her leg across his. "You know exactly what I want?"

He chuckled, running his hands down the smooth satiny expanse of her back. "I think it's pretty obvious what you want right now," he murmured.

"Then give it to me."

And he did.

An hour later Karen was sleeping in the outsize guest bed while Colter sat in the needlepoint chair, smoking a cigarette. Around him the elaborately decorated room was shrouded in darkness, and the canopied bed with its chintz hangings resembled a cocoon, Karen's slight form wrapped in the covers as in a chrysalis. He stared up at the cut-glass light fixture above his head and wondered what he was doing in this mansion, with this woman who had so changed his life.

He should have broken it off with Karen while they were still in Ireland. Because he was too gutless then to do what had to be done, she had become a hostage in his latest venture, and he had to make sure that scenario was never repeated.

He inhaled deeply and held the smoke in his lungs, letting it escape slowly. Perhaps it would have been kinder not to return to her, not to raise her hopes. But he had wanted to be with her again more than he'd thought possible, and he'd given in to his own weakness, his desire for her warmth, her companionship, her love. But this night was all they could have together; it had to end here. He couldn't drag her through the wreckage of his life like baggage, couldn't ask her to share more of the anguish and uncertainty she'd just experienced. It was killing him to let her go, but keeping her with him would only cause more pain in the future. For once in his ill-spent life he was going to put someone else first, no matter what it cost him.

He started as a door slammed below the windows, and he heard the sound of voices calling farewell. The guests were going home. He listened to the departures as he smoked slowly, wondering how and when he could bring himself to tell Karen goodby.

Karen stirred, and her hand automatically searched the space next to her in the bed. She found it empty. She sat up, clutching the sheet to her breasts, and spotted Colter sitting in the chair. Naked to the waist, he was a dim outline in the midnight darkness.

"What are you doing?" she muttered groggily, waiting for her eyes to adjust to the gloom.

"Having a smoke," he said. She watched as he exhaled and then stubbed out the butt in a ceramic ashtray.

Karen wrapped the sheet around her and struggled out of bed, almost tripping on the tail end of the bedclothes. He laughed softly as he saw her fighting her way toward him.

"Don't you think such modesty is a little excessive under the circumstances?" he teased her.

"Maybe I'm cold," she retorted.

"Maybe you're inhibited," he replied, and she could see the white flash of his teeth as he smiled.

"How can you say that to me?" she inquired, sitting at his feet and leaning her head against his jeans-clad knee. She yawned and thumbed her hair out of her eyes.

"Because it's true. I can't believe such a prissy little goody two-shoes can be such a wildcat in bed."

"'Prissy little goody two-shoes'!" she said, pretending to be insulted. "I like that."

He bent and put his arms around her. "So do I. I like the fact that no one else knows, that I'm the only one who can turn you into such a greedy creature." He kissed the back of her bare shoulder, and she didn't see the expression of sadness cloud his handsome features.

Karen closed her eyes. She listened for a moment and then said, "Is that everybody going home? I think the noise woke me."

"Probably," he said, sitting back. "The front entry is just below us, all the car doors slamming sounded like a fusillade."

"Linda told me her grandfather imported Carrara marble for those steps," Karen said. "They cost seventy-five thousand pounds. In 1928."

"I hope I left a lot of mud on them on the way in," he answered shortly.

The din below fell off, then ceased completely.

"I guess the party broke up," Karen said dreamily.

"I'm surprised it recovered from my entrance," he answered.

"Oh, come on, you enjoyed it," she said, smiling slightly. "All those stuffy establishment types gathered around, and you standing there in the doorway, the collar of that sailor jacket turned up to your chin, like Clark Gable chasing Greer Garson in *Adventure*."

"What's that, an old movie?"

"Yup. Gable is a wandering seaman who falls for a proper lady, and it really complicates his life."

"That does have a familiar ring," he observed dryly.

Karen got up and crawled into his lap, letting the sheet fall to the floor. He buried his face against her breasts and swung her up into his arms.

"Have I been worth it?" she whispered, closing her eyes as he stood.

He answered her without words, lifting his head to kiss her and carrying her to the bed.

They were roused from sleep in the morning by loud tapping, followed by Linda's voice caroling, "Cherubs, are you awake in there?"

Colter rolled his eyes and vaulted out of bed, heading for the adjoining bathroom. Karen waited until the door closed behind him and then called, "Come on in."

Linda bustled through the hall door, carrying a huge tray. "Here's your breakfast," she announced, then her face fell as she glanced around the room.

"Where's Colter?" she asked, setting the tray on a bed-side stand.

Karen nodded to the bathroom.

"Oh, what a disappointment," Linda mourned. "I was hoping to catch him in the altogether."

Karen giggled.

"You may well laugh," Linda sniffed, "since you've been enjoying the sight for some time now. There are those of us who aren't quite so fortunate."

"How come Doris didn't bring the tray?" Karen asked.

"Doris is a nosy parker and Margaret's spy," Linda replied. "I thought I'd better assume the duties myself and keep her out of here."

They both heard the shower water begin to run, and Linda added, "Sounds like your friend will be occupied for a while. You'd better start on this; it will get cold." She sat on the edge of the bed and picked up a slice of toast, nibbling delicately.

"What did Margaret say after we went upstairs last night?" Karen asked her.

Linda adjusted the sash on her ruffled red satin robe and chewed thoughtfully. "She didn't say much; I think she was flummoxed."

" 'Flummoxed'?" Karen repeated, smiling.

"Stunned and bewildered. Speechless, almost, which in Margaret's case was a beautiful thing to see. It won't last, however. She'll recover and have quite a bit to say, unless I miss my guess, and where Margaret is concerned, I usually don't."

"I hope we haven't caused a lot of trouble for you," Karen said guiltily, reaching for a grapefruit slice and popping it into her mouth.

"Don't be silly, darling. It was worth any amount of static from Margaret to see the expression on her face when Colter walked in. Poor Field will never be the same. I don't know why Margaret thinks that dotty artifact would be able to stop anybody from coming in, much less a hearty specimen like your soldier boy, but that's my stepmother for you. All the help around here is approximately the age of original sin, and she wonders why the place is falling to pot."

Karen chuckled. "Yes, I know, you do have it hard."

"Don't start that, Karen—it's too early in the morning." She stood and dusted her hands on her robe. "Which reminds me, I'd better get after that sluggardly dressmaker. I have a fitting at ten, and I want to confirm the appointment. The last time I showed up there, they had confused the time. I had to wait around like Apple Mary while they inserted panels into a gown for some absurdly fat cow who should have been wearing an Arabian tent."

Karen laughed. "God help them if they keep you waiting again," she said in awed tones.

"I've said it all along; you're no fun." She cast a longing glance at the closed bathroom door. "But Colter, however..."

Karen threw a napkin at her. "Get out of here."

"One would never guess this was *my* house," Linda said imperiously and swept from the room.

A few minutes after she left, Colter emerged from the bathroom, his hair wet and slicked back, a towel wrapped around his hips.

"Where's the duchess?" he said, eyeing the breakfast tray with enthusiasm.

"She has an appointment."

"Did you leave anything for me?" he asked, sitting next to her and grabbing a muffin.

Karen slapped his wrist. "That's mine; can't you see there's a bite out of it? There's plenty more under that cover."

He helped himself, and silence reigned for a few minutes as he ate steadily, demolishing everything on the tray. Karen watched him until he realized she was doing so and grinned sheepishly.

"Gee, I hope you had enough," she said breathlessly.

"My last meal was breakfast yesterday, on the plane," he replied.

"Take my word, you made up for it."

He picked up her hand and kissed it. "I'm a growing boy."

"If you ate regular meals, you wouldn't get so starved," Karen said, throwing back the sheet and going to the closet for her robe. "Should we be changing the tape on your hand, by the way? It's wet. And what about the cut on your head?"

"The tape will dry—it's been wet before. And I don't need the dressing anymore; I took it off. The cut's healing all right."

Karen sighed. She knew that her words were wasted on him. "I'm going to take a shower. Don't eat the dishes while I'm gone."

He waved her on, diving into the plate of fruit. Karen took a long hot shower in the luxuriously appointed guest bath. She washed with glycerine soap pressed into a flower shape and did her hair with an herbal shampoo that smelled like an apothecary shop. She stepped out of the tiled shower stall and wrapped her hair in a thick striped turkish towel, belting her robe around her. Opening the door to the bedroom released a cloud of steam, and when it cleared, she found that Colter was nowhere to be seen.

There was a note pinned to the pillow of the unmade bed.

"Be back in an hour. C."

He was nothing if not succinct. Karen took off her robe and dressed, annoyed. Why did he keep vanishing like a sorcerer's apprentice, and why did he wait until she'd left the room to take off, as if she were his truant officer? She had a sinking feeling that something was up, and she didn't like it. As far as she was aware, he didn't know a soul in London, but of course she wasn't aware of very much where his "other life" was concerned. He must have gone to see someone, because Linda's largesse could have provided anything else that he needed. On a hunch she picked up the house phone and rang Field.

"Yes, madam?" he said in his theatrical accent.

"Did Mr. Colter get a call this morning?" she asked the butler.

"Someone rang for him about ten minutes ago, madam," Field replied, with just the slightest hint of disapproval in his voice. Karen could understand that Colter was not high on his list of favorites and overlooked it. She was relieved to hear that the call had come while she was in the bathroom. His departure wasn't premeditated, then.

"Was it long distance, a . . . trunk call?" Karen asked, feeling guilty about checking up on Colter, but desperate to know what was going on.

"I couldn't possibly say, madam."

Karen realized she was getting nowhere and hung up. Then she paced for half an hour.

Colter returned when he'd said he would. He was attired in the same clothes he'd worn the night before, with the pea jacket over his arm. One look at his face told her that she was in trouble.

"Where did you go?" she greeted him tensely.

He sat down and lit a cigarette, which was always a bad sign. "I had to meet somebody."

"In London? Who do you know here?"

"I have contacts everywhere."

"Contacts?" she repeated, her heart dropping into her shoes. "This was about a job?"

"Yeah."

"How did they know where you were?"

"I left word with Mary Lafferty."

"Oh, of course, excuse me. I forgot about your referral service," Karen said sarcastically.

He let that pass, tapping ash into the ceramic tray.

"Well?" she said. "I hope you told them no."

He avoided her eyes. "I'm going to Lebanon," he said flatly.

"Lebanon," she whispered, staring. She simply couldn't believe it.

He wouldn't look at her.

"You're leaving me again?"

He didn't answer.

"Talk to me, Steven. You're leaving me today, aren't you?"

"Yes."

Karen's breath expelled in a sound that was half sigh, half sob. "Then why did you come back?" she asked, bewildered. "Why did you let me believe we'd be together?"

"I came back to show you I was okay, so you wouldn't worry," he answered quietly.

"And you think I won't worry now?" she asked him incredulously.

He said nothing.

"You never had any intention of staying with me, did you?" she said softly.

"Karen, listen to me . . ." he began.

"No, you listen to me," she countered wildly. Her gaze fell on his bandaged hand. "You're not even waiting until that's healed," she said desperately, trying anything.

"They need me now."

"Oh, why don't you just tell the truth?" she demanded, her anger rising, surmounting the pain. "You can't wait to get away from me."

"That isn't so," he said. His voice was low, almost expressionless, the tone he used when he wanted to disguise his true feelings. But she could guess what they were.

"You have to get on with your life now, don't you?" she said bitterly.

He met her with a stony silence.

"You had your relaxation, right? You came here and used me like one of your prostitute friends, and now it's time to move on to more important things."

He went white beneath his tan, and she regretted the words almost as soon as they left her mouth. For the first time since she'd known him, she felt physical fear.

He picked up a figurine standing on the fireplace mantel and threw it against the wall. The delicate china shattered into a score of fragments. "How dare you say that to me?" he spat between his teeth.

Karen shrank from him, her eyes wide.

He grabbed her shoulders and shook her as she tried frantically to wrest herself from his grasp. Finally he let her go, flinging her away. He sagged against the wall, trembling, his head down.

"Why don't you just hit me?" Karen asked contemptuously, rubbing her bruised arms. "That's what you'd like to do, isn't it?"

"No," he responded, defeated. "I could never hurt you."

"What do you think you're doing right now?" she fired back.

"The right thing," he answered. "I'm doing the right thing."

Karen stared at him. "You are unquestionably the most mixed-up character I have ever met. How can walking out on me, on what we have, be the right thing?"

"I know what's best," he said stonily. "You're too emotional. I have to make this decision."

"You know what's best?" she said in amazement, almost laughing. "You spend your whole life running headlong into the path of what's most likely to kill you, and *you* know what's best?"

"I don't expect you to understand."

"Oh, I understand perfectly. You'd be amazed how much I understand. This is goodbye, right? I'm supposed to forget you now."

"That's the idea," he said flatly.

"You knew this was coming, didn't you? You knew this last night."

"I just got called this morning."

"But you knew when you came here that it was only a matter of time. You knew you would take off on another one of these suicide runs as soon as you got the chance," she accused him.

He confronted her, his fists balled at his side, taking the offensive for the first time. "What did you think would happen, Karen? Did you think I would turn overnight into a CPA or an orthodontist?"

"I guess I thought we would go to your place in Florida. I could get a job; there's a large Spanish-speaking population," she said reasonably.

"Oh, I see; you were going to support me?" he asked scornfully. "And you thought I'd be happy about that?"

"I didn't think that far. I just assumed you would want us to stay together," she cried plaintively, near tears. He looked away, steeling himself to be tough. This had to be done.

"You understood that I had to go last time," he said curtly.

"You had no choice!" Karen countered. "You told me that yourself. And you also said you were coming back." She broke down, crying openly. "You could turn this one down, but you want to go," she went on, wiping her eyes. "It's an excuse; you just want to get away from me." Her voice dropped an octave. "Why did you really come back? To make this break all the more painful?"

"I had to see you again," he admitted huskily.

"I really thought that part of your life was all over," she murmured, as if to herself. "I thought you loved me. You never said it, not once, but I felt it."

She wasn't looking at him, and she didn't see his eyes filling, the wet lashes as he turned his head. "I do love you," he said quietly. "That's why I'm leaving you for good. I'm trying to do you a favor."

"By breaking my heart?" she wailed.

"No. By helping you to save it for someone else."

"I don't want anyone else," she said bitterly.

"You will. You deserve somebody who'll stay with you, who'll make a life with you and take care of you. I can't be that man."

"Yes, you could. But you won't try."

"I can't try. It's too late."

"People can change if they want to badly enough," she said stubbornly. "But you don't want to. You won't make the effort. Is that all I mean to you?"

Colter rubbed the back of his arm across his eyes and took a deep breath, trying to speak calmly. "You mean more to me than anyone ever has, Karen. That's why I'm doing this. Do you think I could stand by and watch you grow unhappy, old before your time with worry and uncertainty?"

"You could leave that life," she protested. "You could try something else."

"I'm no good for you, Karen," he insisted, hitting on what was, for him, the only issue. Then, in a softer voice, he said, "I'm just no good, period."

Karen stared at him. "That's what this is really about, isn't it?" she said softly. "You think you're not worthy of me, or some such nonsense, and you also think I'm a child who has to be protected from herself. So you know better than I do what's best for me. You're not my father, Steven. Can't I make that decision?"

"It's made," he replied flatly. "I'm going to Lebanon."

"And this is your way of showing how much you love me?" she demanded bitterly.

"I know you can't see it, but yes."

"You don't love me," she shouted as she finally realized that he was going to leave no matter what she said or did.

His features hardened, and he turned for the door.

"Go on, summer soldier, live alone, die alone, see if anybody cares, because I sure won't!"

He kept walking.

"Go, then!" she yelled after him. "Go to Lebanon, go to Timbuktu, go to hell!"

The door slammed and she was alone. Karen waited until his footsteps had faded from the stairs before dissolving into tears. She cried for a long time, until she was left drained and dry-eyed on the tangled bedclothes. She fell into a semidoze that lasted until there was a knock on her door at lunchtime.

"Come in," Karen called, sitting up and brushing her hair back from her face. Her eyes were sore and sandy, her cheeks stiff and sticky from crying, and she wasn't surprised by Linda's shocked expression when she came through the door.

"What happened to you?" Linda gasped, looking around the room as if expecting to find the cause of Karen's misery lurking in a corner.

"Oh, it's you," Karen said dully. "I thought it was the maid. She was here before, and I sent her away."

"What's going on? Where is Colter?"

"Gone."

"Again?" Linda said.

"For good," Karen replied.

Linda sat down next to her and searched her tear-stained face. "For good?" she repeated.

"He left me!" Karen wailed, beginning to cry again. "He went out this morning, and when he came back, he announced that he was going to Lebanon. Can you believe it?"

"Oh, dear, that sounds very dangerous," Linda said in a subdued tone.

"Of course it's dangerous. Does he ever do anything that isn't?" Karen said, throwing up her hands. She stood and began walking back and forth in front of the windows, shredding the tissue she held. Linda rummaged in a drawer of the bedside stand and handed her a new box.

Karen threw it on the floor. "Look at me!" she cried, turning her palms up in futility. "Before I met that guy, I never cried, and now I ought to buy stock in a paper-products company."

"But surely he'll see you when he gets back," Linda said carefully.

"No, he won't. He made it very clear that he wants nothing more to do with me."

"Why?"

"Oh, he says it's for my own good, that he would ruin my life or some such drivel, but what he really means is that he won't make the commitment. He won't take the chance on me. It's as simple as that."

"I don't think it is," Linda said slowly.

"What do you mean?" Karen queried, turning toward the other woman.

Linda shrugged. "I saw his face when he came into the dining room last night and spotted you. He's in love with you, Karen, no matter what else he says."

"Then how could he leave me like this?" Karen whispered, pressing her lips together to quell a sob.

"Maybe he was telling you the truth," Linda said. "Maybe he really feels he would only bring you unhappiness in the long run, and it's better to end it now. You have to admit that your backgrounds are very different, and you would both have big adjustments to make."

"Don't start that routine, Linda. It gives me a headache. I know I could adjust to anything for his sake. Why doesn't he feel the same way?"

"Maybe he's more realistic," Linda said quietly.

"Whose side are you on, anyway?" Karen demanded.

Linda stood and came to her side, putting her arm around Karen's shoulder. "I'm on your side, darling, but I know that you're a hopeless romantic. I agree that he's gorgeous and thrilling and brave and all of that, but can you really see him folding the clothes at the launderette and running to the chemist's for a tin of plasters?"

"I could do the laundry," Karen said crossly. "And the errands."

"You refuse to see my point," Linda insisted.

"I see it. I just don't agree with it."

"He's a different breed, that's all, and he recognizes it even if you don't."

"And no socialization between the species is permitted, right?" Karen said cynically.

"I don't know if I'd put it so technically, but yes, that's the general idea."

"It stinks," Karen said, her eyes filling again.

Linda hugged her. "I know it does." She drew back and examined Karen's morose expression. "Did he say what you're supposed to do now?"

"Go home and find someone else."

"Who?"

"He said something about a CPA or an orthodontist. Does he really think that's what I want?"

"Maybe he thinks that's what you need," Linda said wisely.

"Then he's wrong. I need him, and he's gone."

Linda crossed the room and looked out of the window. "He might be back. If he's as miserable as you are without him, you'll see him again."

Karen shook her head. "I said some awful things."

"And?"

"He's very proud. He won't come back."

"What did you say?"

Karen hung her head. "I told him that he'd used me like a whore."

Linda blanched.

"I think he was ready to punch me."

"I'm surprised he didn't."

"He took it out on your figurine instead," Karen said, pointing to the mass of porcelain shards lying in a corner.

Linda walked over to inspect the mess. "Oh, good," she said. "I'm glad someone finally trashed that horror. It was one of Margaret's favorites."

"Was it very valuable?" Karen asked soberly.

"Extremely."

"You'd better send me the bill."

"Don't be silly," Linda said briskly. "I wouldn't think of it."

"Better yet, send him the bill," Karen said bitterly. "If you can find him."

"Where does he live? When he's not traipsing around the globe with a gun, that is."

"Florida. Though you couldn't prove it by me. I've never seen the place."

"Florida. That's somewhere near California, isn't it?" Linda said.

"No, Lin. Wrong direction, wrong coast." Linda's American geography was almost as good as her American history. She'd said once that Abraham Lincoln was famous for winning the Revolutionary War at the Battle of Gettysburg.

"Oh. I seem to remember something about oranges," Linda said, chastised.

"Both states grow them. You're right about that," Karen observed. She glanced at the clock. "It's almost one. How did your fitting go?" She coughed, then blew her nose.

"Oh, the seamstress was all thumbs, but the thing did seem the right size, which is about all one can hope for." She eyed Karen speculatively. "I don't suppose you'll be hanging round now, so you won't be here for the damned showing, anyway."

"I really should go home."

"I can't induce you to stay?"

"No, Linda, I've imposed upon you long enough," Karen said firmly. "I've got to get my life together and stop waiting around for Colter to tell me what to do. I'm going back to New Jersey. I'll get a job and put him out of my mind for good."

"That's the spirit," Linda confirmed, stabbing the air with her fist. "Go in and wash your face, and I'll see about getting us some lunch. All right?"

Karen nodded.

"Are you sure you're okay?"

"Yes, I'm fine. Go ahead."

Linda left, and Karen went to the pediment mirror above the cherry lowboy, gazing at her reflection. She looked like the aftermath of a bad night.

Enough of this, she instructed herself. He waltzed you around for a good turn, but the dance is over. He's gone, and you're on your own.

Feeling, not better, but determined, she headed for the bathroom to fix her face.

The next afternoon she was on a plane for the States.

Chapter 10

Karen's sister Grace was mercifully silent during the trip back to her house from the airport. It wasn't until they were settled in the recreation room, with the kids playing Candy Land on the floor, that she said to Karen, "We missed you at Thanksgiving."

Karen nodded. The American holiday wasn't celebrated in England, and she hadn't even thought about it while she was staying with Linda.

"I'm glad you'll be here for Christmas," Grace went on.

Karen nodded again.

Grace sighed heavily. "Aren't you even going to tell me about it?" she asked.

Karen shrugged resignedly. "There isn't that much to tell. It didn't work out."

"All you said in your phone call was that he'd gone off on another job and you were coming home."

"And here I am," Karen said, hoping Grace would drop it.

She was hoping for too much. "Did you have a fight?" Grace said.

"Sort of. Not really. He wasn't fighting—I was."

Grace stared at her.

Karen made a gesture of dismissal. "He basically told me that he thought he was wrong for me and I'd better forget him and find somebody else."

"That's the first thing I've heard about this situation that I agree with," Grace said darkly. "I just wish he hadn't dragged you all over Europe before coming to that conclusion."

"He didn't drag me. I wanted to go."

"Hmph. And you wound up back here, as alone as when you met him."

Karen stood wearily, putting her hands at the back of her waist and stretching. "Grace, I would consider it a great favor if you didn't feel compelled to say 'I told you so.' It's over and done with, and I just want to put it behind me and get on with my life. And I can't do that with your grilling me like an interrogator in a police procedural."

"I'm sorry," Grace said stiffly. "I didn't mean to intrude." She rose also and headed for the kitchen.

Karen put out her hand and stopped her sister as she walked past. "Grace, wait a minute," she said.

The older woman turned. There were tears in her eyes, and Karen instantly felt guilty.

"I don't want to hurt your feelings," she said gently. "It's just that I can hardly bear to think about it anymore, much less talk about it. Can you understand that?"

"I guess so," Grace murmured. "But I can't abide the idea of anyone mistreating you."

Karen took her sister's arm and made her sit again. "Grace, listen to me. He didn't mistreat me, far from it. I've had time to consider it, and I really think he made the best effort of which he was capable. But he isn't like other people, and he never will be. He said he was going for my sake, and I know he believes that, but there's more to it. He's been alone all his life, first by an accident of fate, then by choice because he was taught early to rely only on himself." Karen gestured earnestly. "His feeling for me was genuine, but it frightened him. He doesn't want to need anyone. He thinks it makes him weak, dependent. He would rather be the person leaving than the one left, and he wasn't taking any chances with me. He got out before I could decide that *I* wanted out.''

"You're very understanding about it," Grace said in a subdued tone.

Karen shook her head, smiling slightly. "I wasn't when it first happened. I screamed and cried and told him to go to hell. But in retrospect I know he didn't mean to hurt me. He tried to avoid that from the beginning, but once I met him, I wouldn't let go, and he... wanted me, so he gave in. But you can't change people in the long run. They remain what they always were." She shrugged. "The bottom line is that if he isn't willing to take a chance on us, I can't make him do it."

"It sounds like you grew up a lot in a short time," Grace commented. "You used to think you could make things happen just because you wanted them to."

"I *had* to grow up, I guess," Karen said. She looked down, avoiding Grace's eyes. "But it still hurts. A lot."

Grace patted her hand. "All right. I won't force you to talk about it."

"Thanks."

"So what are your plans now?" Grace went on.

"Back to the want ads. I'm going to be employed by Christmas if it kills me."

And she was. As if to make up for the other blow it had dealt her, fate smiled in short order, and Karen found a job in a Paterson law office with a substantial bilingual clientele. Translating legal documents involved looking up a lot of unfamiliar terms, and she wound up spending a good deal of her time in the firm's library. There she met Jim Cochran, one of the young attorneys on staff, and as December moved on toward Christmas, he began to ask her out socially. At first she refused, making up excuses that sounded feeble even to her own ears. But then, wondering why she was sentencing herself to lonely evenings in her room with only the company of a book or television, she finally accepted. She was never going to get over Colter if she didn't try to find distractions from thoughts of him. So on a gray, cold Friday afternoon, about three weeks after her return from England, she got home from work and prepared to go out for the evening.

Grace knocked on her door as she was dressing.

"Come in," Karen called.

Grace entered, wiping her hands on a dish towel. "I guess you won't be having dinner with us," Grace observed.

"No, Jim is taking me to Renaud's. It's right across from the skating pond at Rockefeller Center, with a glass wall so you can watch the people on the ice."

"Sounds lovely," Grace said, beaming.

"Get that gleam out of your eye, Grace. I just met the guy."

"That didn't stop you with Colter," Grace pointed out.

Karen shook her head. "No comparison. Jim is nice, but that's all."

"I see. This is 'I have to do something to forget' time. Does Jim understand that?"

"I've told him that I just broke up with someone and want to take things very slow. He agreed."

Grace accepted that in silence, then began to prowl around the room, fidgeting.

"What is it, Grace?" Karen asked patiently.

"Have you heard from him? Colter, I mean?"

"No. I've been getting my mail here; you know that."

"I thought he might have called while we were out or something."

Karen shook her head. "Don't worry about it."

"I can't help it," Grace sighed. She folded her arms and leaned against the wall, watching Karen as she stepped into her pumps and picked up her bag. "How is the apartment search coming?" she asked.

"Pretty good. I've got a list of several possibilities, but two of them are too far from work. The most expensive places are closest."

"You're welcome to stay here just as long as you want," Grace said emphatically.

"I know that," Karen said, glancing in the mirror, "but I have to get back out on my own. I can't let the experience

with Colter send me running to hide at the family home-
stead. I'm getting over it, and I plan to recover completely."

"No more sleepless nights?" Grace asked.

"Less of them," Karen replied honestly.

"Crying fits?"

"Have you been listening at the door?" Karen asked suspiciously.

"I don't have to listen. Something's been causing the red
eyes."

"It gets a little better each day."

"But it's never easy, right?" Grace said.

"Right," Karen answered shortly.

"Do you regret it?"

"What, being with him?"

"Yes."

"Never," Karen said firmly. "Now I know what it's like
really to love somebody and be loved in return. I wouldn't
have missed it."

"Even with the pain?" Grace asked doubtfully.

"Even so. If that's the price I have to pay for the happiness I had, then so be it."

"Don't you think about him now, wonder if he's all
right?"

"Constantly," Karen replied softly.

"How long has it been since you've seen him?"

"Three weeks, four days, and six hours, give or take a few
minutes, and allowing for the time change from England."

Grace shook her head ruefully. "I feel sorry for Jim" was
all she said before she left the room.

Karen got her coat and followed her sister down the stairs
into the kitchen, where Mary, her niece, was sitting at the
table with a giant box of crayons, working on a coloring
book. Her brother was out with his father, so she was seizing the opportunity to color his spacemen purple before he
returned.

Karen went to the stove, where Grace was stirring a pan
of tomato sauce. "Don't worry," she said, giving Grace a
quick hug.

"I won't be too late," Karen added as she turned away.

"Are you sure you're being fair to this guy?" Grace called after her.

Karen looked back at her sister. "Jim?"

"Yes. You're obviously not over Colter, and I just don't think it's right to raise his hopes."

Karen sighed. "I already told you that I explained the situation to him, and he understands. He isn't asking me to marry him, Grace. This is just a friendly dinner, and we're taking it one step at a time."

"That should be a refreshing change from your last relationship," Grace said dryly, moving back from the stove and covering the saucepan.

Karen threw her a dirty look and was relieved when the doorbell rang, announcing Jim's arrival.

Jim was just the "steady" type that Grace loved, and so Karen was not surprised that her sister was quite taken with him and invited him to stop back anytime. Karen ushered him out the door before Grace got a chance to measure him for his wedding tuxedo, and they hurried across the lawn to his car. An arctic wind was picking up, and Karen was glad the interior was already heated from Jim's drive to her sister's house.

She studied her companion covertly as he exited Grace's development and entered the main drag that led out of town. Jim was attractive enough in a pleasant, unassuming way, with short brown hair and medium brown eyes and a quiet sense of humor that often took Karen by surprise. He was really very nice, and she was almost annoyed with herself for her inability to get interested in him. She was hoping that the passage of time would alter her attitude, but she had a sinking feeling that it wouldn't. She suspected that Grace was right. If she still felt the same after a few dates, she was going to tell Jim she'd misjudged and wasn't ready to go out with anyone else. But for now she was going to try to enjoy the evening and forget her recent past with another man.

Jim looked over at her as he pulled to a stop at a light. "You're staring at me," he said, half laughing.

Karen glanced away, embarrassed. "I'm sorry. I was just thinking."

"About what?"

"My life."

He raised his brows. "Oh, oh. Sounds heavy."

Karen smiled ruefully. "Just confusing."

"Really? Don't you like your new job?"

"Yes, I do. It's my personal life that's a mess."

He shot her a sidelong glance. "Still haven't gotten over the old flame, huh?"

Karen sighed. "Everyone tells me these things take time."

Jim nodded. "Though I have to say he must have been somebody special for a great girl like you to carry such a torch."

"That's kind of you to say," Karen replied, feeling guiltier by the minute, as if she were taking advantage of Jim in some subtle, unspecified way.

"Where is he now?" Jim asked, turning onto Route 3 and heading for New York.

"I don't know," Karen said truthfully. Colter had left for Lebanon, but he could be anywhere at the moment.

"Oh. He took off?"

"Yes."

"What did he do?" Jim inquired.

"Do?"

"For a living."

Karen thought about it. "He was kind of an independent contractor, traveled around on jobs, moved a lot, that sort of thing."

Jim realized that she was being deliberately vague and didn't pursue the subject. They chatted about the office where they both worked, until Jim entered the city and parked in an underground garage a few blocks from Rockefeller Center.

Karen hadn't been to New York in years, and she was amazed to see that it had changed hardly at all: it was still dirty, busy, and under construction. They ducked beneath a catwalk and crossed a series of blustery streets, dodging drifting candy wrappers and newspapers, to reach the restaurant. The celebrated Christmas tree towered into the night sky, ablaze with white lights, and they were seated next to a glass wall that afforded a full view of the skating pond. Karen settled in comfortably while Jim ordered drinks and watched clouds of steam escaping from the manholes on the avenue, enveloping passersby in a warm fog from the underground heating system. Christmas shoppers hurried along laden with bags labeled Macy's and Bonwit's and Bloomingdale's, and the skaters glided and looped and twirled, singly and in pairs, their faces flushed and their ears red from the cold. Karen sipped her wine and observed the scene, so different from Almeria, where Christmas arrived in stifling heat and was celebrated with the crèches and piñatas of the native population. She was curiously content and realized, with a feeling of recognition, that she was glad to be home.

They were examining the menu, debating what to order, when their waiter approached the table and said, "Telephone for you, ma'am. Shall I bring it to your table?"

Karen glanced at Jim in surprise. "For me?" she said.

"Yes. The caller said for the young lady with Mr. Cochran. That's you, isn't it?"

Karen nodded, shrugging at Jim.

"Would you like to take it here?" the waiter asked.

"No, don't bother," Karen replied, standing up. "I'll take it at the desk."

Jim pulled out her chair, and the waiter stepped back to let her pass. The hostess at the desk indicated the blinking button on the phone. Karen pressed it and lifted the receiver.

"Hello?" Karen said.

"Oh, Karen, thank God I reached you," Grace said breathlessly. "He was just here, and I don't know what to do."

"Who?" Karen asked, confused.

"Who do you think?" Grace replied, exasperated. "That boyfriend of yours, Colter. I couldn't believe it. We were just talking about him tonight, and then there he was. The bell rang and I answered the door, and he was standing on the porch, big as life, as brown as a leather boot in the middle of winter.''

"He's back?"

"Of course he's back. Aren't you listening to me?" Grace demanded.

"He came to the house?" Karen said, her heart beating faster.

There was a pause during which Grace tried to determine whether her sister had suddenly become stupid or was just so rattled that she was reduced to repeating everything she heard. Deciding on the latter, Grace said carefully, "Yes, Karen. He was here about half an hour ago, and he wanted to see you."

"What did you tell him?"

"I told him the truth, that you weren't home."

"And?"

"He didn't believe me. He thought I was just trying to keep him away from you."

Karen closed her eyes. "Then what happened?" she asked warily, although she could well imagine.

"Well, he was about to push past me, and Ken wasn't home, and I got scared," Grace said apologetically. "That Colter's awfully big, and he looked pretty upset, and..."

"What did you do, Grace?" Karen asked patiently, wincing.

"I told him where you were," Grace said rapidly.

Karen almost dropped the phone. "You didn't give him the address of this restaurant!" she said in a strong voice.

"I had to," Grace whined. "I told him you were out on a date, which was the wrong thing to say, and then he wanted to know with whom, and he was real demanding about it, and I said with a guy at your office..."

"All right, Grace, I get the picture. Is he coming here?"

"I think he is, and that's why I had to call, to warn you. At first I decided not to bother you, but the more I thought about it, the more worried I got. I'm afraid he might make a scene, and maybe you could convince Jim to leave before he gets there."

"I'll try," Karen said firmly.

"I'm sorry I messed up," Grace said with genuine contrition. "I just didn't know what to do. All I could think of was to get rid of him before Ken came home, and they got into it or something. Before I knew it, I had blurted out the name of the place where you were."

"It's all right; I understand. Steven has a way of getting what he wants."

"Are you sure you'll be okay?"

"I'll be fine."

"Karen?"

"Yes?"

"I can see why you had such trouble letting go. He really is very attractive. I mean, he was mad and everything, but I could still tell that he'd be a difficult one to forget."

"Even so, he had no right to just show up there and give you a hard time," Karen said grimly. "I haven't heard from him in almost a month, and he gave me every reason to believe I never would. Now all of a sudden he gets angry because I have the nerve to get on with my life and go out on a date? I hope he does come here. I have a thing or two to say to him."

"But what about Jim?" Grace asked in a worried tone.

"Don't worry—I'll handle it. Thanks for calling."

"Goodbye, and good luck. Let me know what happens."

"I will. Bye." Karen hung up the phone and made her way back to Jim, who was watching her with concern.

"Is there a problem?" he asked.

"I'm afraid so," Karen replied, wondering how she could explain this latest development to him.

"What's the matter? Something with the family?"

Karen sat and met his eyes directly. "You know the old flame we were talking about earlier?"

"Yeah?" he said warily.

"Well, he went to my sister's house tonight, looking for me. And she told him where I was."

It took a few seconds for the import of what she was saying to register.

"You mean he's coming here?" Jim asked in amazement.

"I'm afraid he might."

"Do you want to leave?" he asked.

"I think that would be best. We could go to another restaurant. I'd like to avoid trouble, if it's possible."

"Fine," Jim replied promptly, to her vast relief. "No problem. I'll just get our coats."

"Thanks for being so understanding," Karen said.

"Be back in a minute," Jim said, signaling for the bar bill. He got up and went to the checkroom as Karen looked around for her purse. She had found it and was rising to go after Jim when Colter came through the door.

Karen froze, and her gaze darted to Jim, whose back was to her. He was busy retrieving their coats and didn't see the drama about to unfold.

Colter spotted Karen immediately and brushed past the hostess, who was asking him for his reservation. The hostess, alarmed, signaled to the maître d', who scurried out from behind the phone stand. Colter strode through the forest of tables purposefully, halting at Karen's side as the maître d' almost ran up his heels behind him.

"What are you doing here?" Karen said to him coldly.

"I came to talk to you," he replied.

"Is everything all right, miss?" the maître d' asked anxiously. He clearly didn't want to tangle with anyone Colter's size, but even less did he want a scene in his restaurant, and he could sense that one was coming.

"Everything is fine," Karen said to the maître d'.

"Do you know this . . . gentleman?" the maître d' asked.

"I know him," Karen replied.

The man subsided reluctantly, walking away but casting parting glances over his shoulder, as if waiting for Colter to erupt at any moment. Colter turned his back, dismissing him, and faced Karen, who was regarding him balefully.

Her expression was partially a pose. She was so glad to see him that she had to restrain herself from throwing her arms around his neck, but his outrageous behavior in terrorizing Grace and then showing up in the middle of her date could not be countenanced. Not to mention his sudden reappearance after his theatrical, and seemingly final, farewell. So Karen laced the fingers that longed to caress him in front of her and waited for him to speak.

"You look beautiful," he said.

So did he. He was wearing a gray-and-white checked lumberjack coat, open down the front, his hands thrust into the pockets. A red wool scarf dangled around his neck, offsetting a gray sweater and his perennial faded jeans. He was so tan that his teeth and eyes seemed impossibly pale against the background of his skin, and his hair was blonder than she'd ever seen it, almost white. He looked like an advertisement for a tropical escape vacation. No wonder everybody in the place was staring at him.

"How was Lebanon?" Karen asked crisply.

"Hot. Dry."

"You seem remarkably unscathed. No injuries this time?"

"No."

"How lucky for you. Now do you mind telling me why you found it necessary to scare my sister half to death?"

"How do you know that?"

"She called me here and told me all about it. You haven't answered my question."

"She wouldn't tell me where you were."

"Oh, but she did. Eventually, isn't that right? And that's why you're standing in the middle of this restaurant, making fools of both of us."

"Karen, we have to talk—" he began.

"You did talk," she cut him off. "As I recall, the last time we were together, you said quite a bit, most of which I've been trying to forget ever since."

They both looked up as Jim arrived, with Karen's coat over his arm.

"You ready to go?" he said to Karen, as if Colter weren't there. He'd evidently sized up the situation from a distance and decided to play it cool.

"Who is this guy?" Colter demanded.

"My escort, Jim Cochran," Karen replied, trying to decide how best to avoid a confrontation.

"Your escort?" Colter sneered. "How charming."

Jim turned to him, clearly trying to hold his anger in check. "Look, bud, this lady is with me, and I'm sure she'd be very grateful if you wouldn't embarrass her any more than you already have. Why don't you just run along and leave her alone? If she wants to see you, she'll get in touch."

Colter was livid. He grabbed Jim by the collar and slammed him into the wall. The surrounding diners gasped, and the maître d', taking no further chances, ran for the phone.

"The lady was with me long before you ever met her, *bud*, and I'm taking her home," Colter growled. "Shut up and go away."

Jim struggled to throw off Colter's viselike grip while Karen prayed to disappear or at least transubstantiate into one of the chairs. After a stunned second or two she recovered and grabbed Colter's arm, hissing into his ear, "Let go of him this instant, or I promise you I will never speak to you again."

Colter relaxed his grip reluctantly, and Jim shrugged, straightening his collar.

"Ready to leave?" he asked Karen, as if the previous exchange had not happened.

Karen closed her eyes briefly. This was like a nightmare. Her only concern was to end it as efficiently as possible.

"Jim," she said, with more calm that she felt, "I really do have to talk to him. I think it would be best if you just went home and let me get this straightened out."

"I'm not leaving you with him!" Jim said, as astonished as if she had suggested sacking a church.

"Real brave, aren't you?" Colter said with a derisive smile, and Jim took a belligerent step toward him.

"Be quiet!" Karen said to Colter, and he fell back, scowling. Jim watched him, ready to go at it again if he moved.

"Please, Jim, for me?" Karen said, touching his arm.

Jim looked down at her. "Are you sure that's what you want?"

"I'm sure."

"You know how to get in touch if you need me," he said.

"She won't need you," Colter interjected.

Karen looked at him. He turned his head, flexing his shoulders.

"I don't like this," Jim said.

"I'll be fine."

"All right," he said, sighing, and just as Karen was congratulating herself on getting him to leave, the police arrived. A cruiser pulled up to the door, and two cops got out, one swinging a nightstick. Karen switched from a mental prayer to a full-blown litany.

"What's the trouble here?" the older of the patrolmen said to the group at large.

"No trouble, Officer," Karen babbled, "just a misunderstanding."

"Is that right?" the cop asked Colter, who was clearly an unhappy man.

Colter shrugged. "Whatever she says."

The cop looked at Jim.

"I was just leaving," Jim said. He'd had enough. Defending his date's honor was one thing, but getting arrested was another.

"Why did you call us?" the cop said to the maître d', annoyed.

The little man shrugged. "It looked like a fight was brewing. I didn't want to take the chance."

Karen glanced around at the other diners. They were all watching the scene, riveted. Clearly she and her men friends were more entertaining than the food, or even the nine o'clock movie at home.

"Yeah, well, wait until you see blood the next time, will ya," the cop said wearily and walked off, his partner following him.

Jim and Colter and Karen looked at one another.

"Good night," Jim said shortly and left.

Colter and Karen looked at each other.

"'Please, Jim, for me,'" Colter said in a sugary voice, batting his lashes, imitating Karen.

"Don't you start," Karen told him furiously. "You're lucky I'm even talking to you. How dare you barge in here and make me the feature attraction in this place? We've already had the police; I feel like Mayor Koch will be next, and maybe Eyewitness News."

"At least you got rid of what's his name," Colter muttered darkly.

"I did that so you wouldn't beat him up," Karen responded sharply.

"Good thing, too. He was one step away from an intensive care ward."

"I'm afraid I'll have to ask you to leave," the maître d' said bravely, interrupting their heated exchange.

Colter looked at him, and the smaller man shrank back.

"We're going," Karen said with as much dignity as she could muster, which wasn't a lot. She shouldered into her coat and grabbed Colter's hand, dragging him after her. They were the focus of stares and mutterings until they reached the sidewalk, where Karen closed her eyes and took a deep breath of the frigid air. She exhaled sharply and turned to Colter.

"You have two minutes to explain yourself," she said.

"Do I have to do it in the street?" he asked. "It's ten degrees out here."

Karen glanced across the road. "There's a coffee shop over there."

They ran through the intersection, dodging a taxi that bore down on them with typical indifference, and ducked into the door of a Chock Full O'Nuts. The place was open round-the-clock and packed at that hour with people seeking to escape the winter chill.

Colter took Karen's coat and hung it from a hook outside their booth. He left his on and sat across from her, following her every move. A light snow began to fall, and Karen watched the thin flakes drift past the neon sign outside the window behind his head.

A waitress approached, and Colter ordered two coffees. After she left, he said to Karen, "So who was that guy?"

"Jim?"

He continued to eye her narrowly, as if waiting for an explanation.

"A lawyer I work with," Karen said.

"A lawyer?"

"That's right."

He nodded, as if he'd expected as much. "Didn't take you long, did it?" he asked cynically.

"To what?"

"Hook up with Mr. Wonderful."

Karen stared at him.

"He looks like he just can't wait to take on the mortgage and the kiddies and the whole nine yards."

Karen sighed.

"Are you sleeping with him yet?" Colter asked.

Karen stood immediately, reaching for her purse.

Colter bolted into her path and grabbed her arm. "Wait," he said, holding her still. "Please wait. Stay with me."

Karen tried to wrest free of his grasp. "Why? To take more of this abuse?"

"No more," he said contritely. "I promise. Just sit down, okay?"

Karen sat stiffly, torn between anger at his offensive tactics and joy at the strong emotion that motivated them.

"I was just . . . jealous," he said, not looking at her.

"Why would you be jealous?" Karen demanded. "You told me in no uncertain terms that it was over between us. Did you think I would spend all my time in a state of mourning and not even try to get my life together?"

"It seems you've done that," he said shortly.

"Well, I have a job I like."

"And a new boyfriend."

Karen closed her eyes. "Steven, he's not my boyfriend. If you must know, tonight was my first date with him."

"He took you to a pretty fancy place," Colter said, unconvinced.

"Can we drop the subject of Jim and discuss why you're here?" Karen said, exasperated.

"I missed you," he said quietly.

"Did you think you wouldn't?"

"I didn't think it would be so bad."

The waitress brought their coffee. Karen took a sip of hers as the woman walked away, and Colter added, "The time in Lebanon was like hell."

Karen said nothing, waiting tensely for him to go on.

"The whole place is a desert; the sun is relentless. It was just a featureless inferno, and the job was tedious, and I missed you more than I could believe."

"You mean you missed me this time, until you have a chance to think about it and decide all over again that it wouldn't work."

He looked down at his hands. "I guess I deserved that."

"Yes, you did."

"So you can't forgive me?"

"I already forgave you, Steven. But you just can't pop up every time you have second thoughts and disrupt my life again. You made a decision, and I'm trying to adjust to it. What you're doing tonight isn't helping."

"What if I don't want you to adjust to it?"

Karen studied his face, her breath catching in her throat. "I don't understand."

He put his head back against the wall and closed his eyes. "I've been so lonely," he said softly.

"Me, too," Karen murmured.

"I had the best," he said, looking at her. "I threw it away, and now I'm just trying to get it back."

"What makes you think you have a chance of doing that?" Karen asked him.

"You love me," he answered. "That didn't change in a month."

"How do you know?"

"Because I know you."

"But aren't you worried about me anymore?" Karen asked, unable to resist it. "Aren't you worried that you won't be able to take care of me, that someone else would be better for me?"

"Yes," he conceded.

"Then why are you here?"

"Because I'm more worried about myself," he answered, with an unmistakable note of despair in his voice.

Karen knew this was a difficult admission for him. She waited in silence for him to continue.

"I can't make it without you," he said quietly. "I'll change, and I'll do anything you want, but please don't sentence me to the life I had before we met. I can't go back to it; it's as simple as that."

Karen was curiously calm. She had pictured him saying these words so many times, but now that she was hearing them, there was an air of unreality about the experience, as if she were still imagining it.

"I know I'm not the husband of your dreams," he went on.

"I never said that, Steven. You did," she reminded him.

"But," he continued, as if she hadn't spoken, "I contacted a guy who offered me a job once before, to see if he had anything interesting."

"And?"

"He does. He wants me to head a government counterterrorist unit in Washington. It's a desk job." He hesitated, clearing his throat. "If I take it, will you come with me?"

"As your wife?" Karen asked, her blood pounding in her ears.

He nodded, his jaw working nervously.

"You're asking me to marry you?" she whispered.

He nodded again, his gaze fixed on hers.

Karen bent her head, overcome with emotion, unable to speak. He watched her for a long moment and then said dully, "No, huh?"

She looked up at him, her eyes swimming with tears.

"Too little and too late, right?" he said, his face a sullen mask.

Karen opened her mouth.

He held up his hand. "It's okay; you don't have to explain," he said. "I know what I put you through, and I understand. But it hurts too much to stay, knowing how you feel, so I'm going to take off now, all right?" He paused, swallowing. "Let me just leave you with one thought, Karen. No matter what happens, even if I never see you again, I'll love you as long as I live."

Karen found her voice. "I love you, too, Steven. Of course I'll marry you." She slipped her hand inside his on the table as his face went blank with surprise, then suffused with relief.

He raised her hand to his mouth. "Do you mean it?" he asked, as if afraid to believe his good fortune.

"Yes."

He pulled her out of the booth into the aisle and swept her into his arms. It was the second time that evening they'd made a spectacle of themselves, but Karen no longer cared.

"I was so afraid you wouldn't come back to me," he said brokenly in her ear.

They clung together for a long moment, then he dropped some money onto the table and led Karen out of the shop. The second they hit the street he embraced her again, kissing her wildly, the falling snow wetting their hair and skin and clinging to their eyelashes.

"Let's go someplace," he murmured urgently.

"Someplace?"

"A hotel."

"Where are you staying?"

He shrugged. "I rented a car as soon as I got off the plane and came to find you."

They both looked around. "This is New York City; there must be a million places here," Karen said.

"The Waldorf is just down the block."

"The Waldorf?" Karen said, laughing.

"We'll start the honeymoon early."

They ran hand in hand through the storm and arrived in the hotel lobby, cold, wet, and happy. Colter booked a room at the desk while Karen pushed back her damp hair and tried to defrost her feet, feeling dazzled and supremely grateful.

A few hours earlier she'd thought that Colter would remain nothing more than a memory, and now she was going to marry him.

He returned brandishing a room key like a trophy. "Let's go," he said.

He meant it. When the elevator didn't arrive fast enough, he dragged Karen up three flights of stairs and unlocked the door before she could catch her breath.

"This is lovely," Karen said, glancing around the room when he turned on the light.

"You're lovelier." He pulled off her coat and unzipped her dress in almost the same motion, planting a row of kisses along her spine as he uncovered her back. He set her on the edge of the king-size bed and undressed her like a doll, scattering items of her clothing about until she lay naked on the spread. She watched him through slitted eyes as he took off his clothes, reaching for him when he was still wearing his pants and dragging him on top of her.

Colter offered no resistance, covering her body with his own. He kissed her deeply, caressing her as she fumbled with the fastening of his jeans.

"Help me," she finally said in frustration. "This thing is worse than a chastity belt."

He laughed, a low intimate sound that sank into her bones and told her that she had won him forever.

"Can't wait?" he murmured.

"No," she moaned.

And she didn't have to. He freed himself from his pants and drove into her so deeply that she gasped with gratification.

"Better?" he said.

"Oh, yes." She closed her eyes and wound her legs around him, home at last.

When it was over, they lay curled up together, Karen's head on his shoulder, her arm thrown across his middle.

"Where in the Southwest?" she asked dreamily, breaking a long silence.

"What?"

"Where's the job? I'd like to know where I'm moving."

"Oh. New Mexico, I think."

"You think?"

"All I needed to know was if I had the job. I can iron out the details later. There are several spots available, but I'm sure New Mexico is one of them."

"Lots of work there for a Spanish translator," Karen observed.

"What about your job here?" he asked.

"Since I can't be in two places at once, I guess I'll have to quit it," she said dryly.

"Goodbye, Jim Cochran," Colter said with satisfaction.

"Poor Jim. I'm sure he thinks we're both insane, and who could blame him?"

"He'll get over it."

"And Grace. I'd have to say you got off on the wrong foot with Grace."

He winced. "I'll apologize."

"You'd better, if you expect her to attend the wedding. Can we have it here?"

"Have it anyplace you like. You're the one with friends and family; I'll just bring myself."

Karen kissed his collarbone. "You're not alone anymore, darling."

He squeezed her. "Thanks to you."

"I can't wait to tell Linda," Karen said suddenly, struck by the thought.

"How is the scourge of St. John's Wood?" Colter asked, referring to the section of London where Linda lived.

"You won't believe it."

"Where she's concerned, I'll believe anything."

"In her last letter she said she was dating that guard who was stationed across the street from her house."

Colter sat up and looked at her.

"It's true. The guy came back and rang her bell one day. I told you she was always flirting with him, and I guess he remembered."

"I guess he would," Colter said, shaking his head.

Karen's expression became serious, and she traced the outline of an old scar on his forehead.

"Will you be sorry to give it up?" she asked.

"What?"

"The mercenary business."

"Not if I can have you," he replied. He settled back down, encircling her with his arm. "It was time, anyway. You were right. Sooner or later, my luck was bound to run out."

Karen shuddered. "I'm glad you left before it did."

They heard footsteps in the hall and listened until they had passed.

"Bellboy?" Karen said.

Colter shrugged. "We didn't have any luggage. They probably know enough to leave us alone."

Karen giggled. "I've never done anything like this before."

"Like what?"

"Booked a hotel room to make love. It makes me feel like..."

"A hooker?" he suggested. "Please don't start that again."

"No, no. Like I'm having an affair."

He rolled her under him and pinned her with his weight. "You are. With me. One that's going to last for the rest of your life."

* * * * *

An enticing new historical romance!

Spring Will Come

SHERRY DeBorde

It was 1852, and the steamy South was in its last hours of gentility. Camille Braxton Beaufort went searching for the one man she knew she could trust, and under his protection had her first lesson in love....

Take 4 Silhouette Desire novels
and a surprise gift
⇒❈ FREE ❈⇐

Then preview 6 brand-new Silhouette Desire novels—delivered to your door as soon as they come off the presses! If you decide to keep them, you pay just $2.24 each*—a 10% saving off the retail price, *with no additional charges for postage and handling!*

Silhouette Desire novels are not for everyone. They are written especially for the woman who wants a more satisfying, more deeply involving reading experience. Silhouette Desire novels take you beyond the others.

Start with 4 Silhouette Desire novels and a surprise gift absolutely FREE. They're yours to keep without obligation. You can always return a shipment and cancel at any time.

Simply fill out and return the coupon today!

*$2.25 each plus 69¢ postage and handling per shipment in Canada.

Silhouette Intimate Moments

COMING NEXT MONTH

#205 ALL IN THE FAMILY— Heather Graham Pozzessere

Dan's daughter was going to have a baby, and Kelly's son was responsible. The children were happy, excited and in love, but Kelly and Dan were furious. Their fighting lasted until they realized just how close anger is to passion—and to love.

#206 GAUNTLET RUN—Robin Elliott

Hollis had come home to Texas to take over her father's ranch, but someone was trying very hard to chase her away. Cutter McKenzie had the ruthlessness to hurt her, but her heart wanted to believe that he never would.

#207 PASSAGE TO ZAPHIR—Anna James

Jenna Chapman needed a guide through Africa to help her discover the truth about her father's death, and Sam Matlock was just the man. Together they could risk any danger—even the danger of falling in love.

#208 ASKING FOR TROUBLE—Barbara Faith

Juliana Thornton was a rebel from way back, and Brian McNeeley had always represented the establishment to her. Then they met again on a dangerous tropical island and discovered that love knew no boundaries.

AVAILABLE THIS MONTH: